Children of the Old Stars

"In *Children of the Old Stars,* David Lee Summers has created a wonderful mix of characters and a gripping plot. From the aliens to the whales of Earth, who now communicate with people, each character seems to come to life from the moment they enter the story." Kate Hill, author of *The Chieftain's Bride* and editor of *Parchment Symbols* magazine.

"*Children of the Old Stars* by David Lee Summers has all the best elements of the Great Masters of Science Fiction: Action, Imagination, and Substance. Summers weaves a deft and highly engrossing tale, full of whole galaxies of characters. His world is unique, believable and ultimately sustaining – a story for this time – all times." Denise Chávez, American Book Award winning author of *Face of an Angel.*

"*Children of the Old Stars* has proved an engaging story . . . David Lee Summers has revealed himself to be a master." Alessio Zanelli, author of *Straight Astray.*

Books in the Old Star Saga

The Pirates of Sufiro

Children of the Old Stars

Heirs of the New Earth

Also by David Lee Summers

Vampires of the Scarlet Order

Children of the Old Stars

David Lee Summers

Illustrations by Laura Givens

Hadrosaur Productions
Las Cruces, NM

and

LBF Books
Pittsburgh, PA

Children of the Old Stars

All Rights Reserved

Copyright © 2000 by David Lee Summers

No part of this book may be reproduced or transmitted in any form or by any means, electronic or mechanical including photocopying, recording, or by any information storage or retrieval system without permission in writing from the publisher. Published in the United States by Hadrosaur Productions and LBF Books.

SECOND EDITION

Artwork by Laura Givens
Edited by Jacqueline Druga-Johnston

ISBN 1-885093-38-1

To Bridget Watts

for her love of whales and the stars.

Acknowledgements

Thanks to my cosmology and general relativity classmates from grad school at New Mexico Tech who helped me to dream of how the universe works. Special thanks go to a fellow classmate, the late Daniel Briggs, who saw and pointed out beautiful variations in Einstein's symphony of the cosmos. I hope you are dancing to that symphony now and all of us on Earth miss you very much.

Thanks to William Grother, Marianna Eisenhour, and Michael Ledlow who read earlier drafts of this work and told me what worked and what didn't. Likewise, thanks to Paul Avellar who first pointed out the symmetry between my alien spaceships and globular clusters.

Thanks to my lovely wife, Kumie Wise. You've read this book more than anyone else has; listened to my anxieties and held my hand through the rough parts and laughed at all the right places when it was complete.

Finally thanks to the team that has brought this second edition of the book to fruition: Jacqueline Druga-Johnston who edited the book to a fine polish; Teresa Tunaley who has always been a great source of support and help; and Laura Givens who created the wonderful cover for this edition along with the exemplary interior illustrations.

PART I
The Search on Earth

Like the striving of the people of Firon, and those before them; they rejected Our communications, so Allah destroyed them on account of their faults; and Allah is severe in requiting evil.

— The Koran

John Mark Ellis returns home to Nantucket

The Freedom to Search

Some stories begin with a battle. Even more end with one. Still, there are other stories where the battle occurs before the tale begins. We can only imagine the terrible fight in which Ahab lost his leg to the white whale. We know it was a transforming experience – almost a spiritual conversion. What else could cause a man to lose himself to a quest?

The war-weary planet of Sufiro hung, healing, in the black stillness of space – a blue-green marble spotted with brown continents and white clouds. On Sufiro, Clyde McClintlock sat bored in a pristine white room with perfectly smooth walls and rounded corners. The plastic furniture, a bed, chair, table, and toilet, were as white and featureless as the walls themselves. At the front of the room was a transparent force field, which looked out into an equally pristine white hallway. Clyde picked up a new, crisp book. The book was a mystery novel, but every time he tried to read, images of nearly translucent silver spheres reflecting the planet Sufiro's blue-green oceans would enter his thoughts. People called those spheres the Cluster. It was a benign name for a potent force.

He carefully returned the book to the center of the table, adjusting it precisely. Standing slowly, he put his feet against the back wall. Methodically he paced the distance from the wall to the force field. The cell hadn't changed size; it was still exactly ten paces. Again, McClintlock picked up the book, opened it to the first page, but threw it down almost instantly, activating a button on the edge of the table.

A hologram of a professionally dressed woman materialized on one side of the cell. It was a news holo, originating from Earth. The woman's voice was a forced calm, but held a note of hopelessness. "Humans have now lost over 100 star vessels to the mysterious Cluster. All the races of the Confederation claim losses on the same scale, including the Titans. So far, no Cluster appears to have attacked any planets, though there have been sightings reported over various frontier words, including Earth's key mining colony, Sufiro."

Clyde McClintlock slammed the button, shutting off the hologram. "Don't tell me about the Cluster. I already know more than I want to," he grumbled to no one.

At one time, Clyde McClintlock had been a colonel, leading the armies of the continent of Tejo on Sufiro. Tejo had supplied the mineral,

Erdonium, to Earth to help combat the Cluster, wherever it appeared. As the Cluster appeared more often, demand for the rare material increased. To supply the ever-rising need, the Tejans resorted to using migrant labor from the other major continent on the planet, New Granada. Money was short and competition for trade, fierce. As such, the migrant laborers were paid only enough food to survive and clothing that was little more than rags. Even to Clyde McClintlock, whose job it had been to keep the migrants from rioting, it seemed little different from slavery.

The demand for Erdonium continued to grow. Clyde had been ordered to send an invasion force to New Granada to get more people to mine the mineral. It was during the invasion that a Confederation Commander, John Mark Ellis, had destroyed his supply train. Shortly after that, the Cluster had appeared in the sky. It was while the Cluster was in the sky that he had the vision.

In one instant, he had seen, and more importantly understood, all the pain and suffering his government had caused. More to the point though, he realized how to end it. In one stroke, Clyde McClintlock led a military coup and seized control of his home, Tejo. Peace between the two continents was made and the migrants were sent home. McClintlock had no ambition to run a country. Even more, he did not want to go down in history as another tyrannical militant who ended one type of suffering by imposing another. McClintlock turned control of Tejo's government over to the people. The people promptly arrested him.

Beyond arresting him, though, the people weren't quite sure what to do. Clyde McClintlock had violated the most sacred law of any military officer. He had attacked his Commander-in-Chief and childhood friend, Rocky Hill. On the other hand, no one questioned that it took just that kind of extreme action to save Tejo from the self-destructive path it had been on.

While imprisoned in the capital, Tejo City, McClintlock had heard that Caroline Chung of the mighty Mao Corporation had been elected to lead the people. McClintlock waited impatiently, hoping she would decide on a course of action – any course of action – soon.

Sitting alone in his cell, McClintlock was bothered. He was not bothered by the ultimate outcome of the decision. In a way, he almost didn't care. As far as he was concerned, death would not be too high a price for betraying his closest friend. Instead, he was bothered by the clarity of the vision he had received. It occurred to Clyde that the Cluster might not be the evil that people had claimed it was. Instead, it might be quite different. It might hold answers; answers to many of the deepest mysteries.

Clyde retrieved some paper from the drawer in the table and began to write . . .

* * *

Roly-poly, furred beings with deep, black eyes performed the ceremonial dances and sang the ritual chants that made their vessel traverse space. In another part of the ship, a detection algorithm was danced. The beings, called Titans after their home world, sensed an ancient presence. The presence took the form of silvery, translucent orbs – a large one in the center, smaller ones around the outside. "It is the intelligence," said one of the Titans, continuing to dance.

"Have they detected us?" asked another.

"Unknown. The intelligence is diminished without appendages, but its power is still great," said the first Titan.

The other Titan called to those controlling the ship, "Take steps to ensure we are not detected." With that command, the Titans' spacecraft vanished into a dimension perpendicular to those normally sensed.

* * *

Frail wisps of gray smoke drifted silently past shimmering, iridescent, silver spheres hovering over a tiny foldout desk. The spheres seemed to cling together impossibly. Commander John Mark Ellis of the destroyer, *Firebrandt*, sat transfixed by the image, asking himself questions. The commander sat back in a frail metal chair and lifted the smoldering, brown cigar to his chapped lips. As he sucked in the warm, fragrant smoke, he thought of the terrible damage caused by this lovely cluster of spheres.

Ellis exhaled smoke forcefully and a deep frown etched itself onto his face. With a rumble, deep down in his throat, he sat forward, touched a button on the projector base and changed the hologram. Where the cluster of spheres once hovered, now stood the image of a man who looked very much like him. Both men were over six feet tall and somewhat stocky, each with muscles built up from years of military service. Unlike the commander though, the man in the holographic image was clean-shaven. The image was one of Jerome Mycroft Ellis standing on the bow of a sleek hover boat in the Atlantic Ocean of Earth, his hands on his hips, hair blown back by the wind. Ellis felt his own deep brown eyes grow moist as he thought about his father lost to the cluster of spheres. Ellis' father had not done anything to the spheres – he didn't even try to communicate – yet the Cluster sliced his ship open just as easily as a human would a can of soup.

Ellis, placing the pungent cigar in a small, black ashtray, turned as he heard a knock on the bulkhead next to the alcove where he sat.

"Yes," said Ellis, with an edge to his voice.

The commander heard the soft rustle as the green curtain was pushed aside. The strong, youthful face of his first lieutenant, Frank Rubin appeared. "We're almost at the final jump point for Titan, sir," said the lieutenant in an almost unnaturally booming baritone.

"I'll be on the bridge momentarily," said Ellis, scratchily. He cleared his throat and reached behind him to the tiny bunk and grabbed his blue uniform coat. His attention was dragged back to the image of his father. The commander sighed and turned off the holo projector at its base. In one fluid motion, he grabbed the cigar, took a puff and dumped it down the incinerator chute while folding the tiny metal desk back into the wall. He tossed on the coat without ceremony, without bothering to button it. Taking five steps, he found himself on the bridge of the tiny vessel.

As Ellis entered the bridge, he did not sit down immediately. Rather, he stood just behind his black, leather command chair, his jacket rumpled, the single epaulet on the left shoulder hanging askew. His fingers reached out, almost caressing the top of the chair. For a long moment, he stared at the holographic viewer, then down to the right at the communicator – a thin, pale fellow named Weiss – working at his station. Ellis scanned left where Commissioned Officer (B-Grade) Francis Rubin had just settled in at the pilot's console, slightly forward and to the left of the command seat. Allowing his gaze to wander, he smiled at the gunner, a blonde-haired young woman named Adkins. The smile she returned lit up her face.

The commander returned his gaze to the holographic projector. On it, a course projection seemed to stretch out through the stars to a flashing purple sphere. That was the point at which the ship would inject itself into fourth dimensional reality and return to its home base at Saturn's largest moon, the enigmatically shrouded Titan. Ellis inhaled deeply, smelling new plastic, dust and sweat mingling with old, stale cigar smoke. He examined the light gray metal and plastic of the bridge as though it would be the last time he would ever see it. Finally, he eased around the black command chair, letting his hand trail on the armrest and settled into the not-too-comfortable chair.

"Are you looking forward to going home, sir?" asked Adkins cheerily.

Ellis took a shuddering breath and felt a slight lump form in his throat. "I'm going to miss this ship," he said carefully. "My first command." He sighed to himself.

Rubin turned, looking at his commander. "After our mission at Sufiro, they'd be crazy not to confirm your promotion. The only way to end the war with the Cluster is to be able to talk to them." The B-

Com smiled reassuringly. "At Sufiro, you showed that might actually be possible."

The commander scowled. "As far as I know, my 'communication' with the Cluster might have been nothing more than a bad dream." Ellis' scowl melted into a whimsical grin. "It may have been nothing more than an undigested bit of meat. There might have been more of gravy than grave to that vision."

"More like a nicotine hallucination," chided Adkins, deliberately ignoring the allusion to Dickens.

The commander – a naval traditionalist – scowled at the gunner.

"More like a nicotine hallucination, *sir*," Adkins hastily corrected.

Ellis nodded, grinning mischievously. "All I saw were scenes of the conflict at Sufiro. There was nothing I didn't already know about." The commander shook his head. "I had a few vague impressions."

Rubin took a deep breath. "Quite frankly, sir, it sounds like you're trying to talk yourself out of believing the communication even happened."

Ellis shrugged.

"Sorry to interrupt," cut in the thin voice of the communicator. Weiss turned, holding a hand to the scar on his forehead where a communication's chip had been implanted. "I'm receiving an EQ distress call."

"On speakers," barked Ellis.

Sound from the speakers reverberated suddenly from the walls of the tiny ship's bridge. ". . . stumbled across a Cluster ship in orbit of star 1E1919+0427. We have attempted neither communication nor scans. We request assistance from a Confederation vessel. Repeat – this is the Mao Freighter *Martha's Vineyard* calling for immediate assistance. We have stumbled across . . ." Ellis reached to his own control pad and cut the speakers. He sat stunned for a moment. The *Martha's Vineyard* had been a sister ship to his father's now-destroyed freighter, the *Nantucket*.

"Analysis," called Ellis, sitting up in his chair.

Rubin looked up from his station where he had already been performing calculations. "We can reach 1E1919+0427 using nearly the same jump point as for Titan. It's almost in a straight line between here and our own solar system."

Weiss still looked at Ellis, his hand on his forehead. "Titan control confirms we are the best-positioned ship to make an immediate response. Although there are more heavily armed ships that could be there only an hour later. Titan control says it's your decision."

The commander tapped his fingers rapidly on the armrest of his chair. After only a couple seconds he looked at Rubin. "Proceed to the jump point for 1E19 . . ." Ellis shook his head, not remembering the string of numbers.

"1E1919+0427," stated Rubin, his deep voice giving the impression of confidence. "Aye, sir."

"Full speed." Ellis turned his attention to Weiss. "Inform Titan control that we are going in." As Weiss returned his hand to his forehead, Ellis turned to Adkins. "Better make sure those guns are set, though I hope to God we don't have to use them."

Adkins nodded curtly while Ellis returned his eyes to the holo viewer. In the image, he saw the course projection move over slightly and a new purple sphere appear, slightly closer than the preceding one. After Rubin made the course adjustment, he reached over to the intercom switch. "This is the Executive Officer, we have changed course and are engaged in a rescue mission. All hands to battle stations. Repeat – this is the XO, all hands to battle stations. Prepare for jump in two minutes." Rubin looked at the holographic chronometer readout floating in his workstation window. "Jump in two minutes . . . mark." As Rubin spoke, the computer automatically registered the call to battle stations. An alarm bell sounded as lights went red, drawing people's attentions to their stations.

Automatically, Ellis checked readouts on his own console. He tried, in vain, to remember if he had secured the volume of Emily Dickinson that he had been reading before he had become absorbed in pictures of the Cluster. He shook his head, knowing he didn't have time to worry about it even if he had forgotten.

Rubin looked around at Ellis. "We are at the jump point," he said tersely.

Ellis took a deep breath and gripped the armrests tightly, his knuckles showing white. "Jump!"

Reality exploded as the *Firebrandt* leapt from the confines of three-dimensional existence, riding a gravity wave through the dimension of time. Light swirled in twisting silver intensities becoming loud voices that called Ellis' name. The commander looked around, his mouth agape, to see himself surrounded by Clusters, which melted themselves into the stars of the holo viewer. Ellis was wrenched hard into his seat as reality reasserted itself. Grabbing the armrests tightly, he clamped his mouth and eyes shut getting control of the nausea that inevitably followed the jump.

Ellis slowly opened his aching eyes, looking back to the screen as the other members of the bridge also recovered from the jump. In the center, he saw two yellow stars, nearby. On the surface of the larger, was a vast group of dark spots, covering nearly an eighth of the surface area. The commander pursed his lips, realizing they had jumped in near the star system itself. The screen had automatically damped itself. He shook his head; he thought he had seen many stars on the screen as they came out of the jump.

The commander looked to Weiss. "Where's the *Vineyard*? Are they still okay?"

"Communication's established," reported Weiss. "Transferring coordinates to Mr. Rubin's station. The Cluster is still there, still quiet."

Ellis nodded to the pilot. "Approach," he ordered, his voice hushed. He took a deep breath and fished around his rumpled coat. Finally, he located a cigar, thrust it in his mouth and lit it, ignoring the sour look that appeared on the communicator's face.

The ship pivoted on one axis turning away from the double star. He watched, transfixed as the silver orbs of the Cluster came into view one by one. The Cluster appeared to move hypnotically to the center of the screen. Ellis knew it would be impossible to see the black, Erdonium hull of the freighter. "Mark the freighter's position," ordered Ellis, shaking his head, trying to regain concentration.

Weiss nodded and a bright red dot appeared near the Cluster. As the cluster of spheres grew on the ship's holo viewer, Ellis couldn't help but think of his father, who had, like the captain of the *Martha's Vineyard*, commanded a Mao Corporation freighter. Desperately, he wanted to save this crew. In some small way, he hoped it would quiet some of the guilt he felt over his own father's death.

At the same time, Ellis thought about the Cluster over the planet Sufiro. The Cluster's presence had brought an end to a fierce war fought between the two major continents. The continents of Tejo and New Granada united to defend themselves against the Cluster. It had projected images of the war to Ellis along with a feeling of almost loving warmth. The commander took a long draw on his cigar, trying to reconcile the image of the Cluster as caring peacemaker with the image of the Cluster as a cold, unfeeling murderer.

"Mr. Weiss," said the commander, exhaling smoke. "Tell the *Vineyard* to back slowly away from the Cluster." He turned to the pilot. "Mr. Rubin, maneuver ourselves between the Cluster and the freighter. Let's see if we can get the *Vineyard* safely to a jump point."

Weiss and Rubin nodded in unison. "Aye, sir."

"Shall I train ship's guns on the Cluster, sir?" asked Adkins, running her hand through the short hair on the back of her head.

Ellis thought for a moment, his eyes still fixed on the viewer. "Not just yet," he said thoughtfully. "But be ready. We'll use them if we must." Adkins nodded acknowledgment.

Still transfixed by the image of the Cluster on the holo viewer, a thought came to Ellis. He almost didn't believe it was his own, it seemed so ridiculous. If the Cluster could communicate with him, maybe he could communicate with it. His only clue as to how lay in the fact that at Sufiro, the Cluster seemed to speak to his very emotions.

The bridge crew sat tense, watching nervously as the *Martha's Vineyard* and the *Barbara Firebrandt* performed their excruciatingly slow ballet in space. The freighter gradually became visible on the viewer. A few words appeared in the field, indicating that Rubin had touched thrusters to bring the destroyer in front of the freighter.

As they crept toward the freighter, Ellis began to reason that he might be able to communicate with the Cluster if he emoted hard enough at it. "Bah," he said to himself, smoke escaping his lips. "What am I, some kind of damned actor?" Still, he thought, what harm would come in trying it. Ellis took one last draw on the cigar and reached behind him, placing the butt in the incinerator. He sat forward, staring at the hypnotic image. He filled his mind with sensations of warmth, peace and love. He imagined projecting those images at the Cluster.

A flash of intense green light appeared on the screen followed by blinding white light. "Report," barked Ellis, standing. Suddenly, Ellis collapsed to the deck, his head hitting the metal grating with a sickening thud.

* * *

Mark Ellis found himself in a room, not unlike one in the house in which he grew up. The room was cluttered with things ancient and antique. On shelves, he saw Egyptian alabaster urns next to a brass sextant. A Roman shield leaned against a nineteenth century wooden icebox in the middle of the floor. Ellis turned, feeling a presence in the room.

Sitting on a bright red velvet couch that looked to be French, was a woman with black hair and piercing green eyes. She seemed to be wearing nothing, but for some reason Ellis couldn't get a clear view of her. Straight black hair covered her breasts and antiques obscured the rest. Only the unnaturally bright green eyes stood out clearly.

The commander turned at the sound of someone entering. "Dad!" he whispered, before he saw the figure. He had to steady himself on a treadle sewing machine as he turned. His father stood, just like Ellis last remembered seeing him, a stocky man, his hair cut short, wearing the trim suit of a Mao Corporation captain.

The woman stood and slunk, cat-like, to Jerome Ellis. She felt his arms, as though evaluating their strength. With a nod of approval, she kissed him lightly on the cheek. Mark Ellis sucked in air as he watched his father dissolve into ashes before his eyes.

"No!" he cried. He stood and tried to move toward the woman, but found his feet fixed in place. Instead, the woman turned toward him. Effortlessly, she moved heavy antique furniture out of her way. The commander sobbed, feeling helpless as she approached. However, as she came closer, he felt warmth and tenderness, much like the feeling he had at Sufiro. Ellis calmed down. The woman vanished, but Ellis turned to find her standing right behind him. Lithe arms reached out and embraced the commander. Terrified, he found his hands moving to the small of her back, as though under their own power. Continuing downward, his hands grasped cold buttocks.

By all appearances, her body should be supple and soft as she pressed against him. Instead, it was hard like marble and just as unyielding. A cold chill moved up the commander's spine. He saw her lips approach his, almost in slow motion. As she pulled his head closer, he sensed raw power and intelligence. Desire to help her washed over him. Fear crept back through the desire, though, and he tried in vain to pull back. She planted a cold, firm kiss on his mouth.

* * *

Commander John Mark Ellis found himself flat on his back, blinking at a familiar gray ceiling. He knew the pattern of lines almost by heart. He realized he was lying in his own sleeping alcove. "Careful," came a familiar, feminine voice from the side. "You got a minor concussion when you hit the floor."

The commander moaned slightly as he turned his head. His neck felt as though someone had grabbed his head and jerked it 180 degrees. Sitting next to him was the ship's medic. "I've given you some medication for the pain. You should be functional in a few seconds," she said, closing what looked like a black toolbox.

Ellis gritted his teeth. Suddenly, the image of the green beam and the flash poured back into his mind. "How long have I been out?"

"Only a couple of minutes, sir," she reported. She ran short fingers through close-cropped black hair. "Do you want me to stand by at the launch, sir?"

Ellis felt the medication take effect. His body seemed free of the pain binding him to the bed. With a slight push, he sat up on his bunk. He thought about the flash for a moment, and from the medic's comment realized there might be trouble aboard the *Martha's Vineyard*. "Yes." The sound of his own voice caused his head to throb. "You better stand by." As she stood and stepped through the curtain, Ellis saw Rubin waiting anxiously outside. The commander stood, still feeling some pain, and went through the curtain himself.

"Report, Mr. Rubin," ordered Ellis, rubbing the back of his head.

"Sir, the Cluster is gone," he said grimly. "We almost overtook the *Vineyard* when the Cluster fired its ray."

On the bridge, Ellis looked around at the faces staring at him. There was worry mixed with a bit of fear. Weiss looked from Ellis to Rubin. "Confirmed, sir, we have lost all contact with the *Vineyard*. She's been hulled, but it looks like some interior sections were sealed off. I'm not getting any clear bio readings, but some might have survived."

"Prepare the launch," said Ellis, trying to keep his voice from shaking. "Can you download their computer records?"

Weiss shook his head. "They've been damaged beyond repair. It's hard to say whether or not their black box survived."

"I'll go over with the medic and see," said Ellis, half turning.

Rubin grabbed him by the arm. "That was a nasty concussion, sir. I think maybe you should stay here."

Ellis glared at his first officer. His auburn beard seemed almost to bristle. Rubin quickly removed his hand and Ellis stormed to the launch bay at the stern of the ship.

Brushing past the launch crew, he entered the ship and sat down in the pilot's seat next to the medic, Geraldine Brown. After only a couple of minutes, he received the all-clear signal from the bridge to launch.

Wordlessly, Ellis piloted the launch to the black, cylindrical form of the *Martha's Vineyard*. He scanned the ship and found that one of the airlocks was fortuitously connected to the sealed sections. He scanned the ship again, trying to keep his mind off the faces of his own crew. To them, what had happened was horrifying. The Cluster had attacked a ship he was charged with protecting and he had fainted. The commander could hardly believe it himself.

He maneuvered the rear of the launch to connect with the *Vineyard's* airlock. There was a gentle thud as the ships met and a clang as the launch locked on. Ellis gritted his teeth as he opened the airlock door. Before standing, the commander retrieved a small, clipboard-sized computer that fit into the launch's console. On it, he displayed a schematic of the sections of the ship they could enter. Ellis stood, and went to straighten his uniform coat. Only then did he realize that the medic had removed it. He felt strangely naked, wearing only his tight-fitting gray body suit. Scowling, he led the way out into the damaged freighter.

The large metal corridor was empty and deathly silent. Ellis and Brown turned into one of the cargo areas. Opening the door, they were confronted by a large murky water tank. Ellis thought he could discern some small motion in the tank. Brown opened her black toolkit and found a bio scanner. She waved a wand in front of the cloudy reservoir. "Here are your bio readings," she said grimly. "This tank is filled with plankton-like animals. They probably inhabit an asteroid or planet in this system and are being used as food on one of the colonies."

Ellis nodded, gravely. He examined the small computer and followed the map's directions to another section. He opened the door. Nausea welled up in his throat at the sight that greeted him. The remains of a lone person were next to a sealed emergency door. Blood stood in a grisly pool around the upper half of the body. The lower was nowhere to be seen. Brown came up behind Ellis and gasped. "Oh, my God," she whispered at last.

Ellis stepped in gingerly, half-afraid of what else he might see. There were no people, and thankfully no other bodies. Looking around at the appliances mounted to the wall, Ellis realized he was standing in the galley. The man who died was probably the cook. Looking up at the emergency door, Ellis saw the remains of fruits and vegetables splattered across its once shiny surface. When the section ahead had been exposed to vacuum, all loose items had flown toward the opening. The door had come down, but many objects still would have had momentum, slamming them into the door. Brown stepped up and scanned the remains. "This man didn't suffocate," she said. "There are only minor signs of exposure to vacuum."

The commander kneeled down, next to Brown. "He was being blown out into space when the automatic door came down . . ." The commander's voice cracked.

Brown nodded, agreeing with the assessment.

Ellis checked his computer. "Everything forward of this is exposed to space. So is everything rear of the cargo bay. I don't think there's anyone here we can help." The commander looked into the terrified expression frozen by death onto the face of the cook. A tear escaped his own eye and fell, mingling with the pool of blood.

Ellis swallowed hard and concentrated on his computer pad, checking the sections they were in against known records of this class ship. "The black box is unreachable," he said after a moment. "Another ship will have to retrieve it." Ellis stood. "Let's get out of here."

* * *

Saturn, crowned as it was by a lustrous ring, seemed the perfect home for the galaxy's government. Its largest moon, Titan, had for millennia, been dotted by silver hemispheres. Each of the vast domes was home to ambassadors, military personnel, and government officials from every planet in the Confederation of Homeworlds.

People from Earth, Titan's closest neighbor, often wondered how such an expansive civilization could have eluded their sensors and telescopes as long as it had. The fact of the matter was that the moon's inhabitants, the oldest known race of intelligent beings, simply wanted it that way. They refused to discuss the technology they had used to remain cloaked. At least, most rational humans assumed that technology had been at work. There were, as through the centuries, many humans willing to believe magic had been employed.

The Titans themselves were large creatures, covered with soft pelts. Their arms and legs seemed too short for their bulbous torsos. Humans saw their ursine heads with large eyes adapted to low light, and were reminded of Teddy Bears. Those humans in love with conspiracy theories often said that the image of the Teddy Bear had been placed in the minds of President Theodore Roosevelt's friends to pave the way for humanity's eventual acceptance of the ancient race.

The matron of the Titans, a large being with a silver-gray pelt, named Teklar, turned to her lieutenant. "The intelligence continues to probe, to test, to seek. Another Earth ship has been examined. The human, Ellis, is close to understanding. We must be cautious."

* * *

"You fainted?" Admiral Marlou Strauss was looking at the screen in her office on Titan. She shook her head, pursing thin lips. "The Cluster fired on a civilian freighter and you fainted?" She turned to look Ellis in the eye.

Ellis shrunk back from the strength of her gaze. "I wish I could explain, ma'am."

"I wish you could as well." She sat back, folding her hands into a peak. She took a deep breath, evaluating the commander evenly. "Up until this morning, I was prepared to confirm your promotion to captain." Ellis felt his stomach sink at the words. "While your handling of the Sufiro situation was unorthodox, it got the results we required. Erdonium production has resumed. We will be able to build the ships we need to fight the Cluster. We will need experienced officers to command those ships."

Ellis took a deep breath. "Ma'am, I might have an explanation."

"Very well, Mr. Ellis." The admiral put her hands flat on the desktop.

"I think the Cluster communicates through emotional response. While in orbit around Sufiro, I sensed something. I sensed that they were aware of what had happened on the planet – that they knew about the conflict. I sensed they saw the pain and suffering, but knew that their interference had helped to end the conflict." Ellis looked into the admiral's eyes, but did not see any reaction. He swallowed and plunged forward. "You see, the two continents were engaged in war. When the Cluster arrived, the people were so afraid of what it would do, they stopped fighting and helped each other."

"I've read the report," stated the admiral, coldly.

"But, it's not only that I sensed these things. I also sensed a feeling of warmth from the Cluster, a sense that things would be okay on the planet." Ellis leaned forward hopefully.

Strauss leaned back and eyed Ellis frostily. "You're beginning to sound like one of those communicators who goes around the bend and thinks they're psychic." She shook her head. "I don't see how this helps your case."

"I'm not talking about psychic communication," said Ellis, almost desperately. "I'm talking about emotional sensitivity."

"What the Hell's the difference?" asked Strauss, her patience reaching an end.

"My eyes and ears, perhaps even my sense of touch, tell me you're angry. I don't need any special power to know that my career is in jeopardy."

"You have that right, Mister," snapped Strauss.

"Perhaps the Cluster is like that – only more so. Perhaps emotions are their very basis of communication. Couple that with an elaborate holographic technology – not unlike the Rd'dyggians have – and you have something that looks like visions," Ellis explained. "If the Cluster can sense emotions, I reasoned that they could tell the difference between random signals, so to speak, and those emotions directed at them. As we were approaching the *Martha's Vineyard* I attempted to project my emotions at the Cluster."

Strauss threw her hands into the air. "Now I know you've gone around the bend." She stood and paced behind the desk for several minutes. Finally she stopped and stared at Ellis with Arctic blue eyes. "You are trying to tell me that you tried unauthorized communication with that thing and it responded by destroying the *Vineyard*?"

Ellis looked to the ground. "I suppose I am, ma'am."

She sat down, leaning across the desk. "Well, get this straight and get it straight right now. You are damned lucky I don't believe you. If I did, you would be facing a court martial board for endangering civilians. Do you understand?"

"Yes, ma'am." Ellis' voice was no more than a whisper.

She sat back, folding her arms tightly across her stomach. "Look, Mark," she said, her voice softening slightly. "As far as many of the Admirals here are concerned, the only reason you succeeded at Sufiro was because the leader of one of the warring continents was your grandfather, Ellison Firebrandt." She measured her words. "They believe you used nepotism to reach an end, even if it was a favorable end. They are worried that you might not be able to solve a crisis where you didn't have such an edge."

Ellis wrung his hands. He had wondered exactly the same thing numerous times during the return journey.

"I stuck my neck out for you, Mister. I convinced them you had done a hell of a job." Again, she shook her head. "Then you had to go on that rescue mission. All you had to do was get the *Vineyard* behind you and to safety. For the record, there was nothing you could have done if the Cluster was going to attack. But, fainting when they attack is not acceptable, Mister. What happens when you get into a true battle situation? Will you simply faint away and let your XO take your command?"

"Ma'am," said Ellis, trying not to sound choked up. "I still think there's a reasonable chance of communication with the Cluster."

"Stop pursuing this communication nonsense!" Strauss ground her teeth. "You are in danger of a court-martial!" Her voice became a dangerous whisper. "If you shut up now, I am prepared to reinstate you as first lieutenant on a star cruiser. You have a good record. It's possible I might be able to give you another crack at Commander in a couple of years."

"A demotion," muttered Ellis, heart-broken. "I'm not sure I can accept that."

Strauss closed her eyes, her patience taxed to the limit. "Then you had better be prepared to resign your commission."

Ellis looked up at her, his brown eyes wide, jaw hanging open. He thought for a moment about arguing that the fleet had to do what it could to at least try to communicate with the Cluster before more tragedy struck. The look in her eyes warned him off that path. He sighed, though, knowing he must find the Cluster. He must talk to the Cluster. Somehow, he knew it was the only correct answer. John Mark Ellis took a deep breath and without thinking about it too much longer, lest he stop himself, he let the words fall out. "Admiral Strauss, I hereby resign my commission as an officer of the Confederation Space Fleet."

The admiral closed her eyes for a second, then turned back to her terminal. "I expect your belongings off the *Firebrandt* in 24 hours."

Where No One Knows Your Name

John Mark Ellis stood in a silent hallway outside admiralty headquarters in the human pressure dome on Titan and thrust his hands deep into the pockets of his jacket. The silence should have given him time to think about how to contact the Cluster. Instead, he found himself wallowing in despair, simply wanting to escape. He cursed mildly as he felt around the pocket and realized he had crushed a cigar. He removed the damaged cigar and examined it. Scowling, he thrust it in his mouth and lit it anyway. Smoke issued from a myriad of cracks in the surface.

He looked up just in time to see Frank Rubin stepping his way, waving a computer wafer. "Sir!" called Rubin excitedly. His booming voice echoed off the walls. "I just received a promotion!"

"Congratulations," grumbled Ellis. He bit down hard on the cigar, almost chopping off the end with his teeth.

"Is something the matter, sir?" Concern showed in Rubin's wide blue eyes.

"Calling me 'sir' isn't appropriate anymore, Mr. Rubin," snorted Ellis. He looked down at his wrist chronometer and nodded. "I've got just about enough time to get to the space port and catch a flight to Earth. Would you be so kind as to send my duffel down to my home on Nantucket?"

"Of course, but . . ." Rubin's mouth hung open as Ellis stormed off through the white corridor. The newly promoted A-Com bit his lower lip, feeling frozen in place. Finally he gathered his wits and ran to catch up with his former commander. When he almost caught up to Ellis, he saw him turn to enter the busy spaceport area. Ellis plowed a straight line through the crowd toward the ticket counter, smoke issuing hurly-burly from the crushed cigar like a fog bank surrounding his head. Rubin was nearly out of breath when he finally reached Ellis leaving the counter, ticket in hand.

"Can you believe that?" grumbled Ellis around the forlorn cigar, waving the ticket in Rubin's face. "The only flight to Earth tonight is on one of those tramp freighters that doesn't even have graviton generators."

"What's going on?" Rubin brushed the ticket away from his face.

Ellis was still waving the ticket, unmindful of Rubin. "Have to ride all the way to Earth on some smelly ship that doesn't even have gravity." He looked down at the ticket. "They don't even serve a goddamn meal!"

"Sounds relaxing." Rubin's voice dripped sarcasm. He looked into his former commander's eyes. "Sir, what's the matter? What happened in there with Admiral Strauss?"

Ellis finally removed the cigar, his expression softening a bit toward Rubin. Again, he looked down at his wrist chronometer. "This flight, such as it is, doesn't leave for another hour. Let me buy you a drink and I'll tell you about it."

Again, Rubin found himself following Ellis through the crowd. This time, however, the pace was less frantic. The two sat down at a gleaming silver bar. Ellis ordered scotch. Rubin declined a drink.

By this time, Rubin had guessed what happened. At first, he had been frightened when Ellis had fainted as the Cluster attacked the *Martha's Vineyard*. Knowing the commander as well as he did, it simply seemed impossible. When Ellis had returned from the *Vineyard*, his suspicions had been confirmed. The Cluster had communicated with him a second time. "I don't get it, why wouldn't they confirm your promotion to captain? What about the Cluster? What about Sufiro?"

The drink arrived and Ellis downed it in one shot and ordered another. "They say Sufiro was an accident. They say I couldn't have handled the crisis without my grandfather's help." He stared at the empty glass. "As to the Cluster. They simply won't believe I've been in communication with it. They think I'm making the whole thing up."

"What?" Rubin looked toward the bartender and waved him over. He decided he needed a beer. "I can't believe they're going to cashier you over Sufiro."

"They weren't that upset about Sufiro." Ellis shook his head. "They canned me because I fainted on the bridge of my own goddamned ship."

"But you didn't faint," stammered Rubin. He tried to find words but failed. He might have known what really happened to Ellis, but it could not change how the admiralty saw the situation.

The second glass of scotch arrived at the same time as Rubin's beer. Ellis picked up the glass and stared into the golden liquid. He returned the cigar to his mouth for a moment. Finally, he set it down to let it burn out the rest of the way. "Besides, they didn't exactly cashier me," he said quietly. "I could have returned to active duty as first lieutenant aboard a star cruiser."

Rubin took a long swallow of beer. "You mean you quit?" The lieutenant looked behind the bar, into a large mirror. He looked at his own face, then turned to Ellis again. "Why?"

"I've got to find the Cluster," said Ellis just before swallowing the second scotch in one gulp. "I can't do that as first officer of a star cruiser." He leaned back against the bar. "Besides, what do you suppose the odds would be of my being promoted again?"

"Pretty damn high," said Rubin forcefully. "You're a good officer, any captain would see that. The Cluster can't be that important." He began to turn red. "You can't throw away your career for it!"

"Who says I'm throwing away my career?" Ellis waved off the comment, turning on the stool, so he wouldn't have to look Rubin in the eye. "I'm still on the reserve list. The admiral says that if an emergency comes up, they'll reinstate me."

Rubin snorted frustration. "Mark," he said. Ellis turned as though struck by an electric charge. The use of his first name was almost too much to bear. "Mark, tell me this, how are you going to find the Cluster without the Fleet?"

"The Ellis family has a little money and my mother has some influence," said Ellis thoughtfully. "I'll find a way." Sighing, he returned the glass to the bar. He looked across the crowds of people between the bar and the gate where his ship was docked. "I'd better go," said Ellis, his head down.

Frank Rubin sighed. "Take care of yourself," he said, his normally deep, booming voice quiet.

Ellis took Rubin's hand. "Godspeed Mr. A-Com Rubin." He reached out and embraced his one-time first officer. Ellis reached into his uniform jacket and retrieved his last cigar. "I'll be back," he said with a devilish grin. With that, Rubin watched John Mark Ellis disappear into the crowd.

* * *

Clyde McClintlock wrote furiously. He did not write about anything in particular. Instead he wrote down everything that was on his mind. He wrote about his family moving to Sufiro from Iowa. He wrote about his early years in the Gaean military and his decision to leave to assume a career in the military on Sufiro. With a sigh, he wondered if he had abandoned honor for glory.

Flipping the page in his pad of paper, he started writing down as many of the images the Cluster put into his mind as he could remember. He wrote about a young man, a teenager actually, pulled from his yard in New Granada while teaching his little sister to ride a bicycle. The boy had been forced to work in the Tejan mines. Although Clyde had not been directly responsible for that boy's predicament, he had fought for the country that had stolen the boy from his family.

Clyde stared at the paper after he wrote this scene. He wondered what would have happened if the Cluster had not put that, and other, images in his mind. If not for the Cluster, Clyde would have been unaware of the downtrodden in New Granada. The scenes were packed with emotional energy. Why had the Cluster shown these scenes to him?

Clyde held the paper to his chest, and vowed silently to find the answer.

* * *

John Mark Ellis arrived at the spaceport in Boston feeling grungy. His jacket hung askew over the top of his rumpled jump suit. His auburn hair felt too long and kept falling into his eyes. Not only had there been no gravity on the freighter from Titan, there had been no showers. Consequently, his beard ached, sticky with dried sweat. The one thing there had been on the cruiser was a teleholo. Mark Ellis tried desperately to drive the image of his mother's face as he told her about leaving the fleet, from his mind. Ellis searched his coat desperately for a cigar. He growled when he remembered he had smoked his last cigar on Titan.

Ellis' eyelids felt heavy, despite the fitful nap he had managed to catch on the two-hour trip to Earth. He stood in the dingy port, realizing he was too tired to make the trip home to Nantucket, but too many thoughts buzzed to allow him to sleep. Grumbling, he ran his fingers through his hair, disheveling it even further. His stomach growled.

Ignoring the crowds, he stepped out of the port and made his way to a motel that looked as grungy as he felt. Bright neon meant to be cheery only added to the building's dismal appearance. Inside the lobby, he rang the little electric bell. A bald man with four days' growth of beard stepped up to the counter.

"I need a room for the night," said Ellis wearily.

"No rooms," rasped the man. "Just compartments."

"Great," muttered Ellis, handing his credit chit to the man. The man took more time than necessary processing the chit. Finally, he handed Ellis the chit and key.

"You staying more than the night," sneered the man.

"Not if I can help it," said Ellis, snatching the key. He stormed out to the street without visiting the compartment he had reserved. He knew the space would be no more than a cabinet. He didn't really care, but it did remind him of how crowded the planet was. He would be glad to get back to his spacious house on Nantucket.

Ellis stood in the street trying to sort out his feelings. Mostly, he felt numb, not sure where or how to begin his search. Still, there was some gnawing, underlying feeling. In his mind, he saw Admiral Marlou

Strauss, angry. He saw his mother, disappointed and trying to understand. The green eyes of the woman from Ellis' vision haunted him. The ex-commander's mind was muddled with images of women tormenting him, hounding him, and giving him platitudes. His stomach rumbled again, reminding him he hadn't eaten since well before the meeting. All these feelings combined together, causing a dark memory to surface. Ellis knew where he would go for food.

Numbly, Ellis hailed a hover taxi. "Take me to Cambridge," he said to the cabby.

"Sure you wanna' go there sailor?" asked the hack with a sour laugh. "It's gonna cost."

"Fine," said Ellis as he climbed in the back behind the hepler-proof glass. After a moment, when the cabby didn't lift off, Ellis rapped on the glass. The cabby simply pointed downward. Ellis sighed, looking at the slot for the credit chit. He inserted the chit and the cabby lifted off.

A few minutes later, Ellis found himself standing across from one of the ancient ivy-covered buildings that used to be part of Harvard University. Now, the red brick building covered in rotting ivy was a tenement house for as many people as it could hold.

Ellis thrust his hands deep in his pockets and walked up Garden Street to another large brick enclosure topped by a lurid, gleaming dome. The dome, in turn, was covered in blinking neon proclaiming the name "Hernando's." He nodded satisfactorily, seeing the building that once was Harvard College Observatory. The city lights gleaming brilliantly and exotically off the pollution in the air above had rendered the building useless as a research facility long ago. The photographic plates that had captured images of the heavens now sat collecting dust in the basement of a West Coast museum. Humans, possessing the stars for themselves, were not interested in the antiques. The door opened and a cacophony of voices and music poured out with the people who emerged. Ellis took a deep breath and stepped through the door.

Inside, the walls were black, but glaring spotlights illuminated stages and tables. The erotic sounds of twentieth century rock music throbbed through the very fibers of Ellis' being. The air was filled with pungent smoke. It helped enhance his grungy demeanor. He paid a cover charge to a man standing just inside the door and made his way to a table facing one of the small stages.

A woman wearing enticingly little slunk up to the table and took his drink order. "Scotch, neat," said Ellis, brusquely.

Soon, a short woman stepped onto the stage as new musical rhythms began. Ellis recognized the heavy beat of Arabic belly dance music. He looked at the woman on the stage as she began to move in time to the music, thrusting her hips to the pulsing rhythms. Ellis' drink arrived and he paid the bill.

Ellis looked back to the woman on stage, watching her taut brown skin and dark eyes. She gave him a smile and reached behind her back, undoing the scanty silver bikini top. She swung the top over her head and dropped it to the stage. Ellis found his eyes drawn to her pert, firm breasts, bouncing to the music. He smiled in a kind of delirious amusement as he saw them jiggle and jump. He noted the little bumps surrounding her nipples and how they were just slightly imperfect, not like the even symmetries of the spheres of the Cluster.

Ellis frowned, stunned at the thought. He grabbed his glass of scotch and sipped it, then looked back at the dancer. The beat became heavier and she thrust her hips toward him. Still, Ellis' eyes lingered on her breasts, his thoughts tarrying on how they continued to remind him of the Cluster.

Finally, the music stopped and there was muted applause. Most of the men in the room sat in a stupor. The waitress ambled by and refreshed Ellis' drink. Ellis let his eyes wander over the other patrons. He was stunned to see two beings with orange skin and purple mustache-like growths sitting at one of the other stages. "What would Rd'dyggian warriors find interesting in a place like this?" Ellis asked himself. He stood and stepped over to their table. He saw they were wearing translator boxes.

"Welcome to our humble planet." Ellis tried to sound enthused.

The lead Rd'dyggian grunted, his "mustache" wiggling. Ellis recognized the gesture as polite acknowledgment. They remained facing the stage, though and Ellis wondered why Rd'dyggians would even be interested in human women. Their sexual triggers were quite different. For one thing, Rd'dyggian women did not even have teats of any form. Ellis shook his head and sat down at the table ignored by the seven-foot tall warriors. The next woman who took the stage was pale with black hair and large, ebullient breasts. Her glistening red nipples seemed all wrong against the gleaming surface of her pale white skin.

Ellis swallowed his second drink in one gulp and sighed. He had come to this place to find some sense of release. He tried to let himself be drug into the music and the undulating body on the stage. He was angry, hurt, and lost. In a way, what he wanted was to spend a night viewing women as sex objects and not as colleagues. Yet, these women seemed no more real than the woman in the Cluster vision did. Even more frustrating, he found he could not stop his eyes from wandering to the women's breasts, which also reminded him of the Cluster.

Finally, Ellis gave up trying to find anything erotic in the figure dancing before him. He looked back at the Rd'dyggians and realized that it was not simple curiosity that had brought him to the table. On Sufiro, the Rd'dyggian warrior, Arepno, had helped his grandfather Firebrandt. In a sense, Ellis was looking for a Rd'dyggian to help with his current dilemma. Painfully, Ellis realized that he was not going to receive any help from the Rd'dyggians who were still absorbed in the music. Cursing mildly, he stood and made his way through the room to a table standing alone in a dark corner of the bar. Idly, he picked up the menu, scanning it quickly.

Many minutes later, a waitress arrived and he gave her his order for a hamburger and fries. The throbbing music reawakened the headache that had been pulsing mildly since his head hit the deck grating many hours before. He tapped his foot impatiently waiting for the food to arrive. It was time, he decided to eat and get back to his cabinet for a night's sleep.

When he heard a throat clear behind him, he lifted his arms from the table, assuming it was dinner. He was actually a little annoyed to discover it was one of the dancers. Golden hair tumbled over a black negligee.

"Table dance?" she asked with a smile that was too white.

Ellis eyed her with some exasperation. "No thanks," he sighed. She looked disappointed and turned to leave. Ellis looked at the floor. As she began to move toward another table, he looked up and cleared his throat. She looked around, hopefully. "Do you know where I could find a cigar?"

The dancer eased back to the table, eyeing him with a curious expression. "Cigars are made from tobacco aren't they?"

"The ones I'm looking for are." He smirked.

The dancer shimmied by Ellis and sat at the table. "Tobacco is illegal on Earth, sailor boy."

He looked down at his uniform, then back at the dancer. "May I buy you a drink?"

"Sure," she cooed. "I was beginning to think you were a eunuch. I've never seen a man look so coldly at a woman's body. It's as though you were studying for some kind of exam."

"I guess I'm so used to seeing naked women that this just doesn't faze me much." Ellis gestured around the room. The piping hot food arrived and he ordered a drink for the dancer.

"A sailor through and through," she said. Her too-pink lips framed her too-perfect smile. "They say that men and women aren't even segregated on those Navy ships. You even sleep together."

Ellis took a bite of the greasy hamburger and put it down thinking. "We sleep in adjoining bunks."

She thrust her too-round breasts toward him. "But do any of the sailor women look like this?" Her pale skin was free of all imperfection save a mole on the exposed portion of her shoulder. She looked sculpted in every way. In fact, Ellis realized she must be. This dancer was simply the product of thirtieth century biotechnology. Anyone could have the body they wanted, if they were willing to pay the price.

"When I was a kid, I remember my mother going around the house naked. It used to drive my father crazy." Ellis shook his head. "She's taller and thinner than you, but still..." Ellis took a bite of the hamburger, letting his thoughts trail off, afraid of where they would lead.

"That's sick," she giggled. Her voice did not mirror her words. Instead, she almost seemed amused by Ellis. "But most people who come in here are sick... love sick, that is."

"Lust sick is what my grandfather would say," said Ellis with a wistful smile.

"Why did you come in here?" She eased a little closer to him.

"I guess I'm looking for escape and maybe some answers."

"Ooh," she whispered teasingly. "Sounds mysterious."

"Do you see the news holos?" asked Ellis. "Have you heard about the Cluster?"

"Have I heard?" she laughed outright. "When would I get time to watch a holo broadcast? I have dance practice." She looked at him and let her tongue play over her lips. "I see now, you've come in here to find some escape from all those nasty Clusters."

"It would help if I had a cigar."

"All we sell are marijuana cigarettes. Those are legal."

Ellis buried his face in his hands. "Shit," he whispered under his breath. "Those things will play with your mind worse than tobacco."

"But they won't kill you as fast," she tittered. She pulled out one of the thin cigarettes and lit it. "You don't mind, do you?"

Ellis shook his head. "I suppose not," he said, coughing as she blew curling smoke in his direction. After years of smoking cigars, he found it odd how much the smoke from these legal cigarettes bothered him. His appetite ruined and his headache growing worse, Ellis ordered something non-alcoholic to drink and sat back.

The music changed again. At first, Ellis thought it was ancient classical. Instead, it was something silken and flowing from the mid-twenty-fifth century. He began to sway with the rhythm. "How about that table dance?" he asked, figuring the marijuana smoke must have been getting to him.

She stood and moved to the open floor. Her body undulated in smooth time to the music. Ellis kept his eyes focused on her soft blue eyes, so different from the hard eyes of Admiral Strauss or the piercing green eyes of the woman in the vision. These eyes seemed to call to him, pleading and loving. Again, she smiled and Ellis' stomach seemed to drop as he felt a long denied pressure build at his crotch.

She removed the thin black garment that barely concealed her upper body. Ellis forced himself to look. Again, the two perfect breasts reminded him of the Cluster. He sighed and looked back into her eyes and saw dimples form on either side of her perfect smile.

When the music stopped she returned to the seat at the table. "Finally, we see a human being," she said, wrapping her garment back around her body.

"Maybe love sick is right," said Ellis. "How much do I owe you?"

"That dance is on the house," she said. "It was worth it just to see you lighten up, if only a bit." She leaned forward, putting her hand on his leg. "If it's release you're looking for, I'll blow you for a thousand."

Ellis felt himself flush. With the flush crept an awareness of being on Earth in the zealously religious American sector. Although exotic dancing was tolerated, what she proposed was extraordinarily dangerous. "For someone who's appalled by illegal things, you seem awfully ready to take risks." Ellis' voice was strained. Even so, he was sorely tempted to take her up on the offer. "But why so much?"

"Gotta pay the tax man somehow?" She gave his leg a quick squeeze. Her voice was confident, but her eyes pleaded with Ellis. She too was seeking release.

Suddenly, a chill ran down Ellis' back. He felt hot breath tickle his hair.

"No touching the ladies," came a cold, harsh voice behind him.

The dancer quickly removed her silken hand from his leg. Ellis stood and turned to face a man who was nearly a head taller. He had heard about men with no necks, but this was the first time he had actually met one. He spread his hands wide. "I wasn't touching her, she was touching me."

The bouncer frowned. His trim white shirt outlined perfectly formed muscles. "You callin' the lady a liar?" Then he leaned close to Ellis. "I think it's time you left."

"What? I haven't done anything."

The bouncer spun him around so fast he didn't have time to react. Ellis found himself being picked up by the collar and seat of the pants. Even knowing that he couldn't get out of the position, he struggled to get free as he saw the variety of lights and colors pass by. With a whoosh, he felt cold night air on his face momentarily followed by the stinging sensation of hard plastic smacking him in the face.

Ellis groaned as he sat up on the plastic street and looked back at the bouncer, who turned to go back inside the building that, for centuries, had been a center for education. Ellis' muscles screamed as he tried to stand. He wiped some blood off his chin and spat, feeling far worse than when he arrived. His head throbbed so badly it was difficult to see.

He hailed a cab and returned to the motel near the spaceport.

* * *

Clyde McClintlock looked up at the husky sound of a clearing throat. Standing on the other side of the force field was a guard in a white uniform. "Dinner time, already?" asked Clyde, listlessly.

"You have a visitor," grunted the large, bald guard, standing aside.

A tall, slender woman with black hair streaked gray stepped up. She looked at Clyde with a deeply penetrating gaze. "It's been a long time, Clyde." Her voice was silken, smooth.

Clyde McClintlock stood and straightened the nondescript prison uniform. He ran fingers over his prematurely gray hair, straightening it as best he could without a comb. "Suki Firebrandt Ellis?" His voice was barely a whisper, since he hardly believed the sight of the woman he had known since childhood.

She smiled lopsidedly and turned to the guard, putting her long, but not delicate hand on her hip. "Get lost," she ordered.

Dumbfounded, the guard trudged away and left the woman called Fire alone with the prisoner.

"We have to talk," said Fire. She looked around at the stark, white prison corridor. "But not here."

Clyde laughed nervously. "It's not like I have a lot of choice in my situation."

"Fact of the matter is, Clyde, you're putting the peace between New Granada and Tejo in jeopardy." Fire leaned against the doorframe. "In Tejo, you're a prisoner because you led a military coup. In both New Granada and Tejo, there are those who regard you as a hero. You recognized the atrocities your government was committing against my people." She shrugged. "I think it's too little, too late, myself."

"I imagine most people in New Granada would like to skin me alive though," Clyde said hoarsely.

"Some would," she admitted.

"Would you?"

Fire inclined her head. "I'm not sure yet."

Clyde McClintlock dropped into the unyielding chair. Fire started pacing, her hands on her hips. "If you go to trial and get hit with a heavy sentence, people on both sides will riot," explained Fire. "If you get let off, others will likely riot."

"Your problem, not mine." Clyde looked up.

Fire stopped pacing and stared into the cell. "Either way, you'll be in danger."

Clyde shook his head, ambivalent. "I don't get it. Is this what you wanted to talk about?"

Fire looked at her watch and performed a slight mental calculation. "I said, I don't want to talk about that here." Seeing Clyde's perplexed expression, she explained. "We need to pull you out of the equation, diffuse the powder keg, as it were. The peace between Tejo and New Granada must last."

"That's fine and good," said Clyde standing. "But I'm not exactly in a position to pack up my bags." He looked around the cell.

Fire looked at her watch again. She took a furtive glance down the hall, then reached a hand down the green T-shirt between her ample breasts. Clyde stared, despite himself. She retrieved a small descrambler and affixed it to the door control. "I can get you out of here. We can take you out of the equation. Let you disappear," she whispered.

"Yes, but there are guards, we can't get out that way," protested Clyde.

"Be that as it may," said Fire, grinning. She activated the descrambler, dropping the force field. As Clyde began to step out, Fire shoved him rudely back into the cell and followed him in. "Get down," she ordered, tipping the bed over between them and the wall.

Just then, there was a deafening blast. Alarm klaxons sounded their plaintive, anxious cries even before plastic shrapnel settled to the ground. Clyde looked up from behind the bed to see Manuel Raton holding two rifles, his broad white grin framed by a thick black mustache. "Not a bad jail break, eh?"

Fire grabbed Clyde by the collar and started pulling him through the opening. Clyde stopped and wriggled himself free to sift through the rubble. "We don't have time for this," growled Fire as she took a rifle from Raton.

"Found it!" said Clyde, holding up a pad of paper. He bolted for the ragged hole in the wall.

Return to the Sea

To a geologist, the island of Nantucket is little more than a giant sandbar. To a historian, Nantucket was the center of the American whaling industry for over a hundred years. To John Mark Ellis, Nantucket was home. Even in the thirtieth century, there really were only two ways to get to the island, on the water or over it. To John Mark Ellis, it was virtual sacrilege to travel the forty miles of ocean to the island via hover transport. To him, this was a journey that must be made on the water itself.

Ellis stood on the bow of a ferry out of Hyannis Port, letting the salt air blow past him, cleansing him of the dark emotions he felt. The gray spring day with waters lapping violently at the boat reflected his state of mind perfectly. Neither angry nor cheery, he felt driven by a sense of purpose. He caught his breath as he saw the island appear on the horizon. To the tourists on the boat, it was nothing more than a lump of nondescript earth between gray-green waters and light gray sky. Already, though, Ellis could imagine the bustle of boats at anchor in the port. In his mind, he could see the green of the trees and shrubs atop the sand.

Ellis sighed gently as he saw the old white Brant Point lighthouse at the entrance to the harbor. The one-time space commander smiled broadly as he saw the steeple of the ancient village church rising from the greenery, pointing to the sky from whence he had returned. Ellis hugged himself, knowing he was home.

Mark Ellis was positively giddy as he got off the ferry and turned onto the ancient cobblestone main street. However, as he stepped into the old brick news shop called "The Hub" a great loneliness hit him. His stomach sank as he thought about the times he would come here as a child with his father, newly returned from space. "Hiya Mark," said the man behind the counter, snapping Ellis out of his melancholy. Ellis sighed and purchased a news disk.

"Need any cigars today?" asked the man behind the counter. The grizzled shopkeeper watched Ellis, perplexed as he patted his dirty uniform coat, thinking for a few moments. Finally, Ellis shook his head, no.

"When's your mother gonna be back?" asked the shopkeeper. "They miss her up at the natural sciences museum."

"I'm sure they do," said Ellis. He remembered the odd look she'd given him when she said she had some business to take care of on Sufiro before she came home. "She might be some time still," mumbled Ellis. He knew his mother, Suki Ellis, the director of the Maria Mitchell Association, all too well.

Ellis tucked the news disk in his pocket and stepped out of the shop. He strolled up the street, happy to see the clean red brick mansions and grand white houses among the ancient gray structures. To him, Nantucket was the only purely human place left on Earth.

At last, he reached the door of the old family home. Hidden sensors scanned his eyes and unlocked the door. Turning the polished brass knob, he stepped inside. He was somewhat taken aback to see his duffel bag already inside. On top of the tattered green bag was a note. As he extracted the news disk from the pocket of his uniform coat, Ellis realized Old Coffin probably brought the bags inside. Picking up the note, his suspicions were confirmed.

He nodded to himself, making a mental note to go out and visit the old family friend at his home in Madaket. Unceremoniously, he picked up the duffel bag and hauled it up the creaking wooden stairs into his bedroom. On his way, though, he paused by the door of the master bedroom; the one occupied by his mother. He decided not to violate her privacy, even though he was curious if any of his father's possessions were still in the room.

Down the hall, Ellis tossed the duffel into the old slope-ceilinged room that had long been his own and proceeded to peel himself out of his unwashed navy uniform. Silently, he padded naked across the hardwood floor to the shower. He let the hot, high-pressure water strip away layers of dirt and sweat that clung ungraciously to his body. Finally, he toweled himself off, returned to his room and stood staring at a closet full of outdated clothes. After only a couple of minutes pondering, he picked out a black T-shirt and a comfortable pair of tan slacks.

Feeling reborn, Ellis went back down the old staircase to the living room of the house. His eyes fell on an antique pipe rack. He sighed, thinking how much history there was in those pipes. He grabbed an old curved one that his great great grandfather had owned and stuffed it in his pants pocket.

Stepping out the back door into an overgrown green yard, Ellis found his old black bicycle. He frowned as he saw the state of the chain and cursed the humid salt air. Automatically, he assumed the old homecoming ritual of retrieving oil and rags to revitalize the only transportation, besides feet, he allowed himself on the island.

After an hour of work, he had the bicycle back in operating condition.

Trying not to get the spokes tangled in long grass, he finally got the bike out to the street. Ellis sighed, looking at the cobblestones, but hopped on the bicycle anyway and peddled off, bouncing painfully until he finally reached the smooth plastic roadway that led to Madaket.

Ellis was fond of neither the plastic roadway nor the hovers that buzzed by overhead. Sighing, he applied himself to the job of pedaling, concentrating more on the smells of the greenery and the sounds of the birds around. He was thankful the hovers were, at least, silent. The gray cloud layer overhead was breaking up, revealing a crystalline blue. After ten minutes of pedaling, Ellis was very nearly winded. He grumbled at how out of shape he had become, sitting around in the narrow confines of star cruisers. Gritting his teeth, he peddled another fifteen minutes until he, at last, reached the conglomeration of houses that made up the tiny village of Madaket. Turning down a dirt road, he reached a building that was little more than a shack. Hopping off the bike, he propped it against the weathered, gray wall and knocked on the door.

The man who answered the door looked at Ellis with sharp blue eyes, outlined by crows' feet. He wore a thin, white beard. A black, fisher's hat topped his head. His deeply tanned chest revealed a mixture of muscles and sags that showed this to be a man who had worked hard all his life. Ellis reddened slightly at the thought of his protruding stomach and brow sweating after a brief bike ride. He blushed at the thought of his skin, pale as the underside of a fish.

"John Mark," wheezed the man after several moments. "I didn't recognize you with that beard. For a minute, I thought I'd seen a ghost. You look like your grandfather, Zechariah."

Ellis smiled warmly. "How are you doing, Coffin?"

"Like my name, I feel like death." The old man smiled wanly and motioned for Ellis to come in. "Care for some tea?"

Ellis nodded, looking for a place to sit. The inside of the house was filled to the brim with compasses, sextants, and netting. Seashells were piled in one corner. Ancient starfish were nailed to a wall. Light ship baskets hung from the ceiling along with a carved whale. After a cursory glance, Ellis finally found a couch made of wood and canvas. He pushed aside twenty years worth of sailor's almanacs to find room to sit.

The old man returned from the kitchen with an old ceramic cup, handing it to Ellis. "Your mother called up last night, concerned about you. I hear you've landed yourself some trouble, young man," wheezed Old Man Coffin, turning to scan his pile of maritime artifacts.

"Have you been following the news about the conflict with the

Cluster?" Ellis took a tentative sip of the tea. He made a face when he realized it was Earl Grey. It wouldn't be so bad if it had not been brewed too strongly.

The older man reached behind a net hammock and retrieved a folding deck chair. He took painfully long minutes to unfold the chair. "I can't turn on the holo without seeing something of the war. If it's not a news broadcast, it's a movie," he cackled.

"I was relieved from duty because I tried to talk to the Cluster." Ellis leaned forward slightly.

Old Man Coffin let out a boisterous laugh that dissolved into a coughing fit. Ellis put down the teacup and stood to pat the old man on the back. Coffin looked up at Ellis with tears in his eyes and a grin. "And I used to think it was funny that you and your daddy would go talk to whales!"

Ellis shrugged, returning to his seat on the couch. "People have been talking to whales for years."

"But only you and a few others have broken down the barriers and actually managed to befriend them, really understanding them as individuals." The old man looked toward the ceiling. "It's funny, but here we are two species that evolved on the same planet, but they are almost as alien to us as those amoeba things that come from Zahar." Finally, the old man looked back at Ellis. "If anyone can understand the Cluster, it's you."

Retrieving the tea, Ellis sat thinking about the whales. "Do you think the whales could help me understand how to talk to the Cluster?"

"It's hard to say what the whales can help you understand." The old man scratched silver stubble on his chin. "If anyone can, though, it's Richard. I'd talk to him. Your father was always fond of that old bull."

Ellis sipped the tea. "But even if the whales help me understand," he said after a moment. "I'll need to get back to space to talk to the Cluster. There might be a reasonable amount of Ellis money, but it's definitely not enough to purchase a space ship."

"Oh, you'll find a ship," said the old man. "Like your father, it's in your nature. It would be impossible for you to stay away from space or the sea." Ellis looked at the old man quizzically. "Oh, it might not be a Navy ship, but you'll find something. It won't take long before you'll need to get another job as it is."

Ellis sat up straight. "What do you mean? Last I knew there was pretty much enough money in the family accounts to let me retire even at my age."

The old man opened his arms and gestured around the shack. "At one time, my family could have claimed that as well." Sitting back, the old man rummaged around in a pile of papers and retrieved a jar full of one-inch square brown patches. From his pocket, he pulled an ornately carved meerschaum pipe reddened from age and use. He crumbled one of the patches into the pipe and lit it. "Taxes are going up all the time."

"Surely they wouldn't do anything to the property while mom runs Maria Mitchell," said Ellis.

"Your mother is a talented woman," said Coffin. "However, director of the association is largely an honorary position. If she stays away too long, they'll find someone else connected to an old Nantucket family to take her place. If the Association is too broke, they'll let her go and not bother to replace her. The Maria Mitchell Association is in danger of vanishing as we all are."

"The islanders will band together," said Ellis, a horrified frown forming. "We can't be kicked off our land."

"It's happened almost everywhere else that tourists love. Look at what happened in Santa Fe, centuries ago; Martha's Vineyard not too long ago." The old man held out the jar. Ellis retrieved one of the patches and sniffed it tentatively. "Navy Flake tobacco," grunted the old man.

Putting down the teacup, Ellis retrieved the pipe from his pocket. Thinking about Coffin's words, he awkwardly crumbled the tobacco into the pipe and tried lighting it. It didn't light well at first, but he tamped it down some more and another application of the lighter got it going. The tobacco was somewhat harsh, but that fit Ellis' mood perfectly. He nodded approvingly.

"If you like that, I've got twenty ounces around here somewhere. I could give you some." Coffin smiled.

Ellis nodded. "I'd like that." Finally he leaned forward again. "How long do you think I have?"

"Until what?"

"Until the money runs out?"

Coffin took a long draw on the pipe stem and exhaled slowly. "It's hard to say. At the rate they're raising taxes, I'll probably have to move off the island before you do. I'd say it's more like years than months, if you're lucky and your mother does return."

"What would you do, if you had to move off the island?" asked Ellis, his brow knitted.

"I'd probably die," said the old man, looking out his window at the moors and ocean, beyond. The two men sat, smoking in silence for much of the rest of the afternoon.

* * *

Clyde McClintlock was not completely sure how he ended up in a hover traveling nearly 200 miles per hour over sparkling white sand. More specifically, he knew the sequence of events, but was not sure why Suki Ellis and Manuel Raton of all people would want to break him out of prison. After all, Manuel had been the opposing general in the campaign against New Granada. Likewise, Suki was the mother of the man responsible for his defeat. Having them risk their lives made no sense to him. At this point, he did not value his own life enough for all this trouble. However, he was not in a position to question Suki and Manuel's motivation. Instead, he was busy keeping his head out of range of hepler fire and stray bullets. While he didn't attribute much value to his life, he wasn't about to just throw it away either.

"Only fifty more miles to Roanoke!" called Raton, from the driver's seat.

Fire knelt in the back seat, holding an ancient rifle, pointed to the rear. She was carefully watching three hovers close in, in tight formation. The hovers kicked up great clouds of white sand. Their own hover was wheezing from sand in the intake. "They're gaining, but slowly," she said as a red hepler pulse buzzed beside her head. Clutching the rifle butt tightly in one hand, she grabbed one of the wooden-handled heplers from the seat with her free hand and aimed. Gently, she pushed the trigger with her thumb. As she held down the trigger, several electric-red bolts of light flew from the end of the fragile-looking weapon, striking the left most of the pursuing hovers. A shower of sparks flew up from the impact, but the vehicle kept on coming.

"Damn," cursed Fire. "I wish they'd get close enough so I could fire a round from the rifle. That would slow them down."

Clyde said a silent prayer. At first, he wasn't sure to whom. He had never been a very religious man. As his lips moved, he realized the last time he had said such a prayer. It was when the Cluster had come into orbit around Sufiro, shortly after his troops had been defeated. He hoped the Cluster or someone might perform the same type of miracle all over again, letting Suki and Manuel get to the neutral territory of Roanoke safely.

Clyde's thoughts were interrupted by the loud report of the rifle. "Got one!" called Fire. Colonel McClintlock raised his head just far enough to see the smoking remains of one of the pursuing hovers. He could see two figures thrown to the side, bringing themselves to their feet.

"Ay, carajo, Señora!" shouted Raton. "Just how close are those bastards getting?"

"Close enough!" Fire discharged another round. "Damn! I missed!"

"I think I see the Roanoke border!" Raton put on a burst of speed, throwing Clyde hard into the seat. For several heartbeats he held his breath, then looked up in time to see a hepler pulse whiz by his head.

Fire pushed him back down. "I told you to stay clear!" She reloaded the rifle and fired again.

"It looks like the cavalry's here!" called Raton. Clyde looked up to see a line of rag-tag New Granadan soldiers lining the border to Roanoke. As soon as the hover was past, the militia people fired on the pursuing hovers.

"It looks like they've taken the hint," said Fire as the hovers turned back across the desert. Raton slowed the hover to a reasonable speed and brought it into the small coastal village of Roanoke.

Clyde had never been to the village before, but he had known about the quiet colony that sat across the desert from his own country. A small religious sect had founded Roanoke nearly ten years before Tejo. The land itself was worthless. The coastline was even worse. Consequently, the Tejans never bothered the settlers there.

Raton pulled the hover to a stop by a two-story inn on the seashore. A stout, clean-shaven man wearing a black shirt and black trousers approached the hover. "You know we do not condone violence here," he said, indignant.

"No one was hurt, Reverend Burroughs," reassured Fire whisking her long black hair behind her shoulders.

"What about the hover I saw destroyed?" asked the one-time colonel. "That was pretty damned violent."

"All for show, Clyde," said Manuel, patting the colonel on the back with strong hands.

Clyde stood blinking for several minutes. He began putting pieces of the puzzle together. "That escape did seem awfully easy."

"You call driving like that easy?" Raton put his hands on his hips. His mustache drooped. "Next time, get your own butt out of jail!"

"So, is this what you meant by 'taking me out of the equation?'" Clyde's brow wrinkled.

"Exactly," said Fire, leading Clyde inside the cheerily lit inn. Reverend Burroughs escorted the group to a small round table.

"If you had simply been released," said Manuel, tapping his fingers on the table. "It would have been the same as if you had been given no sentence at all." Manuel's grin grew big and fierce. "Now, you are a bandito, on the run from the law. If you let yourself get caught, it's a whole new ball game. They can throw the book at you without worrying what the people think."

"They'll simply charge you with breaking out of jail," winked Fire. "A pretty serious crime in Tejo, I hear."

Clyde put his head in his hands. "I'm not exactly difficult to find, sitting across the desert from Tejo."

"That's if anyone actually bothers to look," said Fire.

"And if they look too hard, they might wind up in the same mess they were in before." Manuel leaned across the table. "It's easier for them if you stay 'on the run.'"

A waitress came to the table, distributed glasses of water and left.

"I see," said Clyde. "But, why Roanoke?"

"Here," said Reverend Burroughs, "they will have to go through a messy extradition procedure to get you. You are welcome to stay or go as you wish. If you stay, our only price is that you learn something of our faith."

Clyde thought about the Cluster and his prayers. "I could use some instruction in faith, about now, Reverend," he said meekly. He looked back to Fire. "Back at the prison, you said there was something you wanted to ask me?"

"I want to know why you led the military coup," said Fire, drumming her fingers on the table. "I want to know if the Cluster communicated with you."

Clyde McClintlock's bright eyes grew wide, his mouth dropping open, as he sat back in the chair.

* * *

John Mark Ellis careened southward from Nantucket aboard a modest boat, first purchased by his grandfather Zechariah. The little boat had a screw propeller that was designed to make as little noise in the water as possible, but give good speed. The boat also had antigraviton generators and could rise out of the water if there was need for absolute silence, but there was a cost in velocity.

Ellis began to feel like himself as the wind whistled through his hair. He felt the salt sting his face through his freshly trimmed beard. Smoke from his pipe trailed behind him. He felt the exhilaration of Ahab, hunting the whale. Except, this time, he merely wanted a chat.

On the boat's computer, Ellis checked the location of the Atlantic sperm whale feeding grounds and made for them. While he knew the old whale, Richard, was a lone bull, it was likely he would not be too far from any large pods of females.

Setting the boat on automatic pilot, Ellis went into the cabin below. He attached a simple metal pan to a latch on the stove. As he turned on the heat, the boat lurched to the side suddenly, causing him to grab onto the counter. He shook his head, finding it a bit difficult to regain his sea legs. He was, after all, used to space ships and their graviton generators. Unless one was involved in a jump or the ship's momentum was suddenly changed by hepler fire, the ship's decks were rock solid.

After letting the pan heat, he tossed in some potatoes and sausage. He followed that, after a time, with some eggs. Again, the tiny boat lurched, and his hand fell near the heat. Like lightning, he pulled his hand from the fire and sucked on it for a moment. Finally, he removed the small, dented metal pan from the heat. Ellis took the whole conglomeration with him to the tiny wooden table where he sat down to eat.

After eating, he reminded himself to secure the pan under the sink so he could clean it later. From there, he walked across the three-foot wide hallway to the room with his narrow bunk. Sitting on the bunk, he reached across to a white plastic chest. Opening it, he retrieved a translator. He checked the black band and earpiece, making sure it was in working order. Finally, he put the band around his neck, securing it firmly, but not too tightly and placed the earpiece in his ear.

Ellis returned to the wheel, atop the cabin and checked the compass and his latitude. He nodded silent approval as he realized he was near the sperm whale feeding grounds. Using binoculars, he scanned the horizon. He grimaced when he didn't see anything. Waiting five minutes, he scanned again. On the southeastern horizon, he thought he saw a glimmer. Still looking through the binoculars, he turned toward the shimmering. He cursed as the boat lurched again, driving the binoculars against his forehead.

Rubbing his injured head, Ellis, kept his eyes on the sight as it came near enough to see. He was relieved to see the forward-pointing spray of a sperm whale spout. After watching several minutes, he saw, at first five, then seven, maybe eight spouts. A little disappointed that he hadn't found Richard, he was happy to see that he had located those who could help him. The spouts disappeared after a few minutes as the whales dove under the water to search for food.

Ellis slowed his craft as he approached the location of the whales. As he looked over the side at the dark depths, a mighty crash sounded from behind him. Ellis turned in time to be knocked over by the spray of a spout. He heard the patterned clicking of sperm whale speech. The clicking was rapid and arrhythmic almost like radio static. Only an experienced ear could hear the anger in the voice. Struggling to his feet, Ellis turned on the translator device.

"You disturb the children with your motor, human. Be gone!" The translator said the words, but gave none of the finesse that could be heard in the clicks. Looking over the side of the boat, Ellis could see the ten-foot long black head of a mother sperm whale.

"Forgive me," called Ellis. He could hear the clicks issuing from the translator as it rendered his words into the language of the whales. Ellis rushed to the wheel and activated the antigraviton generators of the tiny boat. The whale let out another spout.

Another immense, black head arose from the deep. "The cycle continues," it said. "Be gone!"

"I'm looking for one of your kind." Ellis held his hands over his head protecting himself from another onslaught of spray. The broad head of the first whale disappeared, replaced by the arched form of its glimmering back. Smaller forms began to appear some distance from the boat. Each one spraying. Ellis gasped at the sight.

"None of our kind are interested," said the second whale. "The hunt is the art." She was smaller than the first, not as old. She turned toward the pod of younger whales, spraying as she went.

Just as Ellis' shoulders sank, a third whale head appeared near the boat. Again, he was drenched by spray. This whale had a slightly wrinkled brow, making her look more matronly. "The cycle continues," she said.

"The cycle continues," repeated Ellis solemnly.

"You are looking for one of our kind," she clicked.

"I look for the old bull, Richard." Ellis brushed wet hair from his forehead.

"The one the humans call Richard is 47 miles afin port," said the matronly whale. "The cycle resumes," she said, giving another spout. With that, she dove under the surface, her tail raised in the air, waving to Ellis.

"The cycle resumes," said Ellis as he looked at the general direction of the adult whales. Using their fins as a pointer, he aimed his tiny craft where Richard would be.

Passing by the pod of whales, Ellis heard snippets of stories told to the young whales. The stories were of the old times, when the violent chattering land apes came hunting. According to the stories, the apes were so stupid, it took them nearly seven hundred years to learn to talk. Even then, they had to use devices like the ones Ellis wore. As Ellis continued out to sea, he felt the old twang of guilt that came when he considered that his ancestors made their fortune hunting one of the other intelligent species of Earth.

Continuing toward Richard's hunting grounds, Ellis returned the boat to the water to increase its speed and again stepped below, pondering the fact that Earth was unusually blessed by having three fully self-aware species; the sperm whale, the humpback, and man.

Even in the thirtieth century, most people did not fully understand the subtleties of whale speech. To most, the words "the cycle continues" and "the cycle resumes" were a simple litany, or at best, a greeting. In fact, embedded in the litany were calculations based on temperature, density and salinity factors that determined just where the giant squid and fish were that the whales hunted for food. The hunt is the art.

Humans owed a great debt to both intelligent species of whale. If humans had hunted them to extinction, they likely would not have developed interstellar travel. Just as Newton realized the existence of gravity by being bonked on the head with an apple, Quinn had realized the nature of gravity and its dimensionality by listening to humpback whale speech and understanding the wave patterns produced.

Again, rummaging through his plastic sea chest, Ellis found dry clothes and a yellow rain slicker. Peeling himself out of his dripping clothes, he pulled on a warm, red flannel shirt and blue woolen pants. He replaced his drenched leather shoes with dry socks and rubber boots. Returning to the deck, he scanned the horizon. After only a few minutes, he saw a lone spout, almost nearer than he expected.

As he approached, he saw the great, bifurcated tail go below the surface of the water. Again, he took the boat an inch out of the water, letting it sit silently. Donning the slicker, he waited nearly twenty minutes, watching white clouds build on the horizon.

With a crash, like thunder, he saw a dark gray form lift itself clear out of the water pointing skyward. A waterfall streamed off the glistening body. Ellis caught his breath and held the ship's railing tightly as the body arched and fell back into the water. A spout of water and air buffeted the boat along with a mighty clang. Through the noise, Ellis heard clicking and, "The cycle continues, old friend!"

"It has been a long time, my friend," said Ellis as he watched the 62-foot long spermaceti whale swim alongside the boat.

The whale's eye emerged from the water. "You are alone, young Ellis. Where is your father?"

Ellis took a deep shuddering breath. "Dead, killed in space by something we call the Cluster."

"I shall mourn him," said Richard. His head went below the waves, revealing a wrinkled back. The great tail rose from the water. Richard surfaced after a minute on the other side of the boat. Ellis stepped to the other side and leaned over the railing. Richard rose far enough from the water so Ellis could touch him. He sighed and a tear escaped merging with the water.

"Whales know not the ways of space, young Ellis," said Richard. "Tell me of this Cluster."

"It is a great ball of silver spheres, bigger than you, bigger than your dead brothers, the blue whales. They move through space. Even as we speak, my people and the other peoples of the stars, the Titans, Rd'dyggians, Zahari, all are fighting them."

Richard spouted and clicked, just short of angry. "Why do you fight? Always the same with the tool builders. The art is the death."

Kneeling down by the railing, Ellis swished the water lazily with his left hand. "We tried to talk to the Cluster, peacefully. They began killing all our people."

"Now you know how we feel," said Richard. "Maybe now the tool builders begin to understand." Another great spray came from the whale's spout.

"Maybe *I* begin to understand at least." Ellis pondered the whale's words. "We see the Cluster as evil, but maybe they're not."

"But maybe they are," Richard clicked. "Whales know not the ways of space."

"I don't think the Cluster's evil." Ellis shook his head. "I think one of them has spoken to me."

The whale swished its tail lazily back and forth. "What did it say?"

"I don't know." Looking toward the bright blue sky, Ellis formed his words. "It seemed to speak in emotional metaphor."

"Like the humpbacks," mused Richard. "The art is the song."

Mark Ellis looked at the whale, stunned. "Yes," he said slowly with a newfound understanding. "Just like the humpbacks. The art *is* the song." As Richard dove under the boat again, Ellis stood and ambled back to the other side. Stroking his beard, he pondered the clouds. When Richard rose again, spouting, Ellis looked at him. "Do you think the humpbacks could help me understand?"

"The art is the song, nothing more." Richard's wrinkled form undulated slightly. "They know no more of the ways of space than do I. Besides, young Ellis, to them, man merely chatters. The art is the death."

Ellis sighed. "Can you help me?"

The whale spouted twice, loudly. "I doubt it, the art is the hunt."

"I think the art might be the hunt for the Cluster." Ellis tugged at his auburn beard.

"The art is also the song, you said."

"The art might also be death." Again, Ellis let his eyes wander to the clouds. "They don't leave much behind."

"Then you must find those who understand all three, to understand this Cluster." Richard raised his massive head completely out of the water, bobbing it up and down. "The cycle resumes." With that Richard once again dove below the waves.

Rapping his fingers on the railing, Ellis stood. He walked back to the wheel and retrieved his pipe, tamping the ash into the ocean. He grinned, reminded of the Native American legend that told that Nantucket had been created when god had emptied his pipe into the ocean. Retrieving a deck chair, Ellis tamped a fresh patch of tobacco into his pipe, lighted it and settled in for the wait. The cycle resumed; Richard had gone down to hunt more squid. Using his tongue, he would bait the animals. When he felt them hit, he would clang loudly, stunning them and close the trap. When ready for more air, he would rise to the surface; the cycle continued.

After nearly fifteen minutes, Richard again rose to the surface, less flamboyantly than before. "The cycle continues," he said. Richard let his whole body float to the top. Ellis couldn't help but gasp when he saw the entire 62-foot long scarred and wrinkled body.

"The cycle continues, old friend," said Ellis, nodding appreciatively. "Who would understand the three arts; the hunt, the death and the song?"

Clicking, Richard rolled slightly to his side. "The Rd'dyggians."

"I thought whales knew not the ways of space." Ellis smirked.

Richard turned on his belly again, blowing a waterspout. The water came down in a shower, drenching the smoldering pipe. "Whales know not the ways of space. Whales do know some of the people. Only the Rd'dyggians speak to the humpbacks, the spermaceti, and man. From them you can learn."

Ellis removed the sopping pipe from his mouth. "I only really know one Rd'dyggian," he said, remembering the mission to Sufiro. "A warrior named Arepno."

"Arepno, I know not." Richard was silent for a moment. "Seek the philosopher, not the warrior."

"I don't know any Rd'dyggian philosophers," shrugged Ellis. He put the drenched pipe in his pocket.

"I do," clicked the whale. "Seek G'Liat. He knows the song, the hunt, and the death."

"How would I find him?" asked Ellis, excitedly.

"Whales know not the ways of space," said Richard. "You must use *your* knowledge to find him."

"Thank you, old friend." Ellis noticed that the sun was approaching the tops of the clouds on the horizon. "It's about time for me to be going."

"For me as well," said Richard. "I hope to see you again. The cycle resumes." With that, Richard sunk below the water. Ellis returned to the controls and lowered the boat to the ocean's surface. Just as he did, he heard a great crash of water. Again, Richard rose from the waves, leaping higher than Ellis had ever seen before. The water cascaded off his body and onto the boat's deck. In the air, the whale performed a miraculous spin and turn and returned to the sea forehead first, his tail waving goodbye. Laughing, Ellis turned his boat to starboard and made for Nantucket.

Reverend Clyde's Old Time Cluster Revival

Clyde McClintlock had never considered himself a very religious man. It was true that his parents like many civic-minded Iowans from Earth, went to the mosque and followed the way of Islam. Clyde was familiar with the ways of Allah and his prophet Mohammed. However, his parents seemed to attend the services more out of fashion than out of any actual belief. That seemed true of most people Clyde knew, whether Moslem, Jewish, or Christian. As a citizen of the American Sector, it only mattered that you belonged to one of the sanctioned religions. When Clyde's parents moved to Sufiro, they kept their morality but pretty well dropped the religious trappings. Clyde had been ten years old when that happened.

At the tender age of ten, Clyde was not all that comfortable with the apparent change of belief his parents had undergone. It had confused him and made him wonder about many things adults said. Seven years later, Clyde moved to Earth, to find his roots, figure out just who he was and what he did believe in. Clyde found the Gaean Navy.

In the Navy, Clyde discovered discipline and a world order like none he had ever known before. In the academy, his professors gave him a defined and straightforward sense of what was right and wrong. Quite simply, what his superior officers said was right. Anything else was wrong. This was a world Clyde could understand and, for a time, he was happy.

The first time Clyde's faith in the military was thrown into question was when he was aboard a Gaean destroyer, hunting privateers. His ship, the *Beacon*, was in pursuit of a pirate vessel. The captain had given explicit orders not to fire on the pirate ship. However, the *Beacon's* gunner had scanned a rear-mounted weapon's rack disguised as a thruster pack. Without informing the captain, the gunner had fired, destroying the weapon's mounting as well as the pirate ship. Clyde, who had been piloting the ship, had been shocked at the loss of life and the callous action. However, the sensor logs bore out the gunner's story. The gunner, who had violated the sacred principle of following orders, had been granted a promotion. Meanwhile, Clyde remained pilot of the tiny destroyer for another five years, continuing to follow orders, never coming to notice.

The second time Clyde's faith in the Navy had been hurt had to do with his good friend, John Wong. Clyde knew that Lieutenant Wong was the son of an admiral, but never thought much of it. Clyde, like John, was a lieutenant. Unlike John, Clyde had more years of service. He also knew that Lieutenant Wong had never particularly distinguished himself in the line of duty. Thus, it was clear to Clyde that he would be promoted well ahead of his friend. Instead, John's mother called in some favors. Within four years, John Wong was captain of his own ship while Clyde still served as a lieutenant. That was when Clyde decided he would resign his commission and return home to Sufiro.

On Sufiro, Clyde's faith took a third blow. His childhood friend, Rocky Hill, was lieutenant governor of the continent of Tejo. Rocky was looking for a leader of a new Tejo military. His choice was Clyde McClintlock. It was then that Clyde, who had never risen beyond the rank of lieutenant, who had never particularly distinguished himself in the line of duty, suddenly found himself leading the army of an entire continent. Quite frankly, Clyde didn't feel that he deserved the honor.

Clyde's faith was utterly demolished when he led a military coup and took over the Tejan continent. To do that went against everything he had been taught. It went against every instinct, except for one. That instinct was the basic morality his parents had raised him with.

In essence, when Clyde arrived in Roanoke, a freed political prisoner, he had come full circle. He was a reborn man, looking for something, anything actually, to believe in.

The people of Roanoke believed in a religion that Clyde knew only slightly. Rather than believing that the carpenter of Nazareth, called Jesus, was a mere prophet, these people believed he was, in fact, the Messiah. What made them different from the Christians Clyde had known on Earth was their devotion to their faith.

Clyde McClintlock found the religion and the faith of these people attractive. The structure of the faith was casual. There were few rituals. They had a strong sense of discipline and they spoke to God all the time, whenever they wanted.

There was only one problem Clyde saw with the faith of the people of Roanoke. They claimed that God spoke to them. In the weeks that Clyde had been in Roanoke, learning the ways of the people, learning to pray, never once had God seemed to speak to him. The way these people felt about God was more akin to the way he felt about the Cluster than anything else.

Clyde McClintlock had written down the impressions he had received from the Cluster. Those impressions had given him a moral certainty like none that he had ever felt in his life. The Cluster had put images directly in his mind. What he saw from the Cluster was far more real to Clyde than what he felt from the God of Roanoke.

On the day of his rescue from prison, Suki Firebrandt had asked whether or not the Cluster had communicated with Clyde. This shook him. "You see," she had said, "the Cluster seems to have communicated with John Mark." Clyde thought back to the conversation with Fire.

* * *

"It what?" asked Clyde, almost falling out of the austere, wooden chair in the little inn.

"Mark says he saw what amounted to visions." Fire leaned across the table. Her brown eyes glistened with moisture, but she kept the rest of her face rock steady. "I have to know, Clyde, did the Cluster communicate with you as well?"

Clyde told about his visions. He told Suki how they had led him to the decision to lead the military coup against the leaders of Tejo. "The experience was almost, religious," said Clyde, a gleam in his blue eyes.

Fire put her head down. Manuel Raton reached out a rough hand and took hers. "You see," said Manuel softly. "Mark has been kicked out of the Gaean Navy because he suggested they try communicating with the Cluster rather than destroy it."

Clyde's cynicism about the Gaean Navy ran so deep by that point that the news did not surprise him in the least. Still, the fact that he was not the only one who had seen the visions reassured him. For the first time since he had led the military coup, Clyde began to feel at peace.

"I just had to know," said Fire looking up at last, "whether or not the communication was real. I had to know that if Mark had been kicked out of the fleet, it was not for something imaginary."

"Not only was it real," said Clyde, "it was something noble."

For the first time in her life, Fire saw why her father had believed so strongly in the McClintlock family. "Thank you," she said. She and Manuel stood. Clyde stood as well. All three embraced.

"What is Mark going to do now?" Clyde asked.

"I think he's going to try to find the Cluster," said Fire. "He wants to talk to it."

"If anyone can succeed," said Clyde. "It's Mark Ellis."

* * *

On that particular Sunday, Clyde was sitting in the tiny white, wooden church in Roanoke. Reverend Burroughs was preaching from the Revised Dead Sea Version of the Old Testament book of Ezekiel. He spoke dramatically, gesturing wildly with his hands. Clyde was not too fond of the Old Testament. In it, God seemed far too vengeful; more someone to be feared rather than loved and confided in. However, something in the words the Reverend read caught Clyde's attention.

"This is the vision that Ezekiel saw: There came the likeness of a chariot with wheel inside wheel and the wheels did not turn as they approached. When the being rose, the wheels rose like a bird with two wings." As Burroughs read, his voice rose to a crescendo. Clyde listened to the description of the vision and his mind's eye worked on wheels inside wheels that did not turn. He imagined spheres hanging close together. The Reverend continued to speak about how the wheels were attached to each other and something about faces.

The preacher's voice dropped to a near reverential whisper. "And wheel joined to wheel when they moved. And their appearance and their working were as if it were a wheel in the middle of a wheel. As for the likeness of the living creatures, their appearance was like burning coals of fire and like the appearance of lamps." This caused Clyde to sit upright, listening intently, now. He thought about the silver orbs of the Cluster, brightly reflecting the light of Sufiro's sun as it had orbited the planet.

"Now there was over their heads an expanse, like an awesome gleam of crystal and a voice came from above the expanse..." Clyde wiped sweat from his brow. The spheres spoke to Ezekiel.

Ezekiel was speaking of a vision of God. Clyde retrieved the notepaper with a sketch of the Cluster. Next to the sketch, he drew wheels within wheels. To Clyde McClintlock, it was clear that Ezekiel had described the Cluster in beautiful, poetic language.

Images of the Cluster visiting Earth in ancient times came to Clyde's mind. Many of Earth's religions were based on various portions of the Old Testament. Could it be that everyone had it wrong? Clyde began writing feverishly on his pad of paper. What if the Cluster was not really an alien intelligence? What if it was the one great Intelligence? Clyde stopped for a moment, afraid of where his thoughts were leading. However, the conclusions he was reaching were inevitable to him. Quite simply, Clyde McClintlock began to see the Cluster as God incarnate.

Not only that, but the Cluster had spoken to him. That made Clyde, the prophet of the Cluster, just as Ezekiel was the prophet of God. Clyde put his trembling hand to his mouth. The Cluster had also spoken to John Mark Ellis. Ellis, like many prophets, had been persecuted for trying to spread the word.

Sitting there in the church, Clyde's hands shook violently. He felt like throwing up. No matter what, he needed air. He stood, and nearly tripping over the feet of one of his fellow parishioners, he stumbled out of the church and into the open air.

Clyde McClintlock stood outside, blinking at Sufiro's blue-green sky. He was both exhilarated and terrified. He was not sure what to do. Feeling his knees go weak, he simply dropped to a crouch on the cool stone steps in front of the church. Half an hour later, Reverend Burroughs appeared at the door to greet the parishioners as they prepared to leave the building.

"I've had people fall asleep on my sermons," said the minister with a gleam in his eye. "But I've never had any run out in a cold sweat, before."

"I'm sorry." Clyde unfolded aching limbs and looked around a little nervously. "I'm afraid I got a good close-up look at God Himself." He stopped himself from saying more as the first of the people began to pour out of the tiny white church building. The former colonel slumped into the shadows as people shook hands with the minister. He stood there, a cool breeze playing across his face, trying to figure out what to do. He looked to the sky and realized that the first thing he should do was find John Mark Ellis. Ellis would have a good idea of what to do.

Clyde ducked around behind the church and made his way back to the tiny house the people of Roanoke loaned him. Green shrubbery and a beautifully manicured lawn surrounded the house. In many ways, it was the nicest house Clyde had ever lived in.

Stepping inside, he dialed up a shipping schedule on the computer terminal. There would be a ship going from Roanoke to the minor continent of Little Sonora in a couple of days. From Little Sonora, he could catch a ship to Earth.

Using the Gaean Navy Veteran's index, it took no time to find out that Ellis lived on Nantucket Island. Clyde's jaw hung open as he read that. For Ellis to be able to afford even a shack on the island would have to make him rich beyond belief. What was he doing as a commander of a destroyer?

A knock on the door caused Clyde to jump. He stood, walking across the soft beige carpet, and opened the door. Reverend Burroughs stood, wearing a concerned frown. "Sorry to impose, Colonel McClintlock, but I was worried about you after the service."

Clyde took a deep breath and held his hand open, inviting the Reverend inside. Burroughs stepped in and sat down at a simple square Formica-topped table. Clyde offered the minister a cup of coffee. Burroughs politely declined, but Clyde poured some in a fine porcelain cup and sat down at the table with the minister. "I'm sorry if I gave you a start." Tentatively, Clyde sipped the dark, thick coffee. "It's just the words you read from the book of Ezekiel." Taking a deep breath, he ran his fingers through gray hair. "It just began to sound like you were describing the Cluster."

"It was a vision," said Burroughs reassuringly. "It was God's way of showing himself to the prophet, Ezekiel."

"Is it possible that the Cluster is God's way of showing himself to us in this century?" Clyde looked where the cream-colored wall met the gently curving white ceiling. "Perhaps as a prelude to something. Maybe even the Second Coming of Christ."

Burroughs folded his hands carefully, looking down at the table. He spoke slowly, choosing his words carefully. "Quite frankly, nothing is beyond possibility." Clyde brightened somewhat at this, but the Reverend raised his hand in warning. "But visions like Ezekiel's tend not to come to groups of people. They only visit the anointed ones."

"There are so many more people today, though," said Clyde, slowly. "It seems like God would need to be much more convincing than he ever had to in the past."

"It just doesn't work that way. Look how many times Christ was asked to put on a show to prove himself and didn't. He didn't need to. God doesn't put on demonstrations. He expects you to have faith." Burroughs chewed his lower lip. "Besides, the Cluster is made of spheres. Ezekiel's vision was wheels and faces and such. Frankly, I don't see the similarity."

Clyde frowned and took another sip of his coffee. "I think it's about time for me to move on," he said at last.

"As you wish," said the minister gently. "But you will be in danger if you leave. The people of Tejo and New Granada would arrest you if you went there."

"I'm thinking of going to Earth," said Clyde.

"Then," said Burroughs steadily, "may God protect you, for the Earth is a far more dangerous place than either of the two major continents of this planet."

Clyde nodded somberly. The Reverend pulled a small book from his jacket pocket and handed it to the former colonel. "What's this?"

"A gift for you," said the Reverend. Clyde looked down at the Revised Dead Sea Version of the Bible the Reverend had handed him. "A gift to help you remember His teachings." The Reverend smiled, stood and shook Clyde's hand, warmly. "God go with you, brother."

"And with you, Reverend," said Clyde. He stood, holding the book close to his heart, watching the stern, yet vital man depart. Once gone, Clyde sat down, took a sip of coffee and turned to the first chapter of Ezekiel.

* * *

Clyde McClintlock found no resistance on the trip to Little Sonora or the subsequent trip to Earth. He was somewhat surprised that he had full access to his bank accounts back at Tejo City. While in Little Sonora, he transferred all his money to accounts on Earth, just to be certain it would be safe. Still, the lack of resistance seemed odd. It was almost as if the people of Sufiro wanted him off their world. It saddened him to leave behind the one place in the galaxy he truly thought of as home for what, he knew, would be the last time.

Arriving on Earth, he found the planet as crowded and polluted as he remembered. Landing at the spaceport in Boston, he immediately caught a commuter hover to Hyannis Port. From there he caught another hover out to Nantucket Island. He regretted going out by hover, though. The turbulence over the water buffeted the frail craft. Several times he was sure it would be pitched into the sea, despite its anti-graviton controls.

At the hover port, Clyde asked the man behind the counter whether he knew where the Ellis home was. "One moment," said the man. The man touched his forehead activating a chip implant and scanning the records of island housing. After a moment, the man faced Clyde and gave him directions.

Clyde stepped lightly out of the hover port and felt the soft sea breeze tickle his hair as he looked up into a cloudy gray sky. A plastic road wound its way into the Village of Nantucket. Taking a step, Clyde almost fell flat on his face. He had not been to Earth for several years and was not used to the gravity that was lower than Sufiro's. His stomach felt fluttery. Still, with a heart as light as his stomach, he picked up his leather suitcase and walked the two miles into the village.

Once he arrived in the village itself, Clyde found himself fascinated by the plain structures that surrounded him. In many ways they reminded him of the humble houses of Roanoke, only these houses were almost simpler. The houses of Roanoke had been painted a variety of colors. The houses of Nantucket were covered in plain gray shingles with white trim. Like Roanoke, Christians seeking freedom to worship as they saw fit had built Nantucket. Clyde was relieved when he turned off the crowded main street onto the silent row of gray sentinels where Ellis' house was. Stepping up the street, it only took Clyde a few minutes to find the ancestral home of John Mark Ellis.

Clyde stood in front of the imposing two-story house. The building could have easily held ten apartments the size he grew up in back in Iowa. It boggled his mind that such primitive materials as wooden shingles could have stood up to over a thousand years of rough island weather. He wondered how many times each shingle on the house had been replaced. Reverently, Clyde McClintlock reached up to a brass knocker in the center of the vast white door. His first knock was so tentative he could barely hear it. Gathering resolve, he knocked again.

Clyde's once-light heart grew heavy as he realized that no one was home. His shoulders sank as he trudged downtown and got directions to a motel. Arriving at the motel, he found he had neither enough money for the room nor the night's taxes to stay on the island. Grumbling to himself, Clyde made his way back to the hover port and caught a flight back to Hyannis Port, where he found an affordable bed for the night.

Sitting on the thin steel-framed bed that was covered in a blanket that smelled vaguely of mildew, Clyde worried about how he was going to get money to survive on Earth. He tucked his suitcase under the bed and stepped out into the streets of the once-rich town of Hyannis Port. Dirty people wandered by, heads down. People with less money than Clyde began to light fires by their street-side tents.

Clyde McClintlock raised his collar against the wind, thrust his hands deep in his pockets and trudged down to the ocean side. More people camped on the beach. With a deep frown etched on his face, Clyde began to think about the stories the people of Roanoke taught about Jesus preaching by the seashore. He thought about his visions of the Cluster.

On an impulse, Clyde wandered up to a group of rough looking people gathered by a cooking fire with fish skewered on pointed sticks. They huddled away from him, scared of just about any stranger. They protected their fish, which was probably more food than any of them had in days, maybe even weeks.

"Don't be afraid," said Clyde gently. "I'm here to bring you good news, glorious news . . ."

* * *

That night, Clyde McClintlock delighted in the joy he brought to the people at the beach. He brought them news that there was nothing to fear from the Cluster. In fact, he taught them that the Cluster only had good news for the people of the Earth. He read passages from the book of Ezekiel showing them that the Cluster had, in fact, visited Earth in ancient times. Reverend Burroughs might not have seen any similarity between the Cluster and Ezekiel's vision, but these people saw it clearly. Because the people on the beach had not heard the news of how the clusters easily destroyed space vessels, it was easy to tell only the good side. Clyde told them of the visions and how the Cluster had placed him on the path of righteousness. Speaking dramatically, like Reverend Burroughs, he told them the Cluster would set them free.

It all started simply, like that. Clyde made his way up Cape Cod, preaching the good news that the Cluster had come to help humanity. Some who knew of people who had died in the war, turned a deaf ear. Most of the people, haunted and tortured looks in their eyes, listened. After a week, Clyde found he did not need to worry about shelter. The people of the beach took him in and chipped in money, paying his taxes. People loved Reverend Clyde, as he came to be known, because he told them that there was one being that held the answers to a planet in trouble. Better than other preachers and soothsayers, he could show the people holograms of their awesome savior. He told them he had actually talked to it and it had helped him.

Again, sitting on the beach one night, Clyde looked around at the people roasting fish over open fires. "The kingdom of heaven is like a net that was let down into the lake and caught all kinds of fish," said Clyde, recalling the parable spoken by Jesus three thousand years before. "When it was full, the fishermen pulled it up on the shore. Then they sat down and collected the good fish in baskets, but threw the bad away."

"Baskets of fish?" scoffed a man with greasy hair and a livid scar on his forehead. "It's hard to catch even one fish in these waters. Even when you do catch one, it's hardly fit to eat."

"Maybe so," said Clyde patiently. "But this parable demonstrates how it will be at the end of this age we're living in. The Cluster will come and separate the wicked from the righteous by destroying the wicked with its beam. Those who are wicked are the ones who are terrified." Clyde put his hands together. "You, the meek, who have inherited this poor Earth, are the ones who will survive. Do you understand?"

Mouths hanging open, the men and women gathered around the fire nodded. For the first time in over two centuries, the people of Cape Cod, and ultimately the city dwellers in Boston began to feel empowered. They began to feel that there might be some hope of Earth becoming a nice place to live again.

Reverend Clyde McClintlock never asked for money as he went around preaching the good news of the Cluster, but the money found him. He tried to give it to the bureau of taxation to get them off the backs of the poor. The bureau simply credited Clyde's personal account. Clyde would have used the money to build apartment buildings, but there simply wasn't enough land. Besides that, the taxes on those kinds of properties would have taken all the money Clyde had collected.

Clyde decided to use the money he acquired to build a meeting hall. He decided it would be a place where the people could gather to hear his words. As far as he was concerned, people could sleep there as well. The hall he built, six months after returning to Earth proved to be one of the largest structures on Cape Cod. He built the structure up in old Province Town, at the very tip of the cape. Even given the building's size, it still overflowed with people, all of them willing to give all they had to the first man who had ever given them hope for the future.

At the front of the enormous building, Clyde stood behind a giant rostrum. He wore a beautiful white suit. "The way of the Cluster is peace," he said. "The Cluster is here to help the poor and the downtrodden to victory." Clyde would close his eyes and look down at the pulpit, his voice becoming nothing more than a whisper. "Let me tell you how the Cluster helped me see the light. Let me tell you how the Cluster freed the slaves of Sufiro."

* * *

During his six months on Earth, Clyde had not forgotten John Mark Ellis. With his church booming, he wanted more than ever to contact the only other man who had experienced a vision from his savior. This time, he was able to purchase a first class hover ticket to Nantucket. By memory, he wound his way through the streets of the ancient village. Once again, he stood on the front porch of Ellis' home. Like last time, McClintlock wondered at the size of the house. This time, though, McClintlock wondered how many of his disciples could live in a house this size. Clyde McClintlock knocked with conviction.

A grizzled old man opened the door. The man wore a white turtleneck shirt and blue pants. White hair stood out at all sides from under a green stocking cap. The old man cocked his head at McClintlock and looked him over as though he were something found on the bottom of a shoe. "This ain't a tourist house," croaked the old man. "Private residence, go away."

As the wry old man started to close the door Clyde called out. "Wait! I'm looking for John Mark Ellis."

"We don't want no salesmen neither," grumbled the old man, again eyeing McClintlock in his nicely pressed and tailored suit.

"I'm not a salesman," said Clyde with a warm smile. "I met Commander Ellis on Sufiro."

"You're a friend?" The old man scratched his beard.

"I don't know if I am or not." Clyde opened his arms. "I'm Clyde McClintlock."

The old man's scowl grew deep. At first, Clyde thought he was going to send him away. Finally, the old man shook his head. "I can't say as I know who you are, but I can tell you that Mark has gone."

"I can get a room at a motel, wait for him," offered Clyde, folding his hands in front of him.

"I'm afraid you'd have to wait for quite a while," wheezed the man. "He's gone off planet."

"Do you know where?" Clyde's brow furrowed.

"I think he's gone to Rd'dyggia, to see some mystic or something. God knows what he hopes to find in that hell hole." The old man's patience had apparently run out, he finally turned back inside, closing the door behind him, muttering something about nosey off-islanders.

Clyde McClintlock's shoulders sank. He realized that he had waited too long to come find Ellis. No, it was not too late. Using the resources of the church, he could follow. Clyde McClintlock smiled to himself. How hard could it be to find a human on Rd'dyggia?

PART II
The Search Within

This is the vision that Ezekiel saw:
There came the likeness of a chariot with wheel inside wheel and the wheels did not turn as they approached. When the being rose, the wheels rose like a bird with two wings. And the faces of the wheels were connected one to the other. There were four faces, the face of a man, the face of a lion, the face of an ox and the face of an eagle. The face of man was joined at the backs of the beasts and the beasts were attached one to another. And wheel joined to wheel when they moved. And their appearance and their working were as if it were a wheel in the middle of a wheel. As for the likeness of the living creatures, their appearance was like burning coals of fire and like the appearance of lamps. Now there was over their heads an expanse, like an awesome gleam of crystal and a voice came from above the expanse.

— The Revised Dead Sea Version of the Bible.
The Book of Ezekiel (published 2766)

John Mark Ellis meets the warrior-philospher, G'Liat

Rd'dyggia

Wan, reddish light found its way to the surface of Titan. The outline of Saturn, turned rusty-orange by the shimmering light, could just be seen through the thin methane fog. Teklar looked out across a black lake of hydrocarbons. She brought any human who questioned that an advanced race could evolve on Titan to this place. The matron would simply wave her hand out across the lake and murmur the word, "home." That simple gesture from the gray-coated creature hushed all cynicism.

Now, she looked across the lake, feeling a much heavier burden than skeptical humans. The Titans, as members of the Confederation of Homeworlds, were sworn to help in the war against the Cluster. However, among themselves, the Titans had sworn never to interfere with the natural development of any less-developed species in the galaxy.

She had told the ambassadors from the homeworlds of the Confederation that Titan ships had been attacked and examined like ships from the other worlds. As such, the Titans were ardently working on a defense against the enigmatic enemy. The truth was that those Titan ships that had been attacked had destroyed themselves to avoid the scrutiny of the Cluster. Not only that, the Titans were not working on a defense. Instead, the attitude of her people was that they should lie low and the other worlds would have to find their own defense. Teklar wondered how long she could conceal the truth from her fellow ambassadors.

Teklar's lieutenant ambled out of the fog. "Ellis has booked passage for Rd'dyggia."

"Good," said Teklar somberly. "There he will find the help he requires."

* * *

John Mark Ellis sat in the nearly empty passenger cabin of a vast transport making its way through the Rd'dyggian-Tzrn stellar system. The seat he occupied stood in a row of three other beige seats. Rounded tan plastic walls enclosed two such rows. It had taken nearly six months to consolidate his finances and help his old friend, Coffin, move into the family home. Suki Firebrandt agreed with her son's plans. If the house remained empty, the village of Nantucket would sell it. Suki needed to return to her job, but she hated to leave Sufiro and Manuel Raton. Ellis' affairs on Earth settled, he was finally on his way to see the philosopher G'Liat.

Only two other people were present in the cabin. One sat near the front, wearing portable EQ communications gear strapped to his head. The man's mind floated in the computer on his lap. He busily conducted transactions of some form or another on the planet ahead and back on Earth. The businessman wore a severely tailored coal-gray suit and stared blankly at the wall ahead. The other person was a jump attendant whose attention was absorbed by a tiny hologram concealed behind a black shield. Probably some kind of exotic dancer, Ellis cynically speculated. She wore a maroon and black jumpsuit designed to accentuate what few feminine curves she had.

Mark Ellis, unlike the other passengers, had dressed for the surface of Rd'dyggia, wearing woolen trousers and a heavy cotton shirt that had been in the attic of the house on Nantucket. The clothes smelled a bit musty and looked ancient, but would be useful in the chill temperatures one could expect to find on the planet ahead. On the seat next to him lay a navy-blue woolen overcoat. The clothes weighed Ellis down and made him itch. The air in the cabin was stale and warm. Consequently, Ellis found himself tugging at his collar and squirming, adjusting his trousers and scratching his legs.

Finally, he gave up and stretched. Doing so, he stood too quickly. The liner had been built principally to haul freight between Gaea-Titan and Rd'dyggia-Tzrn. Expensive graviton generators were a luxury. Instead, rotating the cabin around a central axis simulated gravity. As Ellis stood, he felt a sudden wave of vertigo. His head was lighter than his feet. Not only that, the ship's forward momentum placed the field slightly behind him, putting his center of gravity more in his buttocks than his middle body. He reached forward and stabilized himself on the seat in front. "A ten year space veteran, and I can't even stand on a star vessel," muttered the ex-commander.

In fact, Ellis was thankful that the ship required gravity for its cargo. Like many space veterans, Ellis despised weightlessness. He imagined the condition was analogous to eighteenth and nineteenth century sailors who hated swimming. As he stood, he realized he needed to go to the restroom.

Getting the feel of the differential gravity, Ellis eased his way forward, toward the tiny restroom. As he passed the jump attendant, Ellis' ear caught faint tinkling music, not unlike that he had heard in Boston. He looked back to see that the attendant was, indeed watching a holo of a male stripper.

Ellis sighed as he stepped into the restroom and closed the door, bolting it behind him. For a moment, he stood thinking about his own recent experience with strippers. Although the image of the Cluster was still etched in his memory, he felt an even stronger sensation. Put simply, John Mark Ellis was lonely. He missed his comrades aboard the destroyer, *Firebrandt*. Right then, as he pulled down his trousers and sat on the all-too-small toilet, he realized that he had never been this alone in all the time he had been in the Gaean Navy.

Ellis thought about the businessman, his head entrapped in communication's equipment. He wondered if such a person ever knew real companionship or camaraderie. At the same time, that kind of person was always tied into the network with many billions of minds. A man in the net was never alone, but how often had the businessman known the kindhearted smile of a friend? The image of Adkins' warmly smiling face came to Ellis at that moment. He flushed hotly as he felt his penis stiffen slightly. The sensation only lasted a moment, though, as her expression turned to one of fear, in his mind. He remembered her reaction to the sight of the Cluster. Ellis closed his eyes against the sudden onslaught of images of daughters and sons who had lost parents to those horribly reflective silver orbs.

Finally, Ellis finished, washed up and stepped gingerly back to his seat. It's time, he thought, to find the person who can help me understand this thing. He pulled down a little keyboard from the seat in front. Using the on-board holographic interface, Ellis tapped into the Rd'dyggian directory structure, switching on an automatic translation to English. He then performed a search for the name G'Liat. The computer produced over ten thousand Rd'dyggians whose names could be rendered into generic as G'Liat.

Ellis looked at the myriad names swirling by on his screen, nodding. He narrowed his search to those, so named who had the vocation of philosopher. The computer softly informed him that there was no one with that name and vocation.

Ellis growled to himself. Of course there was no one with that name and vocation. Philosophy, as a profession, was practically unknown on Rd'dyggia. By and large, Rd'dyggians only believed in things they could observe. They only ever acted on things that had foreseeable, practical results. "Natural Philosophy" did exist but was translated as "Science." Ellis cursed himself for wasting his money on a trip to Rd'dyggia on the advice of a whale.

Running his hand through his beard, which was again growing a bit shabby and in need of a trim, Ellis pondered his next course of action. He had to think like a whale, not a human. Richard had called G'Liat a philosopher. Immediately, Ellis, thinking like a human, had assumed that was the Rd'dyggian's profession. However, whales didn't have professions, they only had interests. More precisely, whales believed that they were their destinies.

Using that reasoning, Ellis realized that G'Liat could be a philosopher by hobby; perhaps an interest gained by working with other species as a diplomat or military person. That led Ellis to consider his old acquaintance, Arepno. However, Arepno was a privateer. While that was an honorable profession among Rd'dyggians, it was certainly not among many of the planets of the galaxy. The ex-commander thought it was doubtful the Rd'dyggian computer would give an off-worlder any information about privateers. Still, it was worth a try. After all, Ellis' own grandfather had been a Gaean privateer.

Entering the information, Ellis was stunned to find that the computer did give him information. It listed Arepno, Commander of Fleet St'rac, Retired. For a moment, Ellis wondered whether or not he had found the right person. After all, as far as he knew, Arepno was commander of a lone ship. Still, Ellis printed out a copy of the information and put it in his shirt pocket. It might, at least, be a lead.

"Sir," came a squeaky voice to Ellis' right.

The ex-commander looked up, pulled out of his reverie by the jump attendant's voice.

She wore a wry grin. "The captain will be preparing to dock at Rd'dyggian Station Seven in a few minutes. Please, shut down your computer link and return the touch pad to its upright and locked position."

"No problem," muttered Ellis, shaking his head. He'd have to continue his search a little later.

Ellis watched her move toward the front of the cabin, her narrow hips moving in a forced sway. There were several gentle nudges and he felt his weight shift from slightly behind him to more directly under his seat. The ship was decelerating. The shift was so subtle, he doubted the businessman, still absorbed and adorned in his flight-approved communication's gear, even noticed.

The jump attendant fastened her shoulder restraints, just as a singsong voice came over the microphone. "This is your captain, speaking. Please fasten your lap belts and shoulder restraints, there will be a momentary lessening and ultimate loss of gravity for a few moments until we move into the station docking bay, where we'll be under the influence of graviton generators." Ellis felt his jaw tighten at the jovial sound of the "captain's" voice. Still, he did as commanded and fastened in.

"Oh God," moaned Ellis as he felt the seat drop from beneath him. The loss of gravity was a little less momentary than Ellis was comfortable with. Soon, though, he watched as the jump attendant, then the business man were pulled into their seats as the ship moved into the Rd'dyggian station. Doing so, the station's graviton generators took hold of the ship section by section. Within a moment, Ellis felt a more natural, uniform gravity take hold of his own form. The ex-commander grimaced, missing the simplicity of establishing planetary orbit, then merely climbing into a launch and descending. Even so, he consoled himself with the thought that it was now only a matter of going through customs at the station and then catching a launch to the surface.

Soon, there was a faint nudge followed by a bump. The ship had docked at the station. When the jump attendant undid her restraints, Ellis knew it was safe and undid his even before the "captain" came on the intercom to tell them they had arrived.

The captain reminded the passengers that they had docked at a section of the station designed for human habitation. Any sensitive people going down to the surface of the planet would want to purchase breathing apparatus while still on the station. Ellis shook his head as he retrieved his lone flight bag from the overhead compartment, thinking a seasoned space veteran has no need for breathing apparatus in perfectly breathable air. So what if the soil had a high sulfur content, giving the air a rotten-egg smell. It would be invigorating, thought the ex-commander smugly. He looked forward, in time to see the thin, pallid businessman leaving the ship, looking vaguely like an android or cyborg out of some cheap science thriller. Ellis laughed inwardly as he retrieved his overcoat from the seat.

The jump attendant spoke her overly rehearsed good-bye and wishes that Ellis would please fly with them again. Fat chance, he thought initially. He had only taken this particular jump to Rd'dyggia because it was cheap and relatively fast. However, he had to be concerned about his finances. It was sad, he thought, how his family's fortune was coming to an end so abruptly, especially when he hadn't squandered any of his wealth. So, he would probably be back, whether or not he wanted to be.

The trip through customs was comparatively painless. A six-foot tall, dumpy Rd'dyggian in a gold uniform, wearing a breathing mask, scanned his bag. The Rd'dyggian's purple mustache-like growth wiggled under the clear plastic mask. Soon, a mechanically synthesized voice spoke. "Are you just doing business on the station, or do you plan to visit the planet?"

"I'm planning to visit the planet," stated Ellis. "Can you direct me to the shuttle bays?"

The Rd'dyggian nodded in a simulated human gesture. "How

long will your stay be?"

"I plan to visit an old friend." Ellis shrugged. "I really hadn't thought about it. Indefinite, I suppose."

"Your visa is good for a month," said the Rd'dyggian flatly. "If you stay longer than that, you will need to get it renewed at the human embassy." Without another word, the Rd'dyggian pointed down a bare metal corridor toward some booths where shuttles could be hired to go to the surface.

Ellis made his way down the strangely empty corridor and stood in front of three booths. Two were empty. The lone human attendant was sound asleep in a large padded chair behind the counter. Ellis approached and knocked on the shiny metal counter top.

The attendant was an elfin woman with brown hair cropped close to her head. She opened one eye. "What do you want?" Her voice was drowsy.

Ellis gritted his teeth, still used to being a commander. "I want to go to the planet."

The woman grinned petulantly, seeing his annoyance as she opened the other eye. "A lot of people think they want to go to the surface," she said smugly. "Usually they take one breath of the air, turn around and get back aboard my ship, begging me to bring them back here where they can do business over the hologram. Rd'dyggia's not a pretty world by human standards."

Ellis tapped his foot impatiently. "Look, I just want to get down to the planet, so I can meet up with an old friend. Now, will you sign me up for a shuttle, or do I have to go somewhere else?"

The woman looked first at one of the adjoining booths, then at the other. "Seeing as I'm the only game in town, I suppose I'll give you a ride."

"I could always get a flight from the Rd'dyggian part of the station," said Ellis, trying to match her biting sarcasm.

The woman sighed, her grin becoming more sincere. "Sorry," she said, her tone softening. "I'm always grumpy when I wake up. Besides, the company of Rd'dyggians doesn't do much for my mood." She shrugged and looked at Ellis with wide, dark eyes. "Sure, I'll give you a ride to the planet."

"So, you're both the pilot and ticket clerk?" Ellis softened a bit himself.

"It pays the bills." She gestured toward the nearly empty room. "And, as you can see from our teeming space port, I need all the money I can get."

Ellis nodded and paid a fare. She informed him that she would take the shuttle to the surface in about an hour. "There's another passenger ship coming in then, we'll see if anyone from that ship wants to go down."

"You don't sound too hopeful."

"Hey," she said with a wink. "I've already gotten more business today than in the past week. Maybe I'll get lucky."

"With your attitude," grumbled Ellis, "you'll need all the luck you can get." With that, he turned to locate someplace to grab a bite to eat. He didn't see the gesture she waved at his retreating back.

* * *

As it turned out, Ellis was the only passenger aboard the shuttle. Thus, he was able to sit in the cockpit of the tiny shuttle along with the pilot, whose name turned out to be Guadalupe Cordova. "But you can call me, Captain," she said with a smug grin as she powered up the engines for the decent to the planet. Ellis groaned and rolled his eyes in response.

His stomach's rumbling, trying to digest Rd'dyggian food, did not help his mood. Ellis shook his head and sighed, thinking it had taken him years of working his tail off in the military to even make lieutenant, and eventually commander. Guadalupe Cordova had only needed to buy a shuttle.

Even though he was perturbed, Ellis was glad to be sitting in the cockpit. The passenger cabin did not have windows. This way, at least, he would get to see the planet as they approached.

Once she was given clearance, Cordova detached the ship easily and spiraled away from the Rd'dyggian space station. After being in the nearly deserted human sector of the station, Ellis was surprised to see that there was actually quite considerable traffic in orbit.

Cordova turned the ship to give Ellis a view of the planet below. The ex-commander caught his breath. No inhabited world in the galaxy could match Rd'dyggia for sheer abstract grandeur – at least to a human's eyes. Vast red and green continents, streaked purple with vegetation jutted out of vivid turquoise oceans tinged with dark yellow highlights. A gossamer ring, sparkling ruddy silver encircled the planet. As the shuttle moved around the planet, Ellis noticed that the world was wrapped in a shroud of atmosphere dispersing the orange light of the local star.

As they rounded the planet, Ellis caught sight of a vivid blue star. The star seemed a little too big and disk-like. Ellis realized that this must be the system's other inhabited planet, Tzrn – not a star. The peoples of Tzrn and Rd'dyggia had discovered space travel within ten years of one another. Upon their mutual discovery, war began devastating the surfaces of each planet. The war was only ended by the intervention of the Titans. Unfortunately, the peace process did not go as planned. The spider-like Tzrn and giant orange Rd'dyggians united their forces against the highly advanced Titans. Fortunately, the Titans were able to stop the suicidal assault of the two primitive peoples. It was then, the Titans vowed never to interfere with primitive cultures again.

Cordova turned to Ellis. "So, where do you want to go?"

"I thought that was obvious," said Ellis, pointing out the window to the planet. "Drop me wherever you normally take passengers going to the planet."

"Since you're my only passenger, the field's open. Name your pleasure."

Ellis retrieved the slip of paper from the pocket of his cotton shirt and unfolded it. "Do you know anything about the Fleet St'rac?"

"What?" Cordova shrugged. "You think this is some kind of quiz?"

Ellis heaved a deep sigh. "It will help answer where I want to go."

"It's an inside joke." Cordova smiled showing teeth that seemed too big for her small features. "St'rac is an animal a little like raccoons on Earth, except they're feathered and can tear the arm off of your average human. They have a reputation for stealing food and just about anything else not nailed down."

"I see," said Ellis slowly. "So, someone with Fleet St'rac is a thief . . . a privateer, perhaps?"

"Perhaps," admitted Cordova. "They use it to throw off outworlders. So you want to see a privateer?"

"Retired," admitted Ellis. "He's a friend of my grandfather's."

"Your grandfather has some interesting friends," said Cordova suspiciously. "You ain't transporting any stolen goods?"

"In that bag?" Ellis gestured to his tiny traveling bag strapped next to him.

"I've seen some pretty dangerous explosives in even smaller bags," said Cordova straight-faced. "So, now that I've answered your question, where do you want to go?"

"I just have some coordinates and info I copied from the computer on the transport."

"Hand them over," sighed Cordova, growing slightly impatient. She scanned the slip of paper and then entered the coordinates into her computer. Some words appeared on her console. "Your grandfather really does have some impressive friends," whistled Cordova.

"What do you mean?" asked Ellis, all innocence.

"Those're the coordinates for the home of Arepno, the hero of Sufiro."

You sure you want to go down without an invitation?"

Ellis blinked a few times. He grew curious about how the Rd'dyggians viewed Arepno. "Hero of Sufiro?"

"Yeah, you know that little backwater planet out on the far edge of the galaxy? The one threatened by the Cluster? Arepno was there. They say he saved it from certain destruction." Cordova shook her head. "Don't you read the papers?"

"I guess I missed it," muttered Ellis. "Anyway, yes, that's Arepno, friend of my grandfather's."

Cordova told the computer to implement the coordinates she had entered. The tiny ship spun on two of its axes and began to move toward the planet. Ellis saw that they were en route to the reddest of the continents. The descent through the atmosphere went smoothly. They careened through dark gray, almost green, clouds. Soon, they were swooping over tall, unmoving purple vegetation. The mountains, made of oxidized iron, looked almost soft by comparison. Within minutes, Captain Cordova settled the shuttle gently to the red ground.

Ellis craned his neck, looking through the windows trying to discern where they were. They were sitting on an empty patch of red ground in the middle of a grove of purple trees. The trees were vaguely reminiscent of palms, but more arched and foreboding.

"Where the hell are we?" asked Ellis.

"We're right outside Arepno's compound."

Again, Ellis peered through the glass trying to find evidence of any sort of habitation. "The nearest city must be miles away."

"You really didn't do your research, did you?" asked Cordova. "Rd'dyggians don't have cities the way humans have cities. They have family compounds, spaced as far apart as possible. They don't like intruders," she cautioned at last.

"You don't recommend going up and knocking on the door then," asked Ellis, tugging on his beard.

"I'd use the teleholo in the back to see if your 'friend' wants to accept visitors," recommended Cordova.

Ellis did as suggested and stepped back to the rear of the shuttle, where the teleholo console was. The ship's computer had found the number of the compound based on the coordinates fed into the flight computer. Soon an image, like a Grecian bust, shimmered and appeared on the dais in front of the ex-commander. The head had the familiar orange skin, black eyes and purple mustache. Still, the features were not as worn as he remembered, nor did this Rd'dyggian have Arepno's trademark eye patch. Ellis took a deep breath. "May I speak to Arepno, please?"

After a moment, the "mustache" moved. A second later, words issued from the speaker. "Who, may I ask, is calling?"

"Commander John Mark Ellis. Arepno and I met at Sufiro."

"One moment please." The head shimmered as the person who answered the holo stepped out of view.

After nearly two minutes, another head appeared. This one had the wrinkled brow, slight twinkle to one eye, and an eye patch over the other, which Ellis remembered. "Young Ellis," boomed the speakers. "How nice to see you."

"I was wondering if you would mind a visitor," asked Ellis, sheepishly.

"When?" asked Arepno. Despite his time with humans, the Rd'dyggian was still the complete pragmatist.

"Actually," said Ellis, wringing his hands. "I'm in a shuttle, near your compound."

"Ah, I see," mused Arepno. "You are the one who landed. I will meet you in a few minutes, outside. Welcome to Rd'dyggia." With that, Arepno's image vanished from the teleholo.

Ellis retrieved his bag and coat, then stuck his head through the door to the cockpit. "My friend will be out to meet me, thanks!"

"You paid in advance," said Cordova, slight dimples forming around her smile. "That's all the thanks I need." She looked out at the planet. "I'll wait long enough to make sure you haven't changed your mind about having a breathing mask."

"The air's breathable enough," grumbled Ellis. "Thanks, again." With that, Ellis donned his greatcoat and pushed the button next to the shuttle's door. He was immediately assaulted by the smell of rotten eggs. Ellis closed his eyes against their watering for a moment, trying not to gag and glad he had only eaten a meager meal before coming down to the planet's surface.

"Hey, you're letting the air in," called Cordova.

Ellis waved his apology and stepped out of the craft onto deceptively soft and powdery soil. As he stepped onto the soil, a layer of dust swirled up. The smell was heavy in ammonia. It was like being hit in the face by cat urine. Ellis held his breath as long as he could, then cautiously inhaled some air, but almost threw up.

With a grimace, he looked up to see Arepno, adorned in golden robes tied with a red sash. "Let me help you, my friend," he said, with the assistance of a translator box.

"I think I'll be okay," gasped Ellis. Suddenly a chill passed through his bones. The air was only about 10 degrees Celsius. He pulled the coat closed around him.

Arepno came to Ellis' side and put out a helping hand. Ellis took it. As they passed by the front window of the shuttle, Ellis forced a calm smile and waved to Cordova. Soon, the shuttle ascended into the sky, kicking up a spray of the cat urine-smelling sand. Ellis looked toward the shuttle lifting up into the orange sky, thinking he had been deposited right in the middle of hell itself. "Great planet," he commented to Arepno.

"Now you know how I felt, being on Sufiro," said Arepno.

"People keep saying that to me." Ellis shook his head slightly.

"Let's go inside," said Arepno with a tilted head. "We can get you warm and you can tell me what brings you to my humble world."

Warrior Philosopher

Arepno's house was a squat, circular structure. The building had a reddish hue like the surrounding dirt. At first, Ellis thought it was small, but that was only a matter of perspective in this alien landscape. It took much longer to walk from the landing site to the house than Ellis had expected. Among other things, his estimate had been based on the sizes of the trees that came almost to the roof of the house. As it turned out, those squat-looking trees were nearly ten meters tall.

After his initial difficulties breathing Rd'dyggian air, Ellis found his respiration returning to normal. At least the smells of sulfur and ammonia no longer made him gag. Actually, the air itself was quite breathable. It was almost the same ratio of nitrogen to oxygen as was on Earth and the atmospheric pressure was just slightly higher than that of Earth. The water vapor content seemed high to Ellis, even though he had grown up on an island in the North Atlantic.

Being able to breathe more normally, Ellis found he could walk without Arepno's help. Looking at the warrior, he realized that his bright orange skin did not seem quite as overwhelming in the light of his own planet. His skin looked more a ruddy tan here. In fact, his purple mustache looked nearly black. In this light, Ellis thought Arepno looked almost handsome.

Wordlessly, the seven-foot tall warrior invited Ellis into his house. Inside sat three other Rd'dyggians. It was impossible for Ellis to distinguish male from female. All three had the prehensile purple mustaches. One was slightly taller than Arepno. Two were slightly shorter. They were lounging on the floor. One of the shorter ones appeared to be scanning a ledger of some form and wore a loose fitting copper-colored gown that draped around the entire body. The taller one was writing and wearing more of a long tunic adorned with some floral pattern Ellis did not recognize. The other of the shorter ones was working on some cloth with what appeared to be a staple gun. This Rd'dyggian wore a silver jerkin and pants cut to resemble the shape of Arepno's robes.

The room itself seemed Spartan. Unlike a human living room, nothing adorned the walls. Other than the objects used by the people, the room was empty. The walls seemed made of the same dirt as the ground outside, though the air seemed devoid of the ammonia smell.

"Allow me to introduce my two wives, Arepnon and R'landan,

and my co-husband, R'landa," said Arepno, first in Rd'dyggian so his family could hear, then with the translator so Ellis could understand.

"Pleased to meet you," said Ellis nervously. He cursed inwardly that he had not brought any kind of translation device along. It seemed rude to make his host restate everything he said.

Arepno introduced Ellis as another hero of Sufiro. Arepno's family nodded courteously. The warrior then turned to Ellis. "Let us retire to my chambers where we may talk freely."

Arepno led him through the large common room to a room at the side. Like the common room, the side room had no corners; it was completely round. There were no chairs. However, there was a table of sorts in the center of the room. On it was a plate that Ellis recognized as a Rd'dyggian computer. Next to it were several of the ledgers like the type one of the shorter people was reading in the common room.

Before Arepno said anything, the taller Rd'dyggian appeared in the doorway with two glasses of water. Ellis noticed that this Rd'dyggian's tunic was not actually floral, but a mishmash of colors that resembled the flowers of Earth. The Rd'dyggian handed one glass to Arepno and the other to Ellis, then nodded to Arepno. "Thank you, R'landa." Arepno nodded. Again, he spoke in Rd'dyggian, but used the translator to speak for Ellis' benefit.

As R'landa left, Ellis turned to his host. "I am terribly sorry I forgot to wear a translator."

"Apology accepted," vocalized Arepno with a lift of his hand. "You seemed in a great hurry to be here. You did not contact me before coming to my world."

Ellis nodded. "The problem is . . . that ever since Sufiro, I can't get the vision of the Cluster out of my mind."

"I have heard," said Arepno, slowly, almost measured, "that you encountered another Cluster on your way home to Earth. They say a ship was destroyed."

"I was charged with cowardice," confessed Ellis, bluntly. He took a deep breath, then picked up the glass of water, sniffed its vaguely rotten-egg smell and put the glass back on the table. "The fact of the matter is that the Cluster communicated with me through a vision of some sort. The power of the vision caused me to pass out." Ellis, his throat almost too dry to speak, grabbed the glass, held his breath and swallowed the water. "Unfortunately, I passed out right as we almost had the civilian ship under our protection."

"So, why come to Rd'dyggia?" Arepno folded his arms.

"An old friend, on Earth, recommended that I seek out one who knew communications, understood the hunt and its consequences. He recommended I talk to a philosopher named G'Liat."

Arepno's dark mustache wiggled momentarily, though he made no sound. Finally, he sat forward. "There are no philosophers on Rd'dyggia," intoned Arepno, at last.

"I know that," growled Ellis. He shook his head, then silently gathered his thoughts. More composed, he continued, "but, I have to know whether or not I committed an act of cowardice and fainted on the bridge of my ship during a crisis situation, or whether I really and truly communicated with the Cluster in some way that is not understood."

Arepno sat silent, his mustache wiggling. Ellis got the impression that the warrior was holding something back.

"Damn it, Arepno! I was booted out of the fleet! I've been dishonored." Ellis put his face in his hands. "I don't even know if it was my fault. If so, I'll have to learn to live with what I did. If not, though, I'll have to seek justice."

"Why should I help a coward?" asked Arepno. He picked up the glass and let his mustache-like protrusions slide into the water.

"Because, I might not be a coward. My honor is at stake. The honor of my family," pleaded Ellis.

Arepno looked over the glass at Ellis. "Honor can be a dangerous concept. Humans do not have a sense of family honor. Not like Rd'dyggians."

"I do," said Ellis firmly. "The Cluster took the life of my father. Despite that, I risked my career on an attempt to talk to the Cluster rather than destroy it. That attempt might have succeeded. I don't know. Is there a G'Liat? Could he help me?"

Arepno lowered the glass and made a noise, not unlike a human sigh. "There is a G'Liat," he said at last. "He is not a philosopher, but a warrior. He is a giant among Rd'dyggians – perhaps the greatest warrior of all. Some say he is a sorcerer. He was my teacher for a short time." Arepno turned down the speaker volume on the translator box. "He knows the hunt. He knows death. Most of all, he understands the abstract world of the mind. Not just Rd'dyggian minds, but the minds of off-worlders. He taught me of humans and Tzrn, but he understands them all. If he learns of a species, he goes to meet it, to understand it."

Ellis licked his lips. "Has he met the Cluster?"

Arepno shook his head, in an imitation of the human gesture. "He has tried and failed."

"Perhaps I can give him some insight," pondered Ellis.

"So like your grandfather." Arepno sat back. "Such arrogance you humans display. Although you might give him some insight, I suspect it will be you who gains insight, *if* you are not a coward." Arepno's mustache formed a shape, not unlike a smile. "I will take you to him this afternoon, but first, dine with me and my family, grandson of Firebrandt."

Ellis nodded, recognizing that Arepno had paid him a great compliment in referring to him by the name of a respected friend. "Thank you, I will." As they stood to join the others, Ellis asked, "So, what's this about you being retired?"

"I have been retired many seasons," said Arepno.

"What about your ship? What about Sufiro?"

"Whoever said I had acted in a, how do you humans say, official capacity?" Ellis thought he detected a hint of laughter from the translator's speaker.

* * *

Later that afternoon, Mark Ellis groaned as Arepno's hover bounced in air turbulence. The hover, unlike human built vehicles, was more an aircraft, traveling high in the Rd'dyggian atmosphere. The dinner so graciously prepared by Arepno's wives, combined with the meal from the space station caused his stomach to do flip-flops. Although the vegetables, meats, and teas were perfectly edible by human standards, Rd'dyggians' digestive systems were far more efficient than his.

The punch line of an old human joke said, Rd'dyggians don't have a brain in their head. That was literally true. Rd'dyggians had evolved such that their brains were in their upper chest cavity behind a nearly impervious wall of bone. Their stomachs were in their heads, with an organ that did much the same thing as intestines located just below the shoulders. Ellis' stomach did another turn as he remembered the sight of the first headless Rd'dyggian he had ever seen on Titan. The being was a communicator; no sight or hearing was necessary. He only needed to use his brain to speak to ships coming and leaving. A bag hanging limply from his shoulders had replaced his stomach.

"How much farther is G'Liat's compound," groaned Ellis.

"Not much," said Arepno. "Only a few hundred more kilometers."

Ellis put his head back against the hard, high-backed seat of the hover and sighed. He ran his hand over the cool, unyielding leather-like material of the armrest at his side, then looked out at the lush alien landscape. The purple vegetation and red sand made him long for his gray island home. The sparse housing suddenly made him long for the closeness of humans.

Ellis looked back toward Arepno, whose hands rested firmly on a square silver plate embedded in the console. His face showed concentration as he steered the craft – his brain tied directly into the computer. Ellis had spent most of the journey, so far, in silence, afraid to distract Arepno. He pursed his lips though, thinking it might be more than that. Their conversations so far had been stilted, and uncomfortable.

"So," began Ellis, cautiously, "I didn't know Rd'dyggian women took the names of their spouses."

Arepno inclined his head.

"I'm sorry, am I distracting you?" Ellis' voice held a nervous twinge.

"No distraction," came the voice from the translator box. "Not with this simple craft." Arepno faced Ellis. "I simply do not understand the inference."

"Your wives were named Arepnon and R'landan." Ellis' brow creased. "Didn't your wives take the names of you and R'landa?"

"Ah," said Arepno, looking back out the window. "The problem is a difference of perspective. If I understand, on Earth your wife would be Mrs. John, am I right?"

"Close," conceded Ellis. "She would be Mrs. Ellis – in my culture, at least. Though most humans don't change names to match their mates anymore. Actually," he mused, "most humans don't even know their mates anymore. The actual physical act is considered something of a taboo for many."

Arepno imitated a human nod. "Yes, the human capacity to reject love has been well documented since the whale epics of your nineteenth century." His mustache wiggled, then he continued. "In my culture on Rd'dyggia, husbands assume the names of their first wives. It is a sign of deference that I have taken a shorter version of Arepnon's name."

Ellis wrung his hands, somewhat annoyed at himself that he had made an assumption based on what, even many humans, considered an outmoded system of mating. "I guess I'm just an old-fashioned guy." Ellis ran his hands through auburn hair. "What was your name before you were married?"

"That is irrelevant," stated Arepno blandly. Ellis imagined the warrior was irritated, though the translator betrayed no such emotion. "That name has evaporated into the past. It is forgotten." The Rd'dyggian's face seemed to go blank for several minutes. "We are nearly at G'Liat's. Prepare for descent."

Almost instantly, Arepno put the craft into a dive. Ellis closed his eyes tightly as he felt the bile build in his throat. He gripped the armrest of the seat and willed himself not to vomit in Arepno's craft.

Abruptly, the tiny craft bumped hard against unyielding ground. Once it came to a stop. Ellis leaned into the glass of the craft's bubble top. "We have arrived," announced Arepno.

"We certainly have," grumbled Ellis. "Should we call the compound and announce our arrival?" He scanned the almost completely bare console of Arepno's craft, not even knowing if there was communication's equipment, much less how to operate it.

"I already have," said Arepno, matter-of-factly as ever. "G'Liat is expecting you." With that, the bubble top of the aircraft opened, causing Ellis to nearly tumble out onto the ground.

Remembering that he did not have any translation equipment, Ellis sat up and looked at Arepno. "Could I impose upon you, and ask a favor?"

"You may ask." Arepno's unblinking black eye stared forward.

"Could I borrow your translation gear? After all, I am going to meet with a great warrior."

"No imposition," stated Arepno. "No need. G'Liat speaks the language you call Generic." Ellis' eyebrows came together. He was not aware that Rd'dyggian vocal chords were structured in a way that would allow them to speak terro-generic.

After only a moment's hesitation, Ellis climbed out of the cockpit and straightened his coat. "Thank you, for all your help and hospitality," he said, leaning over the edge of the hover.

"I will have your payment, when the Cluster has ended its killing," said Arepno. Ellis had to move his hands out of the way quickly before the bubble top came down. He was pushed rudely aside as Arepno activated the anti-graviton generator. Within seconds, the aircraft was gone from sight and Ellis found himself standing alone in a clearing of magenta grass.

Looking around, Ellis' queasy stomach sunk as he realized he did not know which direction the compound was in. Trees and tall bushes surrounded the clearing. Overhead, dark gray-green clouds were billowing. Ellis brought the collar of his jacket up and studied the surrounding area.

Most of the vegetation seemed too dense to even move through. However, turning around, Ellis saw a pair of trees, close together. Walking toward them, he saw a round structure behind, not unlike Arepno's house. Ellis shimmied between the trees and found himself standing in a larger clearing, facing the structure. As he made his way toward the house, he heard a shuffling behind him. Turning, he found himself face to chest with a being who towered over eight feet tall. Arepno had always seemed massive, but the warrior now seemed willowy compared with the being standing before him. Looking up, Ellis saw himself mirrored in the great black, unblinking eyes of the alien.

"Who are you?" asked the being in a surprisingly affable, but crisp voice. There was no hint of the Rd'dyggian raspy, singsong style of speaking.

"I am John Mark Ellis." Ellis wrung his hands and blew into them, trying to warm himself. "Are you G'Liat?"

"I am called G'Liat," said the Rd'dyggian, moving around Ellis, looking down at him. "Though, you are not simply John Mark Ellis."

Ellis looked down at himself, then looked back up, his brow wrinkled. "I don't understand."

"No, you don't," agreed G'Liat. The being wore a one-piece black suit, tailored to fit his body. On his feet were glossy black boots. Around his neck was a silver choker. The attire looked odd given Rd'dyggians love of wearing loose-fitting clothing. The being motioned for Ellis to follow with a large, six-fingered hand, adorned in brightly colored rings.

They walked to G'Liat's compound. The room was a study in contrasts. As opposed to Arepno's house, the main room was extremely full. Ellis saw evidence of travels to nearly every inhabited planet he knew and some he did not. Unlike old man Coffin's house back on Nantucket this room was not cluttered. Instead, it seemed extremely well organized almost like the storeroom of a museum or library. Titan data cubes were in one section. In another section, he saw books stacked neatly. Oddly, above the books he saw painted on the wall the human symbol for yin yang. Next to that hung a crucifix. What really caught Ellis' attention though was a nearly white piece of bone with a black etching of a tall ship.

Ellis stepped up and looked at the bone. He touched it lightly. "It's scrimshaw," he declared. "This has been illegal to purchase even before whales were known to be intelligent."

"Once their intelligence was determined, mere ownership of antique scrimshaw was also considered unethical." The Rd'dyggian seemed to eye him closely.

Ellis' eyebrows came together. "Killing whales for their baleen has been unethical for centuries. I didn't know any scrimshaw still existed."

"You surprise me," said G'Liat evenly. "Hunting whales is not ethical now, yet you feel nostalgia for the days when your ancestors hunted whales."

"How do you know my ancestors hunted whales?" Ellis blinked at the Rd'dyggian teacher several times.

"It was the look in your eye, when you saw the bone. It was the look of the predator." G'Liat folded his arms. "It is a look that most humans would not get. They would not recognize the bone for what it is."

"Why do you have a piece of scrimshaw?" Ellis asked, suspiciously.

"It reminds me that humans, like many other species in the galaxy, are dangerous to those they do not understand," explained G'Liat.

Ellis returned his gaze to the whalebone, then looked back to G'Liat. "I do feel a certain nostalgia for this piece of bone." He shook his head, as though trying to clear a thought. "I know I shouldn't. One of my closest friends on Earth is a whale."

G'Liat nodded. "I have yet to meet a species that wasn't racist to some degree or another." The warrior paused and looked toward the ceiling. "Perhaps, specist would be a better word, if it existed."

Ellis inclined his head. "I would debate that."

"Indeed! Specism is part of evolution. We can't have competitors as intelligent as us. Most of us, who have grown to high intelligence, have learned to control it. The whales, who do not interact, don't bother to control their racism. Those who are powerful, do not need."

"Powerful? Like the Cluster." Ellis moved toward the teacher.

"We are getting ahead of ourselves. May I offer you a drink? I have filtered water that should be more palatable than well water."

"Thank you." Ellis smiled, truly grateful. "I would appreciate that."

"Please forgive the state of the house," explained G'Liat. "My co-husband died only a year ago. My wives have been gone for some time. I was never the housekeeper of the group." Ellis watched as G'Liat went into the other room. The teacher's movements were almost feline. His manner was so gentle, his voice so practiced, that he did not seem alien. G'Liat returned and handed Ellis a glass of water.

"Did Arepno tell you I've come trying to find a way to communicate with the Cluster?" Ellis took a sip of the water. He wrinkled his nose, detecting the flat taste of distillation.

"First things first." G'Liat held his finger up to his nose. "Before you can know the Cluster, you must know yourself."

"Who am I?" Ellis tugged at his beard with his free hand.

"Exactly. Who are you?" G'Liat again motioned for Ellis to follow. The teacher led Ellis into a room where there were two chairs. One was little more than a functional stool. The other was a leather-bound recliner from Earth. G'Liat sat on the stool and held his open hand toward the recliner. Ellis sat, but resisted the temptation to lean back in the comfortable chair. "John Mark Ellis is a label. Who is John Mark Ellis?"

"Right now, I really don't know," said Ellis, uncomfortably. "Before I left the space service, I would have answered, a ship captain." He sat the glass down by the side of the chair. "Now, I'm not even an officer."

"Ah." G'Liat put his hand on his chest. "But ships are part of your self-image. It was evident when you looked at the scrimshaw. Are you sure you are not still a captain?"

"A captain without a ship?" Ellis shook his head.

"Captain of your destiny, perhaps. A warrior, at least," suggested G'Liat. "To have embarked on this quest, you must still feel responsibility to yourself and to your planet."

"Perhaps," admitted Ellis. "Perhaps it's just self-interest. I don't want to die at the hands of the Cluster."

"Why would self-interest be bad?" asked G'Liat flatly. "Especially if it's not destructive. But to be that interested in yourself, you must know who you are."

Ellis picked up the glass of water and peered into it for several minutes. "What if I found that the Cluster must be destroyed?"

"You are ahead of the game again," said G'Liat, calmly. "You assume two options. The Cluster is good and could help us or the Cluster is evil and must be destroyed." The teacher inclined his head and folded his giant hands. "What if I were sitting here asking, should I kill Ellis, or should I not kill Ellis?"

Ellis shifted uncomfortably under the gaze of G'Liat. His eyes moved to the warrior's muscular, ring-covered hands. He tugged the collar of his shirt. "I'm not evil," he said at last then swallowed hard. "There's no need for killing."

"Is that true? I don't know who you are? You still have not answered that. Are you good or evil?" G'Liat straightened his back.

"I'd like to think I'm good," said Ellis. He closed his eyes and shook his head trying not to let himself be intimidated. He did not understand the point of the conversation and proceeded cautiously with his answer. "I've done some pretty rotten things in my time, but I don't think that makes me evil."

G'Liat put his hands on his knees. His lipless mouth formed a smile framed by his mustache. "Ever killed a fly or an ant? Ever dissected a frog? Ever dreamed of hunting a whale?"

Ellis began to feel queasy. He remembered pictures he had seen of the great hunts. Whales, like his friend Richard, were speared then lanced. The dead whale was brought to the ship and sliced into pieces. There had been films where seas of blood poured from the animals he called friends. The mental image of the long black carcass being sliced open suddenly seemed uncomfortably close to the image of the long, cylindrical ships being sliced open by the Cluster. "I do not know who the Cluster is."

"Who?" For a moment, Ellis thought he'd caught a glimmer in the warrior's eye. "You make it sound as though the Cluster is an entity unto itself."

"I don't know," said Ellis. "I have a certain sense, but no knowledge."

"Indeed." G'Liat folded his hands into a peak under his nose. Ellis shifted restlessly under the warrior's gaze. "You appear tired," he said after a moment. "I will show you to your sleeping chambers."

G'Liat led him through a number of rooms. All of them were full like the first room Ellis had entered. Finally, after what seemed like a journey around the entire perimeter of the house, they came to a room with a pit dug in the middle. The pit was filled with a soupy, dark substance. At one end of the pit was a smooth depression in the rock.

"I am sorry, but I cannot offer a human-style bed," said G'Liat with a shrug.

Ellis raised both eyebrows, looked from the pit then back to G'Liat. "You're telling me that's a bed?" Ellis pointed at the ooze-filled pit in the floor.

"The mud is highly viscous," explained G'Liat. "Its temperature can be adjusted with the control knob to the left. It will envelop you, but you will not sink. Other humans who have visited have found it quite comfortable."

"Thanks, I think," Ellis muttered under his breath.

"There is a vibrational cleanser to the left as you step out of bed." G'Liat stood silent waiting to see if Ellis had any questions.

"How do I activate the cleanser?"

"Just step out of the pit onto it, it will activate automatically," explained G'Liat. "If you need me during the night, I will be asleep or working in the adjacent room." With that he bid Ellis good night and left the ex-commander alone.

Ellis stared at the pit with some trepidation. He had to admit that he was exhausted and he welcomed the chance to get some sleep. However, the idea of crawling into the ooze did not strongly appeal to him. Finally, he took a deep breath, and took off his boots, woolen pants and cotton shirt.

Standing naked in the chill room, he tested the temperature of the mud with his big toe. He was pleasantly surprised to find that the mud was near body temperature. Reaching down, he turned the knob up a notch, then slipped into the mud.

It turned out that the mud did support him freely. Although the mud enveloped him completely, he felt no sense that he would sink too far. He lay his head in the notched out area of the ground. Except for his head, he felt almost no sensation from the rest of his body, only a delightful warmth. He was asleep in a matter of minutes.

* * *

That night, Ellis dreamt vividly. In his dream, he saw a reddish haze, which looked like a nebula, of sorts. The nebula parted and he saw silver spheroids. He thought he was seeing the silver orbs of the Cluster, at first. The problem was the reddish haze looked like no nebula Ellis knew. It was then that Ellis realized he was looking at the spheroids through an atmosphere. It was not just any atmosphere, though. It was the thick haze that enveloped the surface of Titan. He was seeing the pressure domes that covered the surface of the moon from which all known worlds were governed.

Somehow, at that moment, Ellis realized that it did not matter whether or not he commanded a ship in the Confederation Navy. He was a free human with no allegiance to the Titans anymore. More important, he was the captain, for as long as he lived. He had been waiting for the Admiralty on Titan to give him a ship. He knew now that he must find the ship himself.

Commander, by Nature

John Mark Ellis awoke to smells of bacon and coffee intermingling sensually in the air. The scents were better than incense at blocking out the smells of ammonia and sulfur lurking in the atmosphere. The ex-commander smiled, thinking of his mother's cooking back on Nantucket, and more recently on the frontier world, Sufiro. Without opening his eyes, he stretched his arms into the chill morning air and winced as a dollop of warm mud landed beside his nose and oozed its way to his beard leaving a cold wet trail on his cheek.

With a sigh, Ellis opened his eyes and examined the ceiling above. The adobe ceiling was covered with a smooth white plaster, broken only by the presence of the cleansing unit overhead. Ellis imagined he could see faces in the plaster swirls. For a moment, his attention became fixed on one of the faces. The sweeping plaster over the face reminded Ellis of Clyde McClintlock's white hair. Ellis rubbed more mud into his beard wondering why his mind had conjured the image of the defeated colonel after these weeks away from Sufiro. Ellis had never quite been able to figure the man out. He had no respect for the colonel's undistinguished military career. Likewise, Clyde, while a good man, seemed slow to act. Only the Cluster was a strong enough catalyst to prod him into helping the innocent people he had been sworn to protect all along.

Grimacing slightly, but refusing to let thoughts of McClintlock or the Cluster ruin his mood, Ellis stepped out of the bed, onto the cleansing unit. The unit activated and Ellis felt a tingling sensation as ultrasonic waves vibrated the mud from his body and hair. The waves caressed him luxuriously. For a time, all thoughts of the Cluster left his mind. Instead, he thought of the dancer at the nightclub in Boston and wondered what she could have done for him.

Before his thoughts ran too far, though, Ellis ran his fingers through now-lustrous hair and stepped off the cleanser. His hair was short enough it fell mostly into place on its own. Feeling energized, Ellis looked where he had unceremoniously piled his clothes the night before. He was surprised to see that they had been moved into a neat pile in the corner of the room. Shrugging, he sauntered over and picked up his shirt. Not only had G'Liat fastidiously folded the clothes, he had cleaned them. The shirt was bright white. The woolen trousers were uncharacteristically soft, but pressed to perfection. Looking down, Ellis was impressed by how much the civilian apparel looked like a uniform. Standing straight, Ellis strode out of the room, following the smells of breakfast.

Ellis found the austere G'Liat sitting at a simple, square table. In front of the warrior was a bowl containing a purple gruel, undoubtedly made from vegetables growing around the compound. At the place across from him, though, was a plate with bacon and eggs. Another plate, piled high with muffins, stood in the middle of the table, while a cup of coffee waited nearby. G'Liat gestured for him to take the seat across from him. Ellis smiled and sat. "This looks wonderful," he said. He sipped the coffee and wrinkled his nose slightly at an unusual, but not unpleasant, flavor.

"If I poisoned you, would I be evil?" G'Liat wore an expression, not unlike a mischievous grin. Ellis dropped the mug to the floor. His eyes grew wide. "The coffee contains chicory," explained G'Liat, rising. He retrieved the fallen mug, cleaned up the spilled coffee and set a fresh cup in front of Ellis. "I discovered it while in New Orleans on Earth. It was the only way I could drink this otherwise hideous beverage."

Ellis took a sip from the fresh mug and contemplated the mixture of flavors. "It's good," he said, at last.

"Do you have an answer to my question?" asked G'Liat, his face expressionless.

"I think you're frightening," grumbled Ellis, thinking about the coffee. "I'm not sure that counts as being evil."

G'Liat dipped a spoon-like utensil into his purple gruel. Slowly, he raised it to his face where the mustache like appendages moved the food into his tiny mouth. At last he turned his attention back to Ellis. "Can you tell me who you are?"

"I am John Mark Ellis; a lone human being on a mission. I am commander of my own destiny." Ellis took another sip, savoring the chicory coffee, then set the mug on the table.

"Indeed," said the warrior simply. He raised another spoonful of the gruel to his mouth. "What is your mission, commander?"

"My mission is to seek out the Cluster and talk to it or the people aboard it." Ellis folded his arms and nodded.

"You alone?" G'Liat inclined his head. "What makes you think you are qualified for this mission? I've heard of human hubris, but this is approaching the ridiculous."

"I have communicated with the Cluster," said Ellis, feeling new resolve. "I've done it once, I can do it again."

"Only you?" G'Liat leaned forward slightly. "Be careful how you answer."

Ellis searched his feelings for a moment. He picked up the coffee mug, then set it down again. At last he picked it up and took a sip. "I don't know," he said thoughtfully. "I could probably use help, there might be others who could do this as well." Ellis took a deep breath, then shook his head. "Let them go on their own quest. I can't wait for them."

G'Liat reached out and picked up the plate of muffins, handing it to Ellis. "Eat heartily, commander, we have a busy day ahead."

Through breakfast, Ellis told the warrior about his father having been killed by the Cluster. He went on, detailing both of his experiences with the enigmatic spheres. "While I miss my father desperately, I'm not sure whether the Cluster can be blamed for his death, especially after the second vision," he explained, finishing the last muffin.

G'Liat simply looked out the window, as if daydreaming.

* * *

Later that morning, G'Liat and Ellis were walking outside. A bitter sulfur-smelling fog surrounded them as they walked. Despite the chill, Ellis wore his coat unbuttoned and enjoyed the damp air. G'Liat's form-fitting clothes revealed that his long, lanky body was defined by lithe cat-like muscles. The commander had no doubt that the warrior could move the awkward-looking body with a gymnast's perfection of grace. Indeed, he seemed to glide through the underbrush while Ellis would occasionally stumble on the uneven ground. As they walked, the one-time commander noticed the bell-like chiming of some of the birds and marveled as the light breeze caused the grass to whistle.

"How are you feeling today?" asked the warrior, coming to an abrupt stop.

Ellis had to stop suddenly to keep from running into the warrior's back. "Much better than yesterday. The planet's air seems much more breathable."

"You are becoming acclimated," commented G'Liat. "More importantly, though, I sense that your confidence is high. That is good."

"Is it?" mused Ellis. "I don't know if I understand what you consider good."

"The Cluster has twice impinged your honor," stated G'Liat, simply. "First, when your father was killed. Second, when your military career was ended due to contact with the Cluster. That alone would be enough to destroy most humans or Rd'dyggians. If you are serious in your intention to seek out the Cluster, to communicate with it, you must be free and approach it with as open a mind as possible. You must forget about love of your race. You must forget about your honor and your home."

"You have a home," said Ellis, matter-of-factly.

"It is, as you have seen, merely a place where I keep things. My home is your home, or the home of anyone who stops by, seeking my help." G'Liat's voice, while gentle, seemed to resonate with conviction.

"Your hospitality has been most gracious." Ellis smiled, feeling invigorated. "I just wish I had some way to repay you."

"You do," stated G'Liat. "I want to experience the Cluster as you have experienced it. I want to see what the Cluster has said to you."

"I've already explained as much as I could about the vision the Cluster put in my head," stammered Ellis.

"I know that," said G'Liat. "However, if I am to help you further, I must see the vision first hand, as it exists in your brain."

Ellis cocked his head. "What do you mean?"

"As you might, or might not, know we Rd'dyggians have very sophisticated communications technology." G'Liat put his arms behind his back, as though lecturing. "With the same technology we use to communicate with our ships, we can communicate with each other. We can see each other's thoughts."

Ellis' mouth dropped open. He shuffled his feet and fished instinctively around his coat pockets for a cigar. Instead, he found the pipe. "You mean you can open a direct brain interface with another Rd'dyggian?"

"Routinely, more than one of us interfaces with a common machine. When we do, it is inevitable that we see the other's thoughts. It was relatively easy for us to build a machine that let us view those thoughts directly." G'Liat's unblinking eyes turned toward the jungle.

Ellis stood, silently tearing strips of flake tobacco into the bowl of his pipe. Using his thumb, he tamped them into the bowl. "You propose to use this technique on me?"

"It might allow me to see the very images only you yourself have seen."

Ellis raised the pipe to his mouth and thought for a moment about the smells in the air. Deciding that the concentrations of ammonia and sulfur weren't high enough for spontaneous combustion, he lit the pipe. After puffing on it for a few minutes, he looked back to the warrior. "Would there be any risk to either of us?"

"I have never tried the technique with a human." He looked back to Ellis. "I have, however, used it successfully with Earth creatures; namely spermaceti whales. They proved to be most interesting creatures."

"What's good enough for spermaceti is good enough for this Nantucketer." Ellis savored the smoke from his pipe for a time, preferring it to the smell of the atmosphere.

"That might not be true. Whales have very strong wills." In a very human gesture, G'Liat put his hand on Ellis' shoulder. He flinched slightly and nearly dropped the pipe. "I must warn you that this form of communication can be very intimate. The human race is unique in its fear of intimacy. If you shy from my touch, are you ready for this?"

Ellis took a long draw on his pipe. Exhaling slowly out of the side of his mouth, he relaxed, putting his hand on top of the warrior's. "If it will help me understand the Cluster, I'm ready."

* * *

Clyde McClintlock wore a tailored white suit as he stepped off the transport into the Rd'dyggian space station. He straightened it and brushed back a strand of errant white hair as he approached the customs desk. Two young men in dark suits followed, carrying heavy bags. One man was blonde and called Jonah, the other was redheaded and named Daniel. McClintlock showed his passport to the sleepy Rd'dyggian behind the desk. She stamped the document and then processed the other two men.

McClintlock and his disciples were like a military procession as they marched through the nearly empty station corridor to stand in front of the booth operated by Guadalupe Cordova. She sat provocatively, with one leg draped over the arm of the large chair. Her head was back and a snore escaped at the moment that Clyde knocked on the counter top.

"Miss?" inquired Clyde, somewhat quietly. Cordova stirred a bit, but did not wake. "Miss!" called Clyde, more impatiently.

Cordova opened one of her wide brown eyes, then closed it tightly, swinging her leg down to the ground. Looking at the neglected tile on the floor, she shook her head. "Shit, this is all I need."

"Miss, my name is Clyde McClintlock, I need . . ."

"I know who you are," spat the petite woman as she stood up. "I recognize you from the holo news from Earth." She put her hands on her hips. "If you're here to convert the Rd'dyggians to that weird-ass religion you've cooked up, you can forget it!"

McClintlock's two disciples flushed brightly. The evangelist sighed. "All I need to know is whether or not a man came through here a few days ago."

Cordova inclined her head, examining the reverend. "I don't give out names of my passengers. If someone was trying to escape that kooky cult of yours, I don't blame 'em."

"I can assure you," began McClintlock in a huff, "that I do not run a cult. Besides," he said, softening a bit, "the man I'm looking for is an old friend."

"Yeah, I'm sure you tell that to everyone!" With that, Cordova retrieved a book from behind the counter, flopped in the large chair and carefully examined the pages.

"His name is John Mark Ellis," pleaded McClintlock.

"Ellis?" Cordova looked over the edge of the book. "You know that guy?"

"We both saw the vision of the Cluster while on Sufiro." McClintlock looked toward the ceiling.

"Ah brother!" exclaimed Cordova as she tossed the book back behind the counter. "I knew he was a bit whacked in the head. I didn't know he was a complete loon."

"I would appreciate it if you could help me find him." McClintlock produced a credit chit. "I would appreciate it quite a lot."

Cordova eyed the chit. "I could probably get you going in the right direction."

* * *

G'Liat fed Ellis lunch and then led him around the house to the room where they talked the night before. The warrior instructed Ellis to sit in the large, comfortable chair. After that, he left for a period. During that time, Ellis could hear him banging around in the next room. Finally, the warrior returned, holding a slightly bowed, oblong plate of sorts. The plate appeared to be mother-of-pearl and looked like a good-sized serving tray.

"This device is what we use to communicate directly with the brain," explained G'Liat. He handed it to Ellis who examined the device. There were no controls that Ellis could recognize. He shook his head and handed it back to the warrior.

G'Liat placed the bowed end over his chest. "It is designed to rest over the brain." He removed the device and put his massive six-fingered hand on Ellis' head. "It will be somewhat difficult to use in your case, but despite the differences in brain location, the actual configuration of our brains is quite similar."

"Let's get on with it," said Ellis, growing slightly impatient.

"First, you must relax as completely as possible, clear your mind thoroughly." G'Liat placed the plate on Ellis' head. "Humans are notorious for their lack of ability to relax. Would you like a sedative?"

Ellis pursed his lips, suspicious. "I don't really care for drugs."

"How about a shot of whiskey?"

Ellis sucked in his breath. "It might help." G'Liat stepped out of the room for a moment, then returned with a small glass of amber fluid. Ellis eyed the liquid almost suspiciously, but ultimately downed it. He sucked in his breath then slumped back into the chair. As the warrior balanced the device on his scalp, he looked into G'Liat's eye. "You're sure this will work?"

"We can only try," said G'Liat, hopefully.

Ellis began breathing deeply. He let his mind gently wander to the most relaxing image he knew, the moors of Nantucket Island. He was not even aware of G'Liat, delicately balancing his hands on the device.

* * *

G'Liat was a warrior and a traveler who had seen many places and done many things. Still, the landscape where he found himself seemed as alien as any he had encountered. The sky was a vivid blue with white clouds billowing in the distance. The ground seemed unusually stable for its softness. The warrior knew he was standing on Earth as John Mark Ellis saw it. The roar of the nearby ocean was much louder than he remembered, but comforting. A breeze that would have been too hot seemed pleasantly cool.

G'Liat nodded to himself. He tried to use his will to transport himself through Ellis' memories to the day when the commander had made contact with the Cluster. He was surprised to hear a sea gull screech overhead. He still stood on the sand; the wind still blew around him.

"Commander," called G'Liat. "You must help me. You must show me your contact with the Cluster."

G'Liat found himself lying on a comfortable slab of foam, covered by a sheet of fabric. He felt pleasantly sleepy, having just returned from winning a major victory. Forcing his eyes open, the warrior realized he was aboard an Earth destroyer. Somehow, the scene did not seem right. Still, he allowed himself to relax and be carried by the memory.

As he drifted off to sleep, his mind was assaulted by frightening images. He felt the distress of people as they were captured and taken from their families. He agonized with the torture of thousands of people who were forced to work against their will. Rd'dyggians never believed in slavery. For the first time in his life, G'Liat knew what it was like to be a slave, mining Erdonium on Sufiro.

Feelings of rage began to form. It was almost indefinite at first, but soon the emotion was clear and cogent. The anger built in a spiral of sorts until he was blown off his feet by a violent explosion. At that point, he felt nothing more than curiosity. He tried to say something, but could not be understood. Instead, he felt a sensation of warmth, as though someone shared the bed. G'Liat grew momentarily sad as he remembered the loss of his wives and co-husband.

"This is not the vision of the Cluster I had in mind. It is far too subtle," said the warrior, sadly. "This is the vision you had over Sufiro."

G'Liat recognized the face of Ellis' first officer, Frank Rubin as he peeked around a curtain. Ellis remembered Rubin saying, "Are you all right, sir?" in response to Ellis screaming. Instead, Rubin spoke with Ellis' voice. "It is the Sufiro vision. The visions I felt later are too personal."

G'Liat flung the sheet aside and faced Rubin, putting his hands on the man's shoulders. "You must show me the images you saw later when you tried to rescue the Earth ship."

Rubin evaporated from under G'Liat's grasp. The warrior found himself standing outside a walled fortress nestled against a lake. He heard bagpipes blaring in the distance. The warrior noted with curiosity how almost primal the scene was. "You can't cut me off like this," he complained.

Ellis appeared on the rampart. "I can't let you go further," he called.

"You must," urged G'Liat.

"Part of me wants to let you in, the other part wants you out of my mind."

"Relax!" commanded G'Liat. "Let the fortress to your inner thoughts crumble."

"No," said Ellis, almost sadly. "My memories of the event are linked too closely to things I don't want you to see."

"Then I'll force my way in," called the warrior. "You are only human." He pushed on the wall and it began to crumble. Through a section, G'Liat caught a glimpse of Ellis' father. The fortress wall congealed and became whole again. The warrior's mustache wriggled in annoyance. "Let me in," he pleaded.

Ellis simply shook his head and descended stairs behind the castle wall.

G'Liat looked sadly to the ground. Folding his hands, he began to extract himself from the commander's mind. Just as he was leaving, a view of the domes of Titan superimposed on the Cluster caught his eye.

* * *

John Mark Ellis opened his dark eyes and looked at G'Liat. The warrior sat, slumped, across from him, the device off to his side. "Are you okay?" asked Ellis.

G'Liat looked up with wide, unblinking eyes. "About a year ago, shortly after the first appearance of the Cluster, I went out on a Rd'dyggian war ship to attempt contact." His veneer of humanity seemed to fade away as he spoke. Even the singsong Rd'dyggian accent surfaced for the first time. "Nominally, we went to understand. Secretly, my government wanted to see if alliance was possible. I simply wanted to understand.

"I was outside the ship, in a travel pod. Never once did I sense anything even as strong as what you felt over Sufiro." He looked down to the ground. "The other images you received must have been overwhelming." The warrior looked up again. "The Cluster sliced open my ship and appeared to probe it for a time. Soon after, it moved off and jumped."

"You were left alone in a travel pod," asked Ellis, wide-eyed. "How in hell did you survive?"

"My government had sent a backup ship shortly after we were dispatched. It arrived within half an hour of the Cluster's disappearance." G'Liat straightened his shoulders. "After that, the Cluster was declared an enemy of my people, to be destroyed on sight, if possible."

Ellis rubbed his beard. "So, you're forbidden to try contact again?"

G'Liat shook his head in a deliberately human gesture. "No," he said, forcing his accent to match Ellis'. "My government would not dare. However, I have access to no ships. That makes attempting contact very difficult."

"Why do you think I've succeeded and you've failed?" Ellis' eyebrows came together. "Why can't you see the more recent vision?"

"Perhaps the second question is for you to answer," said G'Liat.

"You saw a fortress," said Ellis slowly, searching his own memory. "I wouldn't let you in. You tried to break in and, somehow, I stopped you."

"You have remarkable will for a human," commented G'Liat. "I'm surprised your people don't make you a communicator."

"They asked. The money is good . . ."

"But you wouldn't be in command," G'Liat finished the sentence, understanding. "Why did you keep me out?"

"I really don't know," said Ellis shaking his head.

"Then you still don't really know who you are. Captain of your destiny is part, but not all. What is your destiny? Where are you going?" The warrior asked the questions rhetorically as he started pacing the room. "As to why you succeeded at communicating with the Cluster, that is even more difficult to guess at. My best guess is that it's simply a combination of things. While in your mind, I could tell that you are a very sensitive individual. In short, I think you are just correctly tuned emotionally, as it were. Furthermore, you were mostly relaxed, but still at a heightened state of awareness after a battle. To be sure, I'd need to try this exercise with another who has contacted the Cluster."

"I thought you said that we would see each other's thoughts," said Ellis. "I only peripherally sensed your thoughts."

G'Liat waved the comment aside. "The experience is different for different beings. Do you know of anyone else who has communicated with the Cluster?"

"My mother tells me that Colonel McClintlock of Tejo had a similar vision." Ellis sighed. "All I can say is that I was at an equally heightened state of awareness during the second encounter, as well." He rubbed his hands together, suddenly feeling the chill of the air around. "Do you think it's possible that the reason the second encounter was more vivid was that I was better tuned?"

"Perhaps," mused G'Liat. "Perhaps it was simply a more vivid vision." He put his hands behind his back. "There was something almost more disturbing in your mind than the visions."

Ellis inclined his head. "More disturbing?"

"Indeed, you have managed to overlay images of the Cluster and the Titans. Are you aware of the significance of that?"

"It was a dream I had last night. The dream helped me find the courage of my convictions."

"Dreams are often dangerous territory," said G'Liat warily. "Where does reality end and dream begin? A lot is written on this subject. Even more is spoken. Do not dismiss the significance of the dream." He paused to let his words sink in. "Where did the Titans evolve?"

"I always assumed it was on Saturn's moon. That's where they say they're from."

"Are you aware there is no archeological or paleontological evidence to support such a claim?" G'Liat looked grave for a second. "I have often suspected that the Titans are not all that they appear."

Ellis took a deep breath. "Are you suggesting that they might be related to the Cluster?"

"I will suggest no more. Over time, I will tell you what I do, in fact, know. I will let you draw your own conclusions. In the meantime, let your dreams guide you."

Ellis' brow creased. "Dreams seem an awfully frivolous thing to trust."

"Dreams are rarely frivolous," said G'Liat harshly. "They are one of the most important ways the human mind processes subconscious information. You have seen the Cluster and the domes on Titan. However, you might not have connected the two if you had not seen them together in a dream. Pay attention to your dreams, Ellis. They are a route to power. You will need all the power you can get when you confront the Cluster."

Ellis dug around his coat pocket for his pipe. He filled it and watched G'Liat pace the room. The commander held up the pipe. G'Liat noticed and waved acquiescence. Lighting the pipe, Ellis fell into silent thought. He began to wonder at the fact that he had done something that a trained communicator could not do. Also, he began to ponder if there was anything he could do without training, especially in light of G'Liat's claim that there was something he should know about the Titans. Taking a puff on his pipe, he looked back to the warrior. "What if the two of us faced the Cluster together?"

"That would be interesting," said G'Liat. "But how could we achieve it?"

"I could sell my property on Nantucket. That might be enough to buy us a ship," speculated Ellis. "I'd have to do it soon, though. The value's dwindling fast. Also, I'd have to get my mother's permission."

"Would it buy us a solid star vessel with enough range to track the Cluster wherever it happened to appear?" asked G'Liat, skeptically.

"Probably not," said Ellis, realizing that the plan would mean displacing Coffin. He closed his eyes against the image of Coffin being forced to leave the island. "However, aside from a Confederate military vessel, the only kind of ship I know that has that kind of range is a mapping vessel."

"Do you think it would be possible for you to get a job with the Gaean mapping service?" asked G'Liat.

"Maybe," mused Ellis. He sucked on the pipe stem for a moment. "I've heard they are always on the search for good captains. The problem is getting an interview . . ."

Ellis was interrupted by the buzz of the teleholo. G'Liat excused himself. The commander could hear two voices speaking Rd'dyggian. To him, it sounded agitated. However, most Rd'dyggians sounded agitated in their own language. After a moment, G'Liat returned. "Your friend Arepno has arrived," he said. "He brings a guest."

"A guest?" Ellis stood, clamping the pipe between his teeth. He followed G'Liat to the door of the house and stepped out with him to the grounds of the compound.

Arepno emerged from the fog, holding a limp body by the collar and seat of the pants. It took a moment for Ellis to realize it was Clyde McClintlock. Arepno threw McClintlock to the ground at Ellis' feet. He knelt down and felt for a pulse. While weak, it was present. Ellis looked up at Arepno.

"We do not abide slavers on this world," growled Arepno's translator box. "Nor do we abide humans who want to convert us to their brand of religion." Ellis was astounded at how the translator box could be made to put a particularly nasty turn on the word, religion. "I have sent his friends back to Gaea, unharmed. He insisted on coming to you. Here he is. I bid you good day, John Mark Ellis." Arepno turned and bowed to G'Liat and then stormed off into the fog.

Return to the Stars

"I presume you know this man," said G'Liat staring down at the prostrate form of Clyde McClintlock.

Mark Ellis, clamping the pipe stem in his teeth still knelt beside the one-time colonel. "He's alive," said the commander around the pipe stem. Looking along the body, Ellis noted that McClintlock's suit was relatively clean, indicating that there had not been much of a fight. Using sensitive fingers, he felt along the spine, checking for any evidence of injury. "As far as I can tell, he's simply unconscious. We should be able to move him."

"Who is he?" asked G'Liat, growing more curious, but seeming unconcerned about human flesh against cold, hard ground.

"He's McClintlock, the leader of the Tejan ground forces on Sufiro I told you about," stated Ellis, his eyebrows crossed. "He's the one who laid down arms and made peace with New Granada." Puffing furiously on the pipe, Ellis remembered seeing the colonel's face in the ceiling that morning. His brow knitted slightly and he looked back at the form on the ground. "We should get him inside where it's warm."

Resuming a more human poise, G'Liat nodded. He helped Ellis pick up the limp body and haul it back to the compound. Inside, they sat McClintlock in the comfortable chair where G'Liat examined his brain using the scanner. McClintlock's head rolled to the side causing the scanner to tip slightly. A soft moan escaped the evangelist's lips. G'Liat set the scanner to the side of the chair.

"Colonel, can you hear me?" asked Ellis.

McClintlock's eyes fluttered for a moment. Shortly after that, the evangelist took a deep breath, then opened his normally bright, blue eyes. Looking groggily around, those eyes seemed, at last, to focus on Ellis. Briefly he opened his mouth, then shook his head, as though trying to clear cobwebs from his brain.

"Bring him a glass of water," ordered Ellis, softly.

G'Liat inclined his head studying McClintlock for a moment, then went off to do as he was bid.

Ellis sat cross-legged on the floor and used his thumb to re-tamp the partially burned tobacco. Looking up, he lit the pipe again and smoked for a couple of minutes, contemplating the groggy form of Clyde McClintlock. At last, G'Liat returned with the water. The warrior helped the evangelist take a sip. With the first drink of water, McClintlock seemed to gain strength. He took the glass gingerly and drank the rest of it down. Blinking a few times, he looked around until he found Ellis again.

"I've found you, at last," whispered McClintlock.

Ellis arched his eyebrows. "Found me?" He held the pipe by its stem and contemplated McClintlock. "Was I lost?"

"Your mother tells me, you had the same vision I had. You had the vision of the Cluster," said McClintlock in a daze.

Ellis nodded. "She told me about your discussion in Roanoke." The commander came slowly to his feet. "I thought you were still on Sufiro."

"The people of Roanoke put me on the path to truth and light," said McClintlock dazedly. "From what your mother told me, I've come to understand that God favors you, as he does me." McClintlock's voice was gaining strength though his eyes, while more focused, still seemed lost.

Ellis looked at G'Liat who shrugged slightly. "I only used the scanner to check that his brain was not seriously harmed. I would have to examine him more closely to determine what, if anything, you have in common."

Looking back at McClintlock, Ellis sighed. "What's this about God? What does it have to do with the Cluster?"

"Surely you see!" said McClintlock, excitedly clapping his hands together. The shock of the clap seemed to startle the reverend. "The Cluster is the hand of God. It brought peace to Sufiro when peace was unobtainable any other way. It sent a vision to you and me. A vision that humanity no longer needs to suffer the tragedy of warfare."

Ellis grew tense. He removed the pipe from his mouth and set it gently on a table. "Colonel, if that's true, what about all the ships it destroyed?" He snorted. "If anything, the Cluster has seemed more the devil than anything else."

"It's God's vengeance," said McClintlock with a slight smile. His eyes drifted off toward the corner of the room. "God always strikes out at evil-doers," he said in a dream-like tone.

Ellis clenched his teeth and ground them slightly. "My father was aboard one of those ships." G'Liat eyed Ellis cautiously. The commander fought to maintain control of his emotions.

Clyde shrugged; his voice still distant. "I cannot speak for the morals of your father, though given what I know of your mother..."

Ellis bolted forward and grabbed the evangelist by the lapels of his coat and shook him. "How dare talk that way about either my father or mother!"

With two quick supple movements, G'Liat sprang between Ellis and McClintlock and pushed them apart. He stood between the two with his hands on his hips. "This is not the time to fight," he said gently. Ellis opened his mouth to protest, but the warrior cut him off with a stare. McClintlock stood, too dazed to deal with his rumpled coat. G'Liat looked at Ellis reproachfully. "The fact of the matter is that McClintlock is valuable."

"Valuable?" asked Ellis, incensed. "It seems to me that he's gone completely round the bend."

"McClintlock's presence only helps us. Instead of only one person who has had contact with the Cluster, there are now two here," explained G'Liat, his voice infuriatingly rational. "I can look for similarities in your brain patterns, find out what's missing in my own to successfully contact the Cluster." G'Liat heaved his chest in an imitation sigh. "From the scan, I know he's suffering from a concussion. Now you're trying to make it worse by shaking him around."

"Why would you want to side with him?" Ellis gestured toward the evangelist. "After all, like Arepno said, he's a slaver. I thought Rd'dyggians hated slavers."

G'Liat turned and helped the dazed McClintlock back to the comfort of the chair. At last he faced Ellis once again. "I thought you said he's the one who laid down arms. Now it's time for you to put aside your feelings."

"But, what about our plans?" Ellis began pacing the room, agitated almost to a frenzy. "I thought you were anxious to go out and try to contact the Cluster personally."

"Indeed, I am," said G'Liat, straightening and putting his hands behind his back. "In fact, I'm more anxious than ever."

"Spending time mapping his brain patterns and mine will delay us. We need to get out there." Ellis pointed to the ceiling. "We need to get out and find the Cluster and stop it."

"I couldn't agree more," said G'Liat. Ellis blinked a few times, as though stunned. "We'll take him with us."

Clyde McClintlock shook his head. The way he stared blankly into the corner of the room indicated that he hadn't quite recovered from either Arepno's or Ellis' assault. "You'll take me where?"

"On a spiritual quest," said G'Liat, his mustache seeming to outline a smile. "We are going to seek God."

McClintlock smiled, his face softened. "I knew I was right to seek out John Mark Ellis." McClintlock looked to the ceiling, his hands upraised. "Praise be to the Cluster."

John Mark Ellis shook his head, retrieved his pipe and stormed outside.

* * *

G'Liat saw to McClintlock's comfort. He gave the evangelist a mixture of herbs that would speed the healing of the head injuries. Once done, the warrior helped the human to the same room where Ellis had spent the previous night. Suppressing his natural revulsion for the small, fragile human form, G'Liat stripped McClintlock of his mildly soiled clothes and helped him into the mud bed. He would clean the evangelist's clothes as he had done for Ellis. The warrior left the dirty laundry near his desk to be dealt with later. That done, the hulking warrior made his way outside.

Standing at the threshold, G'Liat took a deep breath of air. To him, the day seemed warm and a bit dusty, though he knew his human guests were chilled. The sunlight, filtered by the clouds, seemed very cheerful. In point of fact, G'Liat had gotten more than he could hope for, two humans who had contacted the Cluster. The only question he faced was whether or not he could keep them from killing each other while he sought the answers he required.

G'Liat stood silent, not even breathing, and listened to the forest around him. He could hear the faint sounds of Ellis sucking on his pipe. Until G'Liat had been in Ellis' brain, he had never understood what humans found appealing about the drug, tobacco. Even now, the sensation seemed too subtle to explain. Following the sound, G'Liat found Ellis, his head obscured by a billow of smoke, his arms folded, shivering in the glade.

"Do you find McClintlock to be an honorable man?" asked G'Liat, quietly.

Ellis inclined his head, but did not turn to face the warrior. Many humans, G'Liat knew, would be put off by Ellis' refusal to turn. The warrior actually found the posture quite Rd'dyggian. "Honestly, I haven't thought much about that. I don't know much of anything about him."

"Yet, you are justified in judging him almost instantly." G'Liat did his best to imitate the human gesture of a smug nod, though he let himself slip into a native Rd'dyggian accent. He moved around to face Ellis. The bearded human still would not look into his eyes. It only bothered G'Liat because he knew that meant Ellis was still resisting. He waited for Ellis to speak again.

"What do you make of this talk of God's vengeance?" asked Ellis, at last looking G'Liat in the eye.

"It's an interpretation of the visions he saw," postulated the warrior. "They were certainly powerful enough to have religious connotations.

What do you make of it?"

"It gives me the creeps." Ellis removed the pipe and examined it for a moment. "What did Arepno mean about McClintlock being a missionary?"

"You were on Earth more recently than I." G'Liat lowered his neck between his shoulders, a gesture that looked remarkably like a shrug to humans. "I assumed you had heard about Clyde McClintlock's Cluster religion."

"I wasn't exactly in touch with current events," grumbled Ellis. The commander shook his head. "For someone so aware of events on Earth, you seemed awfully ignorant of McClintlock's appearance."

"One human is much like another." G'Liat waved the question aside.

Ellis returned the pipe to his mouth and began to pace. "Do you really think we should take him with us?"

"Indeed," said G'Liat, gently, but firmly.

"Cluster religion," mused Ellis. "Won't his followers, I presume he has followers . . ."

"Quite a number, from what I hear."

"Won't his followers want guidance? Won't they come after him?" Ellis rubbed his beard.

"It's possible," admitted G'Liat. He thought for several minutes. If he did not come up with a convincing argument, Ellis might argue to leave McClintlock behind. "However, they might be willing to help us fund our expedition. In that way, they could be extremely helpful."

Ellis looked toward the sky. "I still like the idea of looking for a job aboard a mapping vessel, though. I think McClintlock could be a hindrance to that."

"His military experience, like yours, could be presented as an asset." G'Liat followed Ellis' gaze, mostly out of curiosity, to see what the human saw in the clouds. "I also think the plan of joining the Gaean mapping service is best. Still, it is good to have a backup plan, if necessary. Any backup plan we have will require money."

Ellis grunted, then shook his head. "I doubt he has more money than I do in my estate."

"Possible," conceded G'Liat. "However, his resources are expanding, while yours are shrinking."

Ellis gripped the pipe with his teeth for several minutes, his hands thrust deeply in his pockets. The trained eyes of the warrior recognized the inner war raging within the human. At last, he turned to face G'Liat again. "Okay, when do we leave for Earth?"

"As soon as McClintlock is well enough to travel." With that, G'Liat felt satisfied that Ellis would stick to the plan. As he turned, Ellis stopped him with a question.

"There's something else that's been bothering me." The commander's brow was furrowed. "What do Rd'dyggian warriors see in human women?"

G'Liat pondered the question for a moment. Finally, confused, the warrior shook his head.

"I saw two Rd'dyggian warriors in a bar, watching human women," said Ellis, carefully measuring his words. "I was wondering what the fascination was."

The warrior thought for a moment about how best to answer. At last he said, "Have you ever seen a beautiful feline or, better yet, an equine running a race?" The warrior only slightly regretted the explanation as he saw the commander shudder. With a slight shake of the head, he turned and made his way back to the compound to see to his other human charge.

* * *

Jonah and Daniel, Clyde McClintlock's disciples sat battered and bruised on the star cruiser returning them to Earth. They prayed that their leader would be able to complete his holy quest to contact the Cluster. They prayed that Arepno had not simply slaughtered their teacher.

A deceptively gentle pinging disturbed their prayers. The captain's voice came over the speakers, attempting to sound calm. "A Cluster ship has just been sighted to our left. I believe it is far enough away that we will be able to evade them and resume our course for Earth."

Jonah and Daniel hurried to the left side of the ship. They saw the Cluster's appearance as a sign that their leader's mission would be a success.

An explosion rocked the after cabin. It was Daniel who pointed out the green beam emerging from the Cluster. "Take us home, oh Lord!" shouted Jonah as the beam sliced into their cabin and the air began to rush out.

* * *

John Mark Ellis watched as G'Liat carefully tended to Clyde McClintlock's injuries. The commander bit his lip. He wondered whether it had been a good idea to come to Rd'dyggia. So far, the warrior seemed to have gained more than Ellis had himself. He thought back to the conversation about the Titan domes. G'Liat knew something about the Titans that Ellis did not. For whatever reason, the warrior was holding back the information. Ellis had to learn more.

He let out a breath he didn't know he was holding, and stepped from the room.

The commander found the warrior's teleholo unit and turned it on, nervously looking over his shoulder to make sure that G'Liat had not followed him. He called Sufiro. Manuel Raton's face appeared. "John Mark! How goes your quest for the Cluster?"

Ellis held his finger up to his lips. "Manuel, I need you to get Mom, quickly."

Manuel looked confused, but nodded. "She's right here."

Raton faded from view and Suki Ellis appeared. "Hi Mark," said Fire. "How are you doing? Where are you calling from?"

Mark Ellis looked around again, biting his lower lip, then turned to face his mother. "I don't have much time to talk, sorry. Mom, what can you tell me about the origin of the Titans?"

Fire laughed and shook her head. "Only that it's one of the most hotly debated topics in academia. The Titans sure don't provide us with anything."

"Could you find out where the Titans came from?" asked Ellis.

Fire's lips curled as though she was about to laugh again, then stopped, seeing the earnest look on her son's face. "Mark, I'm a good historian, but what you asked is like saying, 'Ma, was the Lamb of God on England's pleasant pastures seen?' The preliminary research alone could take years."

"Don't throw Blake at me, mom," sighed Ellis. "Is there anything you could do?"

"It's one of the most fascinating puzzles you could pose to me. Let me go back to Earth and do some poking around there. I should be able to get a couple of weekends on Titan. I can't promise anything." Fire shook her head.

"You don't want to leave Sufiro, do you?" asked Ellis, seeing his mother's frown.

"No, Mark, I don't. But, I can't just let myself be fired from my job on Earth, either. This is a good enough mystery to get me to go home ... at least for a while." Fire sighed. She looked to someone off-screen. Ellis guessed she was looking at Manuel. She turned her attention back to Ellis. "How do I contact you once I find something?"

"I'll let you know." Again, Mark looked over his shoulder to see if G'Liat was eavesdropping. "Mom, I love you. I've gotta go. I'll call soon." With that, Ellis terminated the connection. During his preliminary training as a communicator, Ellis had learned a few tricks with teleholos. He reached under the console and activated a few circuits and quickly erased the record of his call to Sufiro.

* * *

Clyde McClintlock's injuries took about a week to heal. During that time, G'Liat and Ellis spent many hours talking about their experiences with the Cluster. Underlying these conversations was a vague tension. Both the warrior and commander knew that they must develop a strategy for the encounter.

As McClintlock recovered, he began to join the conversations. At first, his input seemed wildly irrational. The evangelist refused to talk about the Cluster directly. Instead, he would speak of the alien as God's hand. Ellis, eventually, grew callused enough to this to ask, "God's hand, eh?"

Clyde, trying to breathe as little of the foul Rd'dyggian air as possible, looked at the commander and grinned. "How do you explain the Cluster, then?"

"To me, it's an alien we've never encountered. It appears hostile. It kills. But there's a contradiction. I get the impression that it likes humans; some humans, at least." The commander shook his head, then looked into McClintlock's warmly smiling face. His bright blue eyes seemed to sparkle. "However, I sense no love from the Cluster."

"I admit, the Cluster is no more than an instrument. It feels no love, no hate. To understand God, I feel I must understand his tools."

Ellis chuckled lightly. "To understand a carpenter, you must understand a hammer?"

"That's the idea." Clyde moved closer to Ellis. At first, the commander tensed but then he relaxed, as he noted no menace in the evangelist's approach. McClintlock lay his hand gently on the commander's shoulder. "If the Cluster isn't an instrument of God, what is it?"

"Simply an alien we've never encountered before," said Ellis, almost reverently.

"Why haven't we met it before?" Clyde's voice held a slight hush.

"It's possible they don't even come from our galaxy. They could be intergalactic travelers from distant reaches of the universe, trying to understand us." Ellis sighed.

"The real question," said McClintlock, removing his hand from Ellis' shoulder, "is which of us is living in the fantasy world?"

With that, the two men walked side by side back to G'Liat's compound where dinner was waiting. That night, Ellis trimmed his beard in anticipation of an interview. G'Liat had booked a commercial flight back to Earth, where the three hoped to get a job on a mapping vessel.

* * *

On Sufiro, Suki Firebrandt Ellis placed her suitcase on Manuel

Raton's bed and started packing her bags for the return to Earth. Manuel Raton stepped up behind her and put his arms around her waist. "I'm gonna miss you," he said sadly.

Fire smiled and turned. "Why not come with me?"

"I hate Earth!" said Manuel, indignant.

Fire snorted. "You haven't been on Earth since you were practically in diapers. Don't give me that." She took Manuel's hands.

"I'm the Sheriff of New Granada. I can't just up and leave," said Manuel, shrugging and turning his feet on the carpet.

"I'm Director of the Maria Mitchell Association and I left for a time. Call it a vacation," reasoned Fire.

"But who'll mind the store while I'm gone?"

"What about Ed Swan, your deputy?" Fire squeezed Manuel's hands and returned to the job of packing.

After a few minutes, Manuel flopped a suitcase on the bed across from Fire's. Silently, he began packing it full of clothes. "Do you think you'll solve the mystery of the origin of the Titans?"

"No," said Fire. "The mystery has been debated for over eight hundred years. You think I'm going to find the answers?"

"If anyone can do it, it's you," said Manuel with a wink.

* * *

Three days later, Ellis, McClintlock, and G'Liat found themselves in the bustling streets of Tokyo. Tokyo of the thirtieth century filled most of the islands of Japan. While many of the other, ancient cities still maintained their names they were little more than suburbs of the mammoth island-city. The three travelers made their way from the spaceport toward the offices of the TransGalactic Mapping Corps via a combination of rail and foot. The TransGalactic Mapping Corps was one of many companies that collected data for the Gaean Mapping Service. Clyde McClintlock, used to the rolling hills and open spaces of Sufiro, was in awe of the city around him. G'Liat simply felt a sensation akin to claustrophobia.

On the trip from Rd'dyggia, they decided it was safest to avoid the North American continent where McClintlock's followers were most numerous. Although Clyde wanted to see his followers and give them encouragement, even he agreed that doing so would slow them down considerably. In fact, Ellis persuaded McClintlock to take on a new persona to avoid such trouble. On the trip to Earth, G'Liat dyed the evangelist's hair black.

Even stronger than Clyde McClintlock's desire, Ellis wanted to see old Coffin and the family home. He wanted to take the boat out and visit with Richard. Like McClintlock, though, Ellis knew that to do so would only hamper the search. Ellis wondered what the stoic G'Liat thought of leaving Rd'dyggia behind.

The home of the TransGalactic Mapping Corps was a skyscraper in the Shikoku Sector. The trio stepped through the front door of the massive glass and plastic structure. The receptionist, sitting behind a simple wooden desk, was a hulking giant of a man. Based on his age, Ellis presumed he must be a retired Sumo wrestler.

"Welcome to TransGalactic Mapping, how may I help you gentlemen?" asked the receptionist.

"We would like to sign up for a mapping expedition," stated Ellis, bluntly.

"So would every other reprobate out on the streets of the city," said the receptionist. Ellis sighed, looking down at the clothes provided by Arepno. They were neat enough, but somewhat casual for the norm in Tokyo. The receptionist put out his hands. "If you hand me your résumés, I'll make sure they are forwarded to the appropriate office."

Ellis started to hold out the disk, but G'Liat caught the commander's hand. "We wish to present our applications to Ms. Meiji in person."

"I don't think so," said the receptionist as he stood. Ellis had horrible visions of the bouncer he had encountered the last time he was on Earth.

"Tell Ms. Meiji that G'Liat of Rd'dyggia wishes to speak with her." With that, G'Liat presented the receptionist with a card. Ellis recognized the writing on the card as Rd'dyggian. The receptionist stared at it for a moment, then nodded to the warrior. He left without a word.

McClintlock stared at G'Liat for several moments. "What was written on the card?"

"Let it suffice to say that having been to Earth a few times, I've developed a handful of connections." G'Liat turned and found an uncomfortable plastic seat.

Ellis followed. To him, the seats were not as uncomfortable as they were to someone of the Rd'dyggian's bulk. "Awfully convenient that you have a friend working for the mapping corps."

"Not a friend, exactly," said G'Liat with a faraway look. "In fact, I've never even met Ms. Meiji. Let's just say, we've heard of each other."

Ellis pursed his lips and folded his arms. He desperately wanted to retrieve his pipe, or better yet, a cigar. However, in Tokyo, the tobacco ban was enforced more heavily than any other place on the planet. In fact, G'Liat had insisted that Ellis leave his tobacco on Rd'dyggia. Ellis had wondered about the request at the time, because most people didn't care about possession. Now, as he sat in an office building in Tokyo, he began to understand. He grew nervous about the pipe and tobacco hidden in his duffel at the hotel.

The receptionist returned after what seemed an hour. He wore a vaguely surprised expression. "Ms. Meiji will see you now," he announced.

The trio followed the receptionist through a hall to a lift, which took them up through the structure. The lift came to a stop on a floor near the top of the building. They were led out into an expansive room littered with waist-high pedestals. Over each pedestal floated stars and grid lines. The holographic projections were the aids used by every human-built star vessel in the galaxy to navigate.

Standing near the center of the room was a well-dressed, slender woman. She came forward, extending her hand to G'Liat. "It's good to meet you, at last," she said with a voice that sounded far too timid. The receptionist bowed slightly and departed through the lift.

"May I present Ms. Meiji," said G'Liat. "Senior mathematician for TransGalactic."

Ellis and McClintlock each shook Meiji's hand. She led them through a veritable maze of holo-maps to comfortable leather chairs in front of a simple wooden desk. "What can I do for you?" she asked without ceremony.

"I've come to ask a favor." G'Liat's Rd'dyggian accent became more pronounced.

"Rd'dyggians don't usually need to ask humans for favors. We'll have to see if this is a favor I can grant." Her face remained nearly expressionless.

"You can, at least, tell us whether or not my request is possible," said the warrior, imitating a smile. The mathematician nodded ascent. "We would like to sign aboard one of your mapping vessels."

"That should not be too difficult," said Meiji. "We are preparing to send out the Ogilby Fleet in about six weeks. We are still looking to fill several key positions." She held out her slender hand. "Let me see your résumés."

Ellis handed the wafer-like disk to the woman. She eyed the old disk skeptically for a moment, then took it away, undoubtedly to a reader somewhere else in the office. Coming back a few minutes later, she viewed the disk contents using the holo terminal on her desk. "Lieutenant John Mark Ellis," she said slowly. "I see you commanded a destroyer. Why should I hire you for a mapping mission?"

"I'm looking forward to new challenges," piped Ellis. "I admit, a mapping vessel is quite different from a military ship, but I'm sure I can learn."

"You've been in a command position," said Meiji, leaning slightly forward. "We likely as not, have no such openings, how do you feel about taking the back seat to someone."

"After commanding a ship, it won't be easy," admitted Ellis. Internally, he debated whether or not he should push for a command position. From the background, it would be extremely difficult to hunt the Cluster. Still, it was better to get into a position where he might encounter the Cluster than not. Certainly it was better than being first officer in the military where his decisions and independent thoughts would, at best, be tolerated. "I took orders a lot longer than I gave them. I can adjust and I want to learn."

Meiji looked at the disk in her hand and her lip turned up slightly. "You are from Nantucket. Did you ever sail with a man named Samuel Coffin?"

Ellis' eyes went wide. "I know Old Man Coffin very well. He was one of my favorite teachers."

Without expression, she continued scanning the disk. She looked at McClintlock. "You look familiar, Mr. McIntosh." Clyde McClintlock shifted uncomfortably under her gaze. Meiji said nothing further. Undoubtedly, she had seen McClintlock's face on the news. Inwardly, Ellis congratulated himself on thinking up McClintlock's alias and phony background. If nothing else, it gave her pause when addressing the colonel. Also, McClintlock's white hair had been such a striking feature, the simple color change seemed extremely effective.

"I'm not sure where you would have seen me," said McClintlock putting on his best Sufiro drawl. "I've been a cook in Nuevo Santa Fe for a number of years."

"Good cooks are hard to come by on mapping ships." Meiji scowled. "The money isn't very good. Why would you want to sign aboard a space vessel?" The real beauty of the alibi, thought Ellis, was that Meiji could call Ellison Firebrandt, the commander's grandfather and he would happily confirm the story without question.

"I want to get out and see the stars." McClintlock smiled his warm, trusting smile.

"Not much to see," said Meiji. "There are few windows aboard interstellar space vessels, Mr. McIntosh."

"Suits me," said McClintlock. "I might get space sick."

Meiji snorted almost indistinctly. Finally she looked at G'Liat. "I think you are a little over-qualified for any position."

"We should talk in private," said G'Liat, deeply solemn. Meiji nodded. With that, she and the Rd'dyggian stood and left for another part of the office. McClintlock looked questioningly at Ellis. Ellis simply shrugged in response. At last, the warrior and the mathematician returned. The Rd'dyggian moved slowly and gracefully so Meiji would not have to move quickly to keep up.

"You three are quite a group." Meiji put her hands behind her back. "Mr. Ellis, you will command the TMV *Nicholas Sanson*, flagship of the Ogilby fleet. I will get you signed up for the appropriate briefings. From your résumé, I see that you understand command. Also, Samuel Coffin is one of the best navigators I know. The fact that you studied with him has influenced my decision. However, you have a lot to learn about mapping vessels." She turned on her heel and faced McClintlock. "Mr. McIntosh, you will be the cook on *Sanson*."

"What about G'Liat?" asked Ellis.

"*Sanson* maintains an official representative of the owners. G'Liat will be on her staff," said Meiji. "All of this is pending the collection of several favors, but all of you have records strong enough to support this decision. That and G'Liat's recommendation make me feel that this is not too stupid."

"Thank you," said G'Liat with a slight bow. With a motion, the warrior led the trio out of the office.

As they stepped out of the building, Ellis noticed it was twilight. Soon the stars would appear. Not long after, Ellis would return to his rightful place among them.

PART III
The Search in Space

At last, the great thunderbird spoke. "What do we do? I like these humans. They respect us and pray to us. When they dream of us, they gain some of our power. That power makes them relatives of ours in a way."

— From the Brule Sioux legend of the Great Thunderbird

Suki Firebrandt Ellis arrives on Titan

A Tall Ship and a Star to Steer Her By

Suki Firebrandt Ellis and Manuel Raton chartered a small sailboat for the trip from Hyannis Port to Nantucket. As they came into port at the island, Manuel shook his head. "Will you look at that? It's almost exactly like Roanoke."

Fire nodded and smiled. She hadn't realized just how much she missed Nantucket until she saw the white and gray buildings superimposed on the greenery of the island. She pointed out a seagull hovering near one of the sails.

Manuel laughed. "Do you know how long it's been since I've seen a real bird? I almost forgot about them."

Old Man Coffin met Fire and Manuel at the pier. He helped them carry their belongings to the old Ellis house. As they unpacked, Coffin seemed to be in a dark mood. Fire took Coffin and Manuel to a restaurant in the village for lobster. As they ate, Coffin looked to Fire. "I'm glad you're back. I guess I'll need to pack my things and move back to the shack."

Fire's glass of wine stopped midway to her lips. She set it down slowly. "Why?"

"Well," began Coffin, "seeing as you are back, I didn't think you'd want me kicking around the old house."

"Nonsense," said Fire. Manuel turned to look at Fire. She kicked him in the ankle making him swallow a bit of lobster too quickly.

"Of course not," sputtered Manuel. "You're welcome to stay."

The next day, Fire walked to the offices of the Maria Mitchell Association. She was met with gasps of surprise. "We were getting ready to put out a new job ad," explained Dorothy Harriman, the observatory director. "We thought you'd decided to stay on Sufiro forever."

Fire sighed and bit her lower lip. "Go ahead and write the ad," she said, almost sadly. "But, don't place it yet. I haven't decided whether I'm back permanently or not."

Harriman whistled. "So, you really like it out there on that frontier planet?"

"It's home," explained Fire.

"So, why'd you come back?" Harriman rubbed liver-spotted hands together. Fire suspected that Harriman secretly coveted the Association Directorship.

"This is home, too." Fire shrugged. She went to her office and turned on the computer and was confronted by more mail than she wanted to deal with. She was tempted to delete the entire list. Thinking better of it, she saved it aside and opened a holographic viewscreen to the Earth Library database. She began a search for books having to do with the Titans.

* * *

Although John Mark Ellis knew the importance of stellar mapping vessels, he had never actually seen one until the day he was to take command of the TMV *Nicholas Sanson*. It was true that he had seen his share of holographic pics and vids, but nothing could compare to the view he had as he approached the ship aboard a TransGalactic shuttle from Earth. The military vessels he was familiar with were little more than functional black cylinders bristling with gun ports; a single glowing, blue Erdon-Quinn generator dominated the back of the ship. The ship Ellis saw through the view port was nothing like that. This new ship simply took his breath away.

During the previous six weeks, John Mark Ellis had spent time studying mapping vessels. As such, he knew that everything he saw had a purpose. Still, the almost feminine curves of this new ship aroused a sense of wonder within the captain. It seemed inappropriate to name the ship, "Nicholas." The ship was still a cylinder, but eight fan-like sensor arrays swept back toward the vessel's stern. Ellis couldn't help but think of sails when he saw the sensor arrays pivoting subtly, sensing the gravitational interactions of many stars. Each of those arrays controlled a seemingly petite EQ generator. The glow from each surrounded the ship like a halo. Military ships were built for powering their way through the fourth dimension to a new location. This ship was built for precision rather than power. It would feel its way along, charting the subtleties of gravity's ever-changing pathways, ultimately allowing all other ships to thrust their way through the void.

G'Liat and McClintlock were already aboard the *Sanson*. McClintlock had spent five of the past six weeks brushing up on his cooking skills. Fortunately, his military training had included some time in the mess hall, learning how to cook for large numbers of people. Growing up on Sufiro, he had learned how to make food taste good. He went aboard *Sanson* about a week before to get familiar with the kitchen.

G'Liat had been summoned aboard *Sanson* by the owner's representative almost immediately. Ellis felt uncomfortable that G'Liat had not been around to help plan for their voyage. The more he was alone, the more agitated Ellis became. One night, while on Earth, Ellis watched a news broadcast about a Zahari ship attacked by the Cluster. Seeing the image of the Cluster, the captain couldn't help but think of the numbing effect it had on his mind. Ellis sucked noisily on his pipe stem, hoping G'Liat would be able to teach him how to cope with the sight. The last thing he wanted was to be paralyzed the next time he saw the spheres. Whether the paralysis was due to fear or some hypnotic effect didn't seem to matter. Still, the captain realized that the training time had been necessary. To carry out their goal, commanding *Sanson* would have to be second nature.

"We're preparing to dock, sir," announced the shuttle pilot.

Ellis nodded ascent, settled back in the chair, and smiled to himself. He had a ship to command. In principle, he could take it wherever he wanted. With it, he would find the Cluster and find out what the visions in his mind were. He would find out why the Cluster killed and try to use that knowledge to stop it. No longer did he have to answer to an admiral. The captain was lost so deeply in thought he didn't feel the shuttle latch onto the ship. He jumped when the pilot tapped him on the shoulder. "You may disembark, now, sir," she said.

Ellis sighed, then nodded. Standing, he grabbed his duffel bag and stepped through the airlock onto the deck of his ship. The graviton generators aboard mapping vessels were set to about eighty percent of Earth gravity. The captain's shoulders slumped slightly when he realized that the only person there to meet him was G'Liat. Ellis rubbed his beard, knowing better than to expect the formality of reviewing his crew upon boarding a civilian vessel.

G'Liat nodded to the captain. Ellis shook his head as he examined his comrade. The Rd'dyggian wore a white shirt with tan trousers and a jacket. The clothes seemed like they would be more in place on a human businessman than on a Rd'dyggian warrior. "I'll take you up to the bridge to meet your officers. Then I'll escort you to Ms. Smart."

"That's Kirsten Smart, the owner's representative?" Ellis looked around noticing the wood trim framing walls painted an off color of white.

G'Liat nodded once and held out his hand, indicating that Ellis should follow. The captain flung his duffel over his shoulder with ease and walked behind G'Liat as the warrior led the way to the lift. As they walked, two men – one big and burley, the other short and lanky – stepped out of a room. Ellis nodded to the two men. The men nodded and continued walking down the hall. Just as G'Liat and Ellis were about to step into the lift, the ship lurched gently to the side. Dropping the duffel, Ellis had to put his hand on the wall to stabilize himself. "What the hell?" he grumbled.

"Watch your step," warned G'Liat. "This being a mapping vessel, we're more sensitive to the structure of space itself. You're used to graviton generators that automatically compensate for these little bumps."

"I know." Ellis scowled. "The graviton generating equipment can interfere with the precise operation of the sensor equipment. I guess I'll just have to get my sea legs back."

* * *

The two men, a programmer named Isaac and a cartographer named Quincy, turned in time to see their new captain miss-step.

"Is that Captain Ellis?" asked Isaac in a hushed voice. He noted Ellis' blue navy jacket, the epaulet still present, hung askew. He also noted the captain's beard. "A little scruffy to be a captain, don't you think? 'Spose Kirsten will make him shave off that beard?"

"He seems like he'd be more at home with sails than EQ generators," said Quincy. "Could be worse, though. Simon could've gotten the captain's job."

"Simon, at least, has experience with mapping vessels," countered Isaac. "Why do I feel like I'm sailing with Captain Ahab?"

* * *

The clean, pale blue walls of the lift impressed Ellis as he and G'Liat rode to the command deck. In fact, the entire ship seemed to have far more color than he was accustomed to from his military days. Though unusual to him, the color did seem to add a level of cheer to the vessel. Ellis wanted to ask G'Liat a dozen questions, but the lift only took a minute to move the four decks from the docking bay to the command level.

As the doors opened, Ellis gasped. It looked as though one could walk the length of the deck and dive into the oceans of Earth. In fact, as he watched, someone walked out and stood on the North American continent with a wand, writing notes in the "air." Ellis pursed his lips and shook his head. All he could think of at the moment was a stanza from Emily Dickinson. "And then a Plank in Reason, broke, And I dropped down, and down – And hit a World, at every plunge," he said. G'Liat simply inclined his head.

In front of the hologram was a rounded, U-shaped console. Two women sat at the console. One, dressed in a simple brown jump suit, was deep in conversation with the man standing in the hologram. The other, wearing a loud, floral print dress seemed simply to be daydreaming as she watched the point where the ceiling seemed to flow into the wall. After the initial shock of the realistic hologram, the most jarring thing about this setting was the fact that no one was in uniform. Ellis tugged at his own turtleneck shirt, thinking the lack of uniforms would be the hardest thing for him to adjust to.

Behind the U-shaped console were two unoccupied chairs. Each had a holographic interface panel. The one on the right was inactive. The left panel had a series of what almost looked to be antique brass knobs and buttons set into a wooden box. "The station on the right," explained G'Liat, "is yours."

Captain John Mark Ellis stepped gingerly toward the command station. He let the duffel bag drop out of his hand and reaching out, he grabbed the back of the chair and held on, as though command itself might escape him again. A tear welled up in the corner of his eye. Looking behind, Ellis saw that he and G'Liat had stepped out of one of two tubes that stood in front of a wall. There were two doors, one on either side of the two lift tubes. A third door stood between the lift tubes. G'Liat stepped forward. "Simon," he called.

The man standing in the holographic interface finished scribbling notes in the darkness around him, and stepped back toward G'Liat and Ellis. "This is your first mate," explained G'Liat. "Simon Yermakov, may I present Captain J. Mark Ellis."

Yermakov sniffed and rubbed his nose on his sleeve. "Good to meet you, Skipper," said the first mate. He held out his hand and Ellis took it.

"I'm not sure how much I like being called 'skipper,'" grumbled Ellis sensing almost instantly that he might be getting off on the wrong foot.

Yermakov grinned lopsidedly. "I'm sure you'll get used to it." With that, the first mate shrugged. Yermakov's puffy cheeks and close-cropped hair gave Ellis the impression that he was talking to a squirrel. "If you'll excuse me, Ms. Smart wanted the initial course projection work done within the hour."

Ellis nodded. "Of course," he muttered under his breath.

G'Liat put his massive six-fingered hand on the captain's shoulder and led him to the U-shaped console. The woman in the brown jump suit, stood at attention. Ellis was taken aback, but pleased after Yermakov's lackadaisical greeting. "This is your pilot, Major Laura Peters," introduced G'Liat.

"Confederation reserve officer?" guessed Ellis, inclining his head.

"Yes, sir," she responded succinctly. "Sir, it is an honor to serve with you. I've read the accounts of your mission to Sufiro." She was interrupted by the sound of Yermakov clearing his throat. The first mate sniffed, then pointed at one of the stars in the hologram with his wand.

"You'd better get back to work." Ellis grinned to himself. He was pleased to have found at least one person on this ship that understood protocol.

"Natalie," said G'Liat, gently. The woman in the flower print dress turned and seemed to look through G'Liat.

"Do you realize just how hard it is to read the mind of a Rd'dyggian, Cap'n Ellis?" she said dreamily. Ellis shook his head, his mouth slightly agape. "Pity, because your mind is even harder to read."

"This is Natalie Papadraxis." G'Liat shrugged apologetically. "She's your communicator."

Ellis reached out to shake her hand, but she shook her head. "You don't want to touch me." Her voice was quiet, perhaps even a little dangerous. "Skin to skin contact could allow me to read too much of your mind at once."

The captain looked pleadingly at G'Liat. He had heard of communicators who believed they were psychic, but he had never met one before. He wanted the warrior to tell him that this really wasn't his only source of contact with Earth, and if need be the Cluster. Instead, he looked back at Natalie Papadraxis' lean face and muttered, "Pleased to make your acquaintance."

G'Liat patted the captain on the shoulder and gestured toward the doors at the back of the command deck. Ellis followed the warrior toward the lift tubes. "So, do you think this is going to work?" asked Ellis.

"We can talk in a little bit." G'Liat looked grim, even for a Rd'dyggian. "First, I'll introduce you to our lord and mistress, Ms. Smart." The warrior stepped up to the sky-blue door at the right of the lift tube and touched a button that activated a chime. They entered when they heard the muffled "come in" from the other side of the door.

Entering, they found themselves in a cozy office. Functional gray carpet covered the floor. Sitting at an antique-looking wooden desk was a broad-shouldered woman. Long brown hair tamed with a barrette framed her round face. "I'll be with you in just a moment," she said. Thick fingers manipulated a portable hologram of stars. "Please be seated."

Ellis and G'Liat took seats in front of the desk. The chairs were simple wire frame structures with minimal padding in the seat and back. This contrasted with the plush green chair that Smart occupied. All three chairs were mounted in tracks in the floor. At last she looked up. "Ah, Captain Ellis, just in time," she said, standing. Her smile was pleasant but guarded. Ellis stood and shook her hand. As he did so, he realized that she was a full foot shorter than he was. Sitting back down, she folded her hands and studied the captain.

"I presume you've met the crew," she said, at last. Ellis nodded. "By now you're thinking this is nothing like a military vessel. If that's true, you'd be absolutely correct."

"It might not be a military crew, but I know enough about corporate mapping vessels to know that they're competent, or you would have fired them." Ellis rubbed his beard.

Kirsten Smart scowled slightly. She stood and stepped over to a panel in the wall. Entering a command in the touch pad, she ordered drinks. After a moment, she pulled open a door. She handed cups of coffee to G'Liat and the captain. She reserved a cup of tea for herself. "G'Liat tells me you like that chicory coffee he drinks."

Ellis glared at the warrior, whose only response was to shrug.

Smart returned to her seat and sipped her tea for a moment. "It is important that you understand the difference between a military mission and a mapping voyage. You've been told that I represent the owners on this vessel. While true, I am also in charge of cartography and astrometry, which is this ship's primary function. In other words, I command the mission."

Ellis sipped his coffee. This coffee was much stronger than that G'Liat had made. He wrinkled his nose when he sipped the bitter liquid. Looking over, he noticed that G'Liat had not touched his own cup. At last, the captain looked back at Smart. "In other words, your function is much like that of a commodore or admiral on a Confederate Naval Vessel."

Smart pondered the comment for a few moments. "That's a fair enough comparison. To be frank, I know very little about commanding ships. That's why you're here." She put down the teacup and sat forward, folding her hands. "I want to make it perfectly clear that I command the mission. If I order a test, that test will be executed. If I order a jump, this ship had better jump. Likewise, you do not have the authority to take this ship anywhere unless I order it. We are not in the business of rescuing vessels in distress. Is that understood?"

Ellis took another sip of the bitter coffee and frowned, wondering how much Smart knew of his history. "I'll follow those regulations to the extent that the ship is not endangered."

Taking a deep breath, Smart sat back. "That's not what the rule book says. I, and only I, will determine when we are in too much danger."

"I respectfully submit," said Ellis, sitting forward. "That you just said that you do not know very much about ships. Only I can make the call when we are in danger. In that situation, you had better not countermand my authority."

Smart nodded. A faint hint of a smile briefly lit her features. "I like a captain who's willing to stand up to me. I suspect that's why Meiji hired you instead of promoting Yermakov." She picked up her teacup again and took another sip. "Oh, Simon is highly competent. He knows this ship a whole lot better than you, and I expect you to take advantage of that knowledge. But if I told him to take the ship into the heart of Sirius, he'd do it."

Ellis nodded understanding. Still, something about that last comment contradicted Yermakov's willingness to stand up to him. The captain retrieved the pipe from his coat. "Do you mind?"

"I mind quite a lot," said Smart, sharply.

"I'm sorry to hear that," said Ellis, taken slightly aback.

"You could be even more sorry." Smart rubbed the bridge of her nose. "There are owners' representatives in the fleet who would have you arrested just for showing them the pipe."

Ellis' brow creased. "Tobacco might be illegal on Earth, but it's not in space."

"Depends on who's interpreting the law, Captain Ellis. TransGalactic regards their ships as Earth territory. Same rules apply here as on planet."

Ellis peered into the bowl of his pipe. "Is that how you interpret the rules?"

Smart heaved a deep sigh. "I live by the spirit of the law, not the letter. It's not my place to say what you do to your own body in your cabin. The rest of this ship is off limits. Understood?"

Ellis put the pipe back unhappily. "Understood."

"Unlike the military, we do not screen for allergies and that sort of thing. The last thing I want you to do is light up your pipe and put poor Natalie into a coughing fit." Smart shook her head.

"Speaking of 'poor Natalie,'" began Ellis, his brow wrinkled. "How good a communicator is she?"

"One of the best in the business," said Smart. "You'll adjust to her thinking communications are psychic. It's more a matter of adjusting your language when you talk to her than anything else."

An uncomfortable silence fell on the room. At last Smart stood. "If there's nothing else, I have to continue getting ready for the first jump. I plan to depart Earth orbit in forty-eight hours. Please have the ship ready to go."

"Aye aye, Ms. Smart," said Ellis as he stood.

Just as Ellis and G'Liat turned to leave, Smart stopped them. "Oh, Captain, would you please have a word with that McIntosh fellow. Whenever I order my eggs over easy, he cooks the yolks through."

Smart's eyes narrowed, seemingly evaluating the captain.

"I'll talk to him." With that G'Liat and Ellis left the room.

* * *

Kirsten Smart watched the doors close behind Ellis and G'Liat. Almost unconsciously, she pulled personnel files up on her holo display. She didn't read any of the text. Instead, she just looked at the faces.

Simon Yermakov's image was taken before his nose had turned a slight red from almost constant congestion. Natalie's image was clear-eyed, revealing a sharp mind and keen intellect. Kirsten wondered what had happened to make her believe she's psychic. Finally, Kirsten pulled up Laura's image. She shook her head. It was bad enough having one militaristic type aboard without Ellis. The new captain seemed to add insult to injury by wearing the uniform coat with the epaulet. *Just the kind of thing to make the crew nervous.*

Kirsten detected a hint of sanity and competence in Ellis despite the beard, the pipe, and the rumpled uniform coat. She hoped that sanity would compensate for any unrest in the crew.

Kirsten brought up the hologram of Ellis, taken only weeks before. She folded her hand under her chin. "What makes you tick, Captain Ellis?" she asked under her breath.

* * *

The captain took a deep breath when he was back out on the command deck. Looking up at G'Liat, he sighed. "You should probably show me to my quarters."

"Better than that," said G'Liat, with an expression that looked like a smile. "I'll show you to your office."

Ellis' jaw dropped. "I have an office?"

"Or a ready room, if you prefer the naval vernacular." The warrior led the captain to the door on the other side of the lift tubes. On his way by, Ellis retrieved the duffel bag.

The office was only a little smaller than Smart's. Instead of the more elegant wooden desk, a gray metal desk stood in the middle of the room. The chair behind the desk was the same frame-type that had stood in front of Smart's desk. Still, Ellis grinned. "I've never been aboard a ship big enough for the captain to have a ready room."

He moved behind the desk and sat down. With slow, deliberate motions, he put his palms down on the desk and took a deep breath, savoring the air. After a moment, he reached over and activated the holographic computer interface.

"You'll find a complete mission profile." G'Liat sat in the chair across from the captain's desk. "I've given you a checklist of the things that Ms. Smart wants the captain to see to personally before the voyage.

As she says, though, Simon Yermakov is plenty competent to see to most of the details of the next two days. That'll give you some time to settle in."

Ellis pursed his lips. "Would Yermakov have command if I hadn't stuck my nose into this job?"

"He was up for it." G'Liat's Rd'dyggian accent slipped somewhat, giving the statement a certain pragmatic tone. "Ms. Smart was telling the truth when she said she didn't want him as captain, though. She was glad when she heard an experienced Navy commander was hired for the job."

Shaking his head, Ellis sat back in the chair. "I'm more worried about how well Yermakov will take my orders." The captain stood and began pacing the room. "Even that's minor compared with questions about how we're going to find the Cluster. It's not like we can take this ship wherever we want."

G'Liat folded his six-fingered hands in a surprisingly human-looking gesture. "If you had your own ship to take where you wanted, where would you go?"

"I'd study the records of Cluster appearances and find out where it had appeared most often. I'd go there," said Ellis, gesturing with his hands.

"I've studied those records." The warrior's mustache wiggled. "There is no such place. The appearances are truly random."

"That being the case, I guess I'd make a random survey of as many systems as I could get to." Ellis folded his arms tightly.

"And you'd spend your family's fortune twice over in fuel." The warrior stood, towering over the captain. "This ship is going to make that survey. We might find the Cluster or we might not. The key, my friend, is patience." G'Liat stood and moved toward the door. "For now, I'd recommend doing what you need to get the ship ready for the voyage. That is the way of the warrior. We'll talk about the Cluster more once we're underway." With that, G'Liat began to step out.

"One more thing," called Ellis, standing. "I've thought a bit more about what you said about the Titans." G'Liat turned sharply and entered the room again, letting the door close behind him.

The warrior held up a long finger, reproachfully. Light glinted menacingly off the ring he wore. "Be careful who you discuss my thoughts on the Titans with."

Ellis waved the warning aside as he stepped toward G'Liat. "If the Titans were tied to the Cluster in some way, why are their ships in as much danger as ours? I've been reading the records of Titan encounters. They've been examined by the Cluster the same as our ships."

G'Liat folded his arms. "Have they? Who prepares those reports?"

"The reports I saw came from the archived news files based on Admiralty reports." Ellis' eyebrows came together.

"Who gives those reports to the Admiralty?"

"The Titans, themselves, I suppose." The captain took a deep breath.

G'Liat leaned close to the captain's ear. His voice was a hoarse whisper. "Rd'dyggian ships have been scouting the remains of all vessels destroyed by the Cluster. The only reported wrecks we cannot find are those of Titan ships."

"So, either the Titans are lying about their ships encountering the Cluster, or their ships are being utterly destroyed by the Cluster."

"There's a third possibility, and that's the one that actually scares me." With that G'Liat straightened and left the room.

Ellis moved to his chair and sat down at the computer to review the mission. He tried to activate the hovering icon for the mission briefing, but found his hand was trembling too much.

* * *

Teklar of Titan was curled up in the nest of her youth in a cave. She knew the caves that Titans called home seemed humble to many species of the galaxy. Despite the humility of their domiciles, the Titans were so technically superior to the rest of the beings in the galaxy that no one scoffed aloud. The hum of the machine, which normally comforted Teklar in times of doubt, brought her only dread. All she could think of was the fact that those machines had been handed down unchanged from the time her ancestors acquired them from the Intelligence. Even so, her mind reached out to the machine and requested a warm drink. The drink materialized where she could reach out and sip with her muzzle. Her paws were curled around, using the warmth of her body to take the chill from her extremities.

She had been convinced that when Ellis and G'Liat joined forces, they would solve the riddle whose answer she could not reveal. More important, she hoped they would find a way to send the Cluster back where it came from without involving her people at all. Instead, they were going to chase through the galaxy with a mapping vessel. Sighing, she took another sip.

Although Rd'dyggians and humans had frighteningly chaotic minds, those minds could often leap to insights far beyond those of the Titans. The more egotistical of her people believed it would be many centuries before the most advanced beings of the galaxy reached the level of technology the Titans possessed. Teklar had her doubts. Deep down, she felt that even the primitive humans would develop technology on a level similar to the Titans in only a few decades. Once that happened, where would the Titans be, whose technology had not evolved in nearly thirty million years?

Teklar knew the answer. The Titans would be where they were at this moment. They would be at the mercy of the humans. Only humans, and maybe Rd'dyggians, had the mental agility to talk to the Cluster. However, she feared the Cluster's response.

* * *

Clyde McClintlock felt ill at ease. He worried about his people back on Earth. While he knew they could take care of themselves, he felt guilty running around the galaxy on a quest for the Cluster without them. He tried to turn his mind to the menu he was preparing for the next day. Looking in the mirror at his hair, dyed black, he felt even guiltier than he did before. Not only was he engaged in a holy quest without his people, he was deceiving the crew of the *Sanson* to do so.

He stood up from the desk and paced the room. With a sigh, he realized how much he felt like he was back in the cell on Sufiro. At least, he thought, John Mark Ellis and G'Liat have some influence over the course of the ship. He was just along for the ride. As he thought, though, he realized he might have some influence over the course of the vessel after all. McClintlock knelt by the side of his bed. The Cluster might only be a tool of God, but it was a powerful tool. He had compared it to a hammer when speaking to Ellis. Nodding to himself, Clyde began to think of it more as a computer where messages could be stored.

"Oh Cluster that roams the heavens," prayed McClintlock. "Your image is exalted! Your dominion is assured and your desires are executed on Earth and in space by my people. You provide our reason for living and forgive our sins. Do not let me be tempted to abandon you. Instead, lead this ship and me to you. Your imperium is coming. Your power and glory will shine throughout the cosmos!"

Shipshape

Aboard naval ships, the space allotted any sailor was at a premium. The crew slept in bunks lining the walls of the ship. The only concession for officers was a curtain that could be pulled across the sleeping space for some modicum of privacy. Even during his tenure as a ship commander, all John Mark Ellis had was a cot, a fold-down desk and a slightly larger curtain.

"So much for being a government employee," said Ellis as he stepped into his quarters aboard the *Nicholas Sanson* for the first time.

Ellis entered alone, after a busy day reviewing crew reports and ship status. The bed, like those aboard naval vessels, was built into the wall. The similarity ended there. The bed was molded into the wall in a way that gave it a certain elegance, making it seem all the more inviting. Not only that, there was a window over the bed, allowing the stars to shine in, giving him a sense of peace, not unlike sleeping on the deck of his grandfather's boat. In addition to the bed were a dresser and two chairs at a round table. Like the bed, they were mounted to the floor in case the graviton generators failed, an occurrence Ellis had a hard time foreseeing on a ship this well maintained. Looking to the left, he saw a door that led into his own private lavatory.

Sitting on the edge of the bed, Ellis eased shoes off his feet and lay back, sinking into the soft, yet supportive mattress. It seemed like it had been a lifetime since the captain had a good night sleep. For the past several weeks, Ellis rented a cubicle in Japan, where the mattress seemed paper-thin. Before that, comfortable as G'Liat's mud bath was, it did not compare to a real bed.

Lying in bed, Ellis thought about the good fortune that had allowed him to command a ship so quickly. One of the senior captains in TransGalactic retired recently, opening a position on a bigger ship for the *Sanson's* previous captain. As Kirsten Smart had said, they were reluctant to promote Yermakov. As Ellis faded toward sleep, he marveled at the remarkable chain of circumstances that allowed him to lie in this bed in these quarters.

The captain's eyes popped open. He thought back to his conversation with G'Liat about finding a ship for their search. He remembered suggesting the mapping vessel to G'Liat. Even so, that suggestion had come after the Rd'dyggian had been inside his mind. The captain's thoughts wandered and he found himself wondering just how long the alien had been planning a trip aboard this particular ship.

Ellis sat up in bed, a cold sweat breaking out on his forehead. It was well known throughout the confederation that the Rd'dyggians had always resented the Titans' interference in their war with the Tzrn. The captain pursed his lips, hoping he wasn't letting himself be a pawn in some elaborate revenge plot.

Ellis growled at himself. The last thing he needed was to be distracted by paranoia, especially when he was scared senseless at the idea of chasing the Cluster alone. Taking a deep breath, Ellis let it out slowly with the words, "I'm in command."

Feeling wide-awake, the captain stood and stepped into the lavatory. Like everything else on the ship, it was spotless. Looking in the mirror, Ellis examined his auburn beard, which he had trimmed just two days before. Small, out of place hairs jutted out at odd angles.

Forcing a smile, Ellis thought his beard reminded him of the crew. By and large, they were efficient and orderly. Still, the bridge crew seemed at odds with that order. The pilot, Laura, seemed the only capable member of the command crew. Ellis vowed to work on shaping up Yermakov and Papadraxis the next day. This was his ship after all, and it was time to take full charge. Using the trimmer he found in the drawer under the sink, Ellis cut the stray hairs in his beard and nodded to himself in the mirror. Pleased that paranoid thoughts were behind him, Ellis shut off the light and returned to the comfortable bed.

* * *

Kirsten Smart stepped into her familiar quarters aboard the *Sanson*. Almost habitually, she turned on the news – audio only – and stepped into the lavatory. Kirsten undid the barrette, letting her hair fall loose. She brushed it methodically while listening to the news. An admiral named Strauss was being interviewed.

"We believe we've detected a pattern in the Cluster attacks," said the admiral. "While many ships have been destroyed, it appears rare that two ships of the same class are ever destroyed."

"You mean, if one human freighter has been destroyed by the Cluster, no other freighter will be destroyed?" asked the reporter.

"No two freighters of the same class," corrected the admiral.

The reporter pressed on. "What about the freighters *Nantucket* and *Martha's Vineyard*?"

The admiral paused an uncomfortably long time. "Our understanding is that the *Vineyard* is an uprated design. It was not identical to the *Nantucket*."

"That sounds like a fine point," said the reporter.

"Fine, but real," stated the admiral, firmly.

Kirsten Smart pursed her lips and wondered whether any mapping vessels had been destroyed. She knew that none of the *Ogilby* fleet had been attacked. With grim hope, she knew that TransGalactic was not the only mapping fleet to use ships of the *Sanson's* design. After a few minutes, she turned off the news, slipped into a nightgown and tried to drift off to sleep. Instead of sleeping, she tossed and turned, unable to get John Mark Ellis' face out of her thoughts.

* * *

The next morning, Clyde McClintlock was up early. He hummed during his shower, confident that his prayers to the Cluster would be answered. He shaved quickly, then donned his white shirt, trousers and apron. The evangelist smiled to himself thinking how much the attire reminded him of the suit he wore when he preached to the people of Cape Cod. Looking in the mirror, his smile turned to a frown as he saw the black-dyed hair standing in contrast to the white clothes. With a sigh, he hurried out of his quarters toward the kitchen where his staff would be waiting for him to present them with the day's menu.

Arriving at the kitchen, Clyde's spirits lifted as he saw the two women and two men who comprised his Monday morning staff getting the kitchen ready for the day. Clyde clapped his hands together and the four looked at him. "Menu for this morning, is bacon, eggs, and buckwheat pancakes," announced McClintlock.

The lead cook, Morganna, stepped up to McClintlock and put her hand on his shoulder. She looked as though a cigarette should be dangling from her mouth. From the heavy tobacco smell that clung to her, McClintlock suspected that she did smoke back in her quarters. The boss, Ms. Smart, forbade smoking anywhere else in the ship. "Mr. McIntosh," she drawled. "This crew is going to mutiny if you make them eat eggs, bacon, and buckwheat pancakes every morning for breakfast."

McClintlock looked to the ground and wrung his hands. While in the Gaean Navy, it had seemed like ambrosia anytime that menu was prepared. The alternatives were always cold, gooey oatmeal or hard biscuits that were served with gravy just to make them edible. The evangelist looked into Morganna's lined face. All his years of command training rebelled against asking a particular question. At a loss for anything else to say, though, he succumbed and asked, "What do you suggest?"

Morganna's concerned expression brightened into a smile. "I can make a green chile and sausage quiche that will knock your socks off. We can serve it with a bit of fruit. The crew will love it."

His stomach feeling hollow, Clyde nodded. "Sounds good."

As the kitchen staff swarmed about, preparing breakfast, Clyde slunk back to his office and turned on his terminal so he could prepare the menus for the rest of the day. Instead, he simply sat wondering how he could continue to pull off this deception perpetrated by Ellis and G'Liat.

Morganna found him like that about an hour later. "Why so blue, boss?"

"Do you think I'm doing a good job?" The question actually made McClintlock's stomach hurt. "I can't even seem to come up with appetizing menus."

Morganna sat down in the chair opposite McClintlock's desk. "It doesn't take a hexadimensional engineer to know you were a cook in the military," she said with a wry grin. "You've just got to learn to ask for advice now and again."

Clyde McClintlock squirmed and looked at the floor. He wanted to shout the fact that he had run the military of an entire continent. Wringing his hands more furiously than before, he wanted to say he had been governor of that continent. On Earth, millions of people followed his teachings about the Cluster. Only momentarily, did he wonder at how a farm kid from Sufiro could have attained all that. With a sigh, he looked up into her brown eyes. "You're right," he said. "You want to help me plan lunch?"

"I thought you'd never ask," she said. "But first, the captain is expecting his breakfast."

Clyde McClintlock laughed inwardly thinking this was the first morning that Ellis had been aboard. "I take it, it's customary for the head chef to take the captain his breakfast?"

"It's good politics," suggested Morganna. "Always good to impress the captain."

Standing, Clyde McClintlock stepped out to the kitchen, where he prepared a tray for Ellis. He had to admit the quiche smelled good. He grabbed a second plate for himself, trusting that Morganna had the situation well in hand, and made his way to the captain's quarters.

* * *

As Clyde left the Kitchen, Isaac and Quincy entered. They grabbed plates and each took a slice of quiche. "Looks like Morganna's cooking again," said Quincy, finding a seat at a table.

"Thank God," sighed Isaac. The programmer's brow knitted. "You know, there's something familiar about our cook."

"You're just being paranoid," said Quincy.

"Who's being paranoid?" asked a stout, balding man, entering the kitchen.

Isaac and Quincy each nodded to Mahuk, the chief engineer. "Isaac keeps telling me he's seen our cook somewhere before," said the burley Quincy. "He even thinks it was on the news."

"Why's that seem so strange?" asked Isaac, holding up his hands in mock indignation.

"The guy's a second-rate cook at best," said Quincy. "He would never get a cooking segment on the news."

"I didn't say it was a cooking segment," said Isaac, exasperated.

"Forget the cook," said Mahuk, waving his hands, already bored with the conversation. "I just want to know if you've modified the code for the EQ drives like I asked."

"I'll have it done right after breakfast," said Isaac.

* * *

McClintlock did not think about consulting the computer, or asking anyone where the captain's cabin was located before he left the kitchen. Despite the fact that Ellis' cabin was only one deck above the kitchen, Clyde wandered the halls long enough for the tray of food to get cold. At last, the one-time colonel found himself knocking on the captain's door.

"It's about time you got here," grumbled Ellis as he stepped out of the lavatory. He sat down at the table. Like the chairs in his office, the chairs at the table were mounted in tracks and could be pushed away and pulled toward the wood-grained table.

"This is a bigger ship than I'm used to," said McClintlock, sitting the tray on the table.

"I know what you mean. I'm still getting used to the idea of having my own quarters, much less my own ready room." Ellis smirked to himself. "I almost feel like an admiral."

"You better not let Ms. Smart hear that. As far as we're concerned, she is the admiral." Sniffing the air, Clyde noticed the air smelled remarkably clean. There was no evidence that the captain had unpacked, much less smoked, his pipes. "Are you feeling okay?"

"I'm feeling fine." Ellis raised his fork and cut into the quiche. Taking a bite, he made a face. "This is good, but it's cold." Shaking his head he looked at the evangelist. "It really did take a long time for you to get here this morning."

McClintlock shrugged. He took a bite. Ellis was right, the quiche was good. "It seems odd that you would go through an entire night without your pipe," McClintlock said, at last.

It was Ellis' turn to shrug. "Ship's rules." McClintlock began to say something, but the captain cut him off. "Even though I can smoke here, the fact of the matter is that Ms. Smart doesn't like it. As you say, she's the admiral. No sense pissing her off."

McClintlock nodded sensing something peculiar in the captain's voice – almost a lilting as though the captain was in love. The evangelist did not care to guess whether it was love with the owner's representative or the ship itself. "So, I hear we're finally heading out tomorrow," said McClintlock changing the subject. "Where's our first destination?"

"The planet Zahar. Ever been there?" The evangelist shook his head. "Neither have I." The captain reached over and flipped on a display. A schematic of a star and nearby planet appeared over the table. The planet seemed impossibly large for its proximity to the star. "Zahar is a terrestrial planet just a little smaller than Jupiter. It's covered with water just the right temperature for a Jacuzzi."

"Sounds like a great place to visit."

"If the gravity wouldn't tear a human to pieces," mused the captain. "It's a rich system, and thus one that people want to get to easily. Unfortunately, the gravitational currents with those two large, close bodies make it a tricky one for small yachts and traders that don't have the computational power of bigger ships. They rely on mapping vessels to provide up-to-date records of the jump points." The captain took a deep breath. "By the way, the last ship attacked by the Cluster was from Zahar." Ellis retrieved a napkin from the tray and wiped his mouth. "It's time I got to the command deck."

McClintlock noticed that the captain's back seemed to straighten with that last statement. He felt a sense of purpose emanating from Ellis. Wishing he could mimic the captain, McClintlock said, "I have a menu to prepare."

* * *

"Mr. Yermakov," barked Ellis as he stepped out onto the command deck. "Status report!"

The first mate was typing commands on a holographic projection of a control console. He sniffed, rubbed his nose on the sleeve of his blue flannel shirt, and then looked around at Ellis. "No problems here, skipper," he said.

The captain took a deep breath and let it out slowly. "Are we ready to get underway, then?"

Yermakov looked toward the screen then changed his holo console to a status readout and back to a console again. After thinking for a moment he shrugged. "Nope."

The omission of the word "sir" irked Ellis. He knew it was not required aboard a civilian ship. It bothered him nonetheless. "Do you care to elaborate, Mr. Yermakov?"

The first mate sniffed again, then shrugged. "We're still taking on supplies, energy packs, that sort of thing. It should all be in your briefing packet. Besides, we've yet to receive destination orders from the boss."

"We know our destination, Mr. Yermakov," snarled Ellis.

"We know we're going to Zahar," conceded Yermakov. "But via which route? It's not a direct jump. Five of the routes were mapped within the last week. Do you know which five?" Yermakov put his hands on his hips. "Which of the ten remaining routes do we take? Or, are we mapping a whole new route?" The mate shook his head and returned to work.

Ellis moved forward and gripped the back of the command chair until his knuckles turned white. He looked forward at the holographic display, showing the Earth rotating below the ship. In the display, it looked as though one could reach out and touch three separate space stations. Forcing himself to relax, he felt the eyes of all the officers on the command deck staring at him.

Ellis turned his attention to Natalie Papadraxis. Her long hair was tied in a braid running down her back. Instead of the floral print dress, she wore shorts and a bikini top. She smiled vacuously. Laura Peters, wearing the same type of brown jump suit as the day before, slowly turned her attention back to her work. Ellis sighed, realizing that his task of shaping up the bridge crew was not going to be an easy one nor was it off to a good start.

Ellis stepped to the front of the command chair and put his hands on his hips. He looked from Papadraxis to Peters to Yermakov. "I think it's important for me to emphasize that while this is a civilian ship, I am still its master. I do require a minimum of discipline. When I request a status report, please give me a complete report." Peters turned her attention from her work back to the captain. Having everyone's attention, Ellis nodded, satisfied, then sat down next to his first mate. Softening his tone a little, he continued. "I admit, I'm new to mapping vessels. When I request a status report, please realize it's to help me keep the ship running smoothly."

Yermakov turned so he was facing the captain more directly. "Start then by realizing that we know our jobs." He put his hands on his knees.

"And I know mine," said Ellis, with an edge in his voice. The captain looked to the floor for a moment, then looked back up into Simon Yermakov's deep brown eyes. While the lighting on the command deck was bright, Yermakov's pupils seemed large. The captain pursed his lips and stood. "If you need me, I'll be in my office." With that, he shook his head and left the command deck.

As the captain sat down behind his desk, he looked up, startled to see that Natalie Papadraxis had followed him in. She stepped up meekly and sat down in one of the chairs opposite the desk. "You have a lot of pent up hostility, Captain."

"Not hostility," said Ellis shaking his head. "What can I do to help this ship run more smoothly?"

Papadraxis' gaze drifted around the room before it settled back on the captain. "Perhaps you could call him, Simon," she said dreamily. With that, she stood and left the room.

Ellis slammed his fist down on the desk. If he were going to get in contact with the Cluster, he would need a disciplined crew, not a bunch of spoiled brats. He would need people who could respond to orders quickly. The captain took several deep breaths and attempted to calm himself. "I *am* the captain," he told himself firmly. The captain's thoughts were interrupted by a knock on the door. "Come in," he called vaguely annoyed.

Kirsten Smart's frame filled the width of the door. "May I come in?" Her tone was curt and formal.

Ellis held his hand out toward the chair opposite the desk. She came in and sat down. "What can I do for you, ma'am?" asked Ellis.

Smart took a deep breath and folded her hands. "I understand you were just out there blustering about discipline. One of the crew says you implied they didn't know how to run this type of ship."

Ellis sat forward. "All I did was request a complete status report from Yermakov," he explained. "I would hope my first mate could produce a more lucid answer than 'nope.'"

"Did you read his status report on the computer this morning?" Smart folded her arms. "If you had, I think you would have found it more complete than anything he could give you verbally."

"The ability to provide a succinct verbal report is necessary in times of crisis," said Ellis, standing.

Smart held out her hands. "What crisis? This is a mapping vessel."

Ellis rubbed his hand through his hair, leaving it tousled. "What is Yermakov taking?"

Smart looked like she had been slapped. "What? What do you mean?"

"The constant sniffling. His eyes are dilated. He seems capable of standing up to me when you say he shouldn't be able to. He's on some kind of medication," said Ellis. "I don't need my officers impaired."

"He's probably taking Proxom. He's not a natural leader. As first mate, he's under a lot of stress." She shrugged. "I may not want him in command, but I don't want him to snap either. You're not helping by yelling at him."

"You asked me 'what danger?'" retorted Ellis, pursing his lips. "What if Yermakov gave me an incorrect report because of the drugs? What if he took too much and passed out?"

"You should talk," said Smart simply, but seemed to check herself. She stood and put her hands on Ellis' desk. "You are awfully uptight about something."

Ellis thrust his hands in his pockets. "Is it so wrong to want discipline on a star vessel? After all, we're surrounded by vacuum. While I'll concede it's a civilian ship, our lives are on the line all the time we're out here."

Smart looked to the deck and wrung her hands. After a moment, she looked up again, her gaze softening. "Okay, I'll agree, some amount of discipline is necessary." She moved away from the desk. "But, your style of discipline may be hard for most of this crew to swallow. You might try ruling with kid gloves, not an iron fist."

Grudgingly, Ellis nodded. "I'll try it your way."

"Good," she said, turning to leave. As she reached the door, she turned back. "Think about losing the beard, it doesn't look very professional."

* * *

Kirsten returned to her office and fell into her chair rubbing the bridge of her nose. She had just blurted out the suggestion to shave the beard. It came out sounding like an order.

On one hand, she supposed she did it to see if he would bend to her will. On the other hand, something about his face seemed familiar and the beard seemed wrong.

She tried to remember the last time she actually watched the holo news, rather than listening to it. Somehow, she thought that if she could remember that date, she might figure out why she asked Ellis to shave.

* * *

That afternoon, Ellis emerged from his office. "Simon," he said, carefully modulating his voice. "I read your afternoon report. It sounds like we're ready to depart for Zahar in the morning."

"That we are, Skipper." Simon Yermakov stared forward at the viewscreen.

Noticing they were alone on the command deck, Ellis sat in the chair next to his first mate. Leaning over, the captain whispered, "I understand you spoke to the boss after I'd asked you for a report earlier."

Yermakov's eyebrows came together. "It wasn't me," he said, flatly. The first mate turned to look at the captain. "I may not agree with your ideas about discipline. More to the point, while I don't like your style,

I figure you'll settle down after a while."

Ellis examined the two empty stations at the front of the command deck. If Yermakov was not the one who went to Smart, he wondered who was. "I'm glad to hear it wasn't you," said the captain. "I prefer my officers come to me if they have a problem."

"I prefer my captains read my reports before they demand them in front of junior officers." Yermakov's eyes were still forward.

Ellis arched an eyebrow and stood to leave.

"If you're here for a bit, I figured I might take a coffee break," stated Yermakov, wryly.

The captain fought an urge to inform his first mate of his place. "Sure," sighed Ellis as he sat down. The command seat had never felt so hard.

* * *

That night, Ellis stood in the lavatory, in his quarters, staring in the mirror. He debated whether he should shave his beard or not. Neatly trimmed as it was, it did not look unprofessional to him. Besides, he thought, who aside from the crew was going to see it? The captain continued to tug nervously at the beard. Finally, he was interrupted by a knock at the door.

About the same time the captain acknowledged the knock, G'Liat stepped into the room. "I understand there have been some teething pains, today."

"You could say that," said Ellis, stepping from the lavatory and taking a seat at the table. He gestured for G'Liat to do the same. "Do you think I should shave?"

The warrior remained standing. "That seems to me to be a personal decision." G'Liat stepped over to the bunk and looked out the view port. "Do it or don't. It makes no difference to me."

"Ms. Smart thinks the beard makes me look unprofessional." The captain's shoulders slumped.

G'Liat moved with feline grace from the window to the chair opposite the captain. "If you think shaving will make you a better warrior, then shave. Some of your kind think it's a necessity. Do it for yourself. Do not do it for her."

Ellis shrugged. "Today, my confidence has been shaken. In the military, I knew how to command a ship." Ellis stopped. "I should say, I thought I knew how to command a ship. Now I'm not so sure I do."

G'Liat's body grew rigid. "Are you saying that when we find the Cluster, this crew won't follow you?"

Shaking his head, Ellis stood. He moved over to the bunk and flopped down on it. "After commanding the *Firebrandt* I thought I had it all figured out. I won the loyalty of that crew by being strong. I'm not sure how to win the loyalty of this crew."

"Perhaps you are trying too hard," pondered the warrior. "Did you win the loyalty of *Firebrandt's* crew by being strong, or by being yourself?"

Ellis pondered the question and looked out at the stars. "Have you ever been to Zahar?"

"It's a beautiful world." G'Liat folded his arms on the table. "The oceans are especially delightful. A mariner such as yourself would be impressed." The warrior lay his head on his arms.

"How would you know?" laughed Ellis. "Rd'dyggians would be crushed on the surface just the same as humans."

"I've seen it through their eyes. I've been in the minds of some Zahari. While unique in their own way, they are not unlike your friends, the whales."

Ellis folded his arms and looked over at the warrior. "Do you suppose the Cluster will be there?"

"At Zahar?" G'Liat shook his head. "I suspect we have much farther to go to find the Cluster."

Ellis tapped his fingers on the table. "Where do we go?" asked the captain, growing more agitated. "How do we get there?" Ellis let out a sigh. "Do I want to get where we're going? I don't know anymore. You keep hinting that there's more for me to learn. What must I learn?"

"You must learn to be a warrior," answered G'Liat simply. "To do that, you must learn to communicate."

"To communicate, I must know who I am." Ellis sighed. "I thought I was the captain, by nature. Also, the military trained me well. They made me a pretty good warrior."

"No," said G'Liat. "They taught you how to be a soldier, not a warrior. The Cluster lies on the path of knowledge. Only a warrior survives on that path. A soldier is merely cannon fodder."

"Where do we start?" asked Ellis with a shrug.

"When we jump, listen as the beyond sings the song of time. When you begin to understand the lyrics you will be ready to confront the Cluster."

Ellis' brow creased. "But you failed in your attempt to talk to the Cluster. How would you know when I'm really ready?"

"I'm still learning the melody. I hope you will teach me the words." With that, G'Liat stood and left the room.

* * *

Manuel Raton was worried. Fire had left for work early in the morning. It was now late at night and she hadn't returned home. He stepped out of the Ellis home into the fog. Raton shivered in the chill, wet air. His bones seemed to ache and his breathing felt labored. He almost thought something would jump out of the fog and attack him.

"Manuel, you forgot to lock the door!" called Coffin's scratchy voice from the fog.

Raton jumped and let out a yelp. "Uh... yeah, thanks," he said. "I just thought I'd take a walk up to Fire's office and see what's keeping her."

"She's probably afraid of your cooking," retorted Coffin. "That stuff's so damn hot, no one could eat it." Coffin closed the door. Manuel heard the bolt slam home.

Raton shook his head. "Can't get any decent chilies on this damned island. Too hot, my ass," he muttered as he felt his way through the fog. After walking for fifteen minutes, Raton cursed, realizing he had ambled up the wrong street. He found a side street that took him around a corner. Ultimately, he found his way to Vestal Street, home of the Maria Mitchell Association. He held on to the white picket fence that surrounded the observatory. From there, he could just make out the faint glow of Fire's office, just off the Association's library. He ambled across the street and let himself in the building.

Fire looked up at Raton when he entered and smiled.

"You're late for dinner," said Raton.

"Oh," gasped Fire. She looked at the clock on her holo-terminal. "I hadn't noticed the time. Sorry." The office was paneled in wood. Wooden shelves lined the walls, filled with ancient, but real books. Fire's desk was an antique that had been modified so that the holo-terminal was incorporated into the top. Around the desk were assorted storage disks and crystals.

"Find anything good?" Manuel threw himself into a chair across from Fire's desk.

Fire shook her head. "Mostly stuff I already know. The Titans have always claimed that they evolved on Titan. However, it doesn't wash. There are no naturally occurring lower life forms. The architecture has always been the same. The only ruins look exactly like the buildings do now. As best as we can tell, their technology hasn't changed in over three thousand years."

Manuel shrugged. "I thought that the Titans said that they foolishly killed off the lower lifeforms when they were more primitive."

"No fossil record of any lower lifeforms," countered Fire.

"How do you know? They rarely let scientists outside their respective domes. There's a lot of Titan that's simply unexplored, except potentially by the Titans themselves."

Fire stood and stretched her arms over her head. She walked around the desk and planted a kiss on Manuel Raton's nose. "The Titans are hiding something. They're lying about their past. If the fossil records were there, they'd show them." She reached back and touched her control pad. An image of the Cluster came up. She touched the pad again. This time, a picture of the domes came up.

Manuel shook his head. "Silver spheres and silver domes. So what if they look the same?"

"The dimensions are identical," said Fire flatly.

"Are they made out of the same material?" asked Raton.

"Who knows?" Fire turned off the display. "No one's scanned the Cluster. But, I'll tell you this. The alloy used to construct the oldest Titan domes is not known in this galaxy."

"Ay, carajo!" Manuel leaned forward. "How did anyone find that out?"

"The Rd'dyggians performed some scans almost a thousand years ago. Seems they've always been suspicious of the Titans."

"Just like humans have been," said Manuel, sitting back in the chair.

"Just like humans," said Fire, nodding.

"So, what do we do now?" asked Manuel.

"All of this only demonstrates why we're skeptical that Titans are really locals. There's maybe just a hint of evidence that they're tied to the Cluster somehow. None of it answers where the Titans came from." Suki Ellis shook her head, her lips pursed. "What do we do now? We go home for dinner." She slid into Manuel's lap.

"Then?" asked Manuel, hopefully.

"To bed," grinned Fire.

"What about the Titans?" asked Manuel.

"They can get their own sex," said Fire, playing with Manuel's long mustache. Manuel pursed his lips. Fire shook her head. "The next question I have to answer is whether I can learn to operate Titan data retrieval systems. If so, maybe we can do a little spying."

"Now that's what I want to hear!" said Manuel, his grin growing broadly.

Fire pouted, letting her lower lip protrude. "Spying on Titans sounds more fun than sex with me?"

"Spying on Titans sounds like more fun than kicking around the house with Old Man Coffin, I'll tell you that," grumbled Raton.

"I'll let you live, this time," said Fire, tugging on Manuel's mustache.

Preaching to the Converted

The next morning, Ellis stepped onto the command deck. His shirt and trousers were pressed to a crispness beyond what he wore in the military. His beard was neat but intact. More than ever, Ellis felt like a warrior. The crewmembers were in their places ready for the ship's departure. Simon Yermakov, wearing a bright red flannel shirt, rested his head on his hand. The captain had carefully made a point of reading the first mate's report that morning. Kirsten Smart's sensing devices were ready for the trip to Zahar. *Nicholas Sanson* was ready to depart on the captain's command and clearance to leave orbit.

Natalie Papadraxis, in a black skirt and peasant blouse, stared in wonder at the hologram. "Earth Central says traffic in the solar system is clear, we can move toward the jump point at will," she reported dreamily.

"Course to jump point is plotted," reported Laura Peters, running a hand nervously through short hair.

"If we know the way," said Ellis in deliberately cheerful tones, "let's get going." He worried that he sounded bitter as he sat down in the command seat.

Peters punched one of the holographic buttons on her console. The panel changed configurations. Instead of a bank of buttons, a three-dimensional representation of the ship floated above a set of directional controls fitted perfectly for her finger spacing. Placing her hand on the controls, she gently massaged the panel. On the holographic screen at the front of the deck, the Earth could be seen slipping to the left and below the ship.

Captain Ellis nodded, pleased with her skill. He brought up a holographic image that showed the course projection and displayed the estimated time of arrival at the jump point. The jump point for Zahar was near the orbit of Mars. The captain stood to stretch. He balanced himself on the armrest as the ship listed slightly; it felt the gravitational convergence of another star system with the sun. Even though their target was to map one of the jumpways to Zahar, Ellis knew that Kirsten Smart's instruments were mapping each of the convergence points as they passed. That information would be added to the net for TransGalactic subscribers throughout the galaxy. In fact, his old ship, the *Firebrandt* used to download data from TransGalactic's competitor, the Andropov Corporation, to update ship's charts.

Getting used to the feel of the gentle sway of the ship, the captain casually walked forward, hands clasped behind his back. He nodded at Major Peters as he passed. Her eyes were focused on the holo of the ship, her brow creased. Stepping on past, the captain entered the hologram and looked around. The holo was set to a scale of one to one, so the stars looked distant. In fact, other than their crispness, the patterns looked no different than they would on Earth. Turning to face the command deck, Ellis was impressed to see that the hologram included a representation of the outside of the ship. Taking a moment, to look around, Ellis let himself get caught up in the illusion that he was standing in the middle of space, looking back at the command deck through a window in his ship.

"Mr. Yermakov," called Ellis. Catching himself, he shook his head. "Simon," he corrected.

"Yes, Skipper," responded the first mate lackadaisically.

"Would you kindly reduce the scale? I'd like to see a course projection in the holo tank." The captain looked to Peters still absorbed in her holo. "If it won't affect your work, Laura."

Peters shook her head, preoccupied. "I don't use the main viewer for in-flight stuff most of the time. I'll let you know if I need it."

Yermakov turned some dials on his antique-looking wooden console hologram. Within a few seconds, Ellis found himself surrounded by nearby stars. A bright red arc jutted out from the sun, toward a yellow-orange star some distance away. The captain noticed that handwritten notes floated near the Zahari star. Those notes were Yermakov's estimates of fuel consumption and estimated times of departure for other systems on their route. Most of those systems were ones that the captain recognized as inhabited. There were others Ellis did not recognize. He assumed those to be uninhabited colony worlds of the Confederation. Looking around at stars to the side and in front of him, he felt like a giant, or even a god of sorts. He contemplated all the empty space between the stars of the galaxy and wondered what was there. Despite all the stars man could reach, most of the galaxy, almost all the empty space between the stars, was completely inaccessible. Star vessels required jump points and there were none that he knew of, in deep space.

"Simon," said Ellis quietly. As he turned around, he saw the officers through a field of stars. "Would you kindly show me the four dimensional representation?"

"Are you sure, Skipper?" asked Yermakov, genuine concern showing on his features. "It can be pretty disorienting in there when we change the view."

"Go ahead," said Ellis taking a deep breath. "I'm ready."

Space seemed to congeal around the captain. In a matter of moments, he realized that he really had not been prepared for this portrayal of space. The hologram was only a projection of fourth dimensional reality into three dimensions. Even so, the black vacuum around him seemed to morph into a bright yellow fabric. The location of the sun and that of Zahar turned into rippling contours like those from rocks dropped into a lake. However, it was not a placid lake. More stars were added like raindrops falling, and Ellis felt like he was standing in the middle of a pulsating, alive thing. The course projection appeared and followed a path where the ripples emanating from the sun intersected ripples from the Zahari star with minimal interference from the undulating waves of other systems. The *Nicholas Sanson* would slowly make its way along that path, updating the map as shown.

Ellis began to get ill, just thinking about the journey. Aboard military ships, the jump would be quick and comparatively painless. While disorienting, it would be over in a short time. On the other hand, this trip would take nearly an hour of being buffeted by the currents of spacetime. Leisurely time, thought the captain, to learn whatever song was to be learned in the beyond.

The captain took a deep breath. "Could you mark the jump nodes for me, Simon?"

"No problem, Skipper," said Yermakov with a sniffle.

Blue dots appeared across the yellow fabric at the points where the ripples met. Those were the points where one could enter fourth dimensional reality. The thing that caught the captain's attention most, though, was that some of the nodes appeared to occur where there was no intersection. "What are these nodes?" asked Ellis, pointing to one of the points that seemed to stand alone.

"Those?" mused Peters. "All the points there are mapped nodes. Some appear in the middle of nowhere. They seem to be transient."

"What do you mean transient?" asked Ellis as he emerged from the hologram.

"They move around. Sometimes they appear in star systems. Other times, we guess they're in deep space. No one who has tried to see where those go has ever returned." Peters turned her attention to her work.

"In the Academy, I was told there were no deep space jump points. All nodes were near stars." The captain's eyebrows came together.

"The military tells you what it wants you to know," said Natalie Papadraxis, her gaze growing frighteningly clear.

Ellis tugged on his beard, longing for his pipe. "Why wouldn't they tell us about deep space jump points?"

"The military doesn't have that much money," explained Natalie. "No one wants a bored ship captain to take an expensive ship through an uncharted node and vanish forever."

Ellis frowned. During his days as a ship captain, he had been so busy that it would be hard to imagine being bored enough to do anything so foolhardy. "How long until we reach the jump point for Zahar?"

"About twenty minutes, sir," reported Peters.

"I'll be in my office. Let me know when we're ready to jump." With that Ellis returned his hands behind his back and stalked off the command deck.

* * *

Clyde McClintlock sat in his office trying to concentrate on the menu for the night. The rolling motion of the ship made him vaguely nauseous and he fought to keep his mind on his work. Every time he looked at the listings of food, though, he felt his stomach turn again.

"For a Navy guy, you look awfully green around the gills," came the voice of his assistant, Morganna.

"Hi," said Clyde, meekly. "Navy ships don't rock like this. In fact, I've been on ocean going ships that made me less seasick. What's going on?"

"It's the ship," explained Morganna. She stepped in the room and pulled up a stool. "They say it's the way it senses gravity waves. Every jump point to another star in the galaxy makes the ship bounce like that."

"Am I the only one aboard that's affected like this?" Clyde took a deep breath, trying to keep his lunch down.

"Most of the crew gets hit at one time or another. Most get over it quickly." Morganna leaned forward. "If you think this is bad, wait until we spend an hour in the beyond."

"I've been on my share of jumps through spacetime." Clyde wanted to sound like the seasoned Navy officer he was, but the queasiness of his stomach dampened his spirits.

"Jumps, maybe," said Morganna, nodding sagely. "This is more like crawling." She inclined her head and examined the head cook. "There are things out there," she whispered. "Some are well known, like jump points where none should be. When you leap out of our natural dimension, you sense things, even when you don't see them." She paused and laughed nervously. "Have you met Natalie, yet?"

Clyde leaned back, letting his head settle into the rest on his chair. "The communicator?"

"Yeah," nodded Morganna. "Everyone says that implant she uses to communicate with other ships makes her think she's psychic. It wouldn't surprise me if she really were psychic though. It'd be from all those years of going beyond space."

"Are you afraid of what you might find in the beyond?" asked Clyde.

"Not so much afraid," mused Morganna. "More in awe. It wouldn't surprise me if that Cluster thing that everyone's afraid of comes from the beyond."

Clyde sat up suddenly. "What do you know about the Cluster?"

"I've felt it out there," whispered Morganna. "That's all."

Clyde grinned and put his hand on Morganna's shoulder. "You shouldn't be afraid of the Cluster. I've seen it."

"You sound like a man who's talked to it, too," said Morganna, reverently.

"I have spoken to it." Clyde McClintlock's blue eyes grew wide. "Besides myself, I only know one other person who has." Clyde folded his hands. "You felt it, but did you hear its words?"

Morganna shook her head. "I've never seen it, much less talked to it. Still, it seemed to be out there with us, in the beyond." They sat in silence for a moment. "You know, I'm not sure it's the evil that everyone says it is. It seems more . . . curious than anything else."

"Curious?" McClintlock didn't notice his nausea any more. "Curious about what?"

"About everything." Morganna smiled. "I've felt at times that it's looking for something or someone."

Clyde rubbed his hands together. This information was almost more than he could ever have hoped for. A secret desire formed as he wondered if the Cluster were searching for him or perhaps even Ellis, whose visions had been stronger than his own. "I've wondered that myself at times," said Clyde. "I've actually even hoped the Cluster was looking for something. The problem is, I'm not positive what it's looking for."

"I'd think you of all people would have an idea," said Morganna.

"What do you mean by that?" asked Clyde, his eyebrows coming together.

"Well, you founded that religion based on the Cluster and all," she said. "That black hair dye doesn't fool anyone, you know."

Clyde McClintlock's mouth dropped open. "You've known I'm Clyde McClintlock all along?" The evangelist sat forward. "How many other people know?"

Morganna shrugged. "All the kitchen staff figured it out right away. I don't know anyone else who's said for sure who they think you are. But, I'm sure there are those who suspect."

Dread filled Clyde, as the ship's rocking became more apparent again. He began to think that Morganna had only said what she had because she knew he was Clyde McClintlock, founder of the Cluster religion back on Earth. "So, you've been telling me all this about the Cluster just to make me feel better?"

"Not likely," laughed Morganna. "I don't like you that much. No, I just wanted to save you from preaching to the converted."

"I see," said Clyde, looking at the floor. "Then you believe that the Cluster is a force of good."

Morganna shrugged. "I'm not sure I'd go that far. I only know it's not evil." She winked at him. "I'm almost sure I wouldn't go as far as saying it's God, like you do. Do you really believe that?"

Clyde McClintlock's gaze seemed to move to a distant part of the room. "On the planet Sufiro, I witnessed a miracle. A man I know very well overcame everything – his upbringing, his years in the military, his inhibitions – to become a force for good because of the visions the Cluster showed him. If the Cluster can bring miracles like that, it's hard for me to say what it is, if it's not the hand of God."

"Miracles don't always come from God," said Morganna. "Sometimes, they just come from people like you and me." Just as she said that, the jump klaxon sounded.

"All hands, prepare for jump," came the calm voice of Major Laura Peters over the intercom. "Jump to Zahari star system will commence in five minutes."

Morganna reached into the pocket of her cooking apron and retrieved a packet. "You might want to take this. This will help you deal with the jump."

Clyde accepted the packet from Morganna. "Thanks," he said as he tore the packet open and dropped two pills in his hand. "What is it?"

"Just a little something that helps prevent space sickness." She stood to leave for her jump station. As she reached the door, she turned and faced McClintlock. "While we're in the beyond, listen for the Cluster."

* * *

John Mark Ellis emerged from his office as the jump alert began. About the same time, Kirsten Smart stepped out of her office. "Is the ship set for its jump," she asked, her attention focused on the captain's auburn beard.

"According to reports, we are shipshape," reported the captain.

Kirsten Smart leaned close to the captain. Her voice was a hoarse whisper. "Next time, I'll thank you to do a walk-around inspection of the ship before the jump. Don't just trust the reports."

The captain's shoulder's dropped. "But didn't you tell me to read Yermakov's reports, rather than ask him for status."

"I know what I told you," she said, exasperated. "But, Simon doesn't have time to tour every section of the ship. I have him doing things for the mission."

Ellis shook his head. "So, before every jump, I'm supposed to tour the ship personally?"

Kirsten Smart just patted Ellis on the shoulder and smiled, almost sweetly. With that, she turned and went back into her quarters. Ellis heaved a deep sigh and made his way to the command seat. He turned toward Yermakov. "I presume everything's in order?"

"We're in good shape, Skipper," said Yermakov as he rubbed his nose on his sleeve.

"Good," said the captain. The tone of his voice did not match the word.

"We are at the jump point and ready to go, as soon as you give the word, Captain," reported Major Peters.

"Very good," said the captain with a little more enthusiasm. He reached over and activated the intercom switch. "Ms. Smart, we're ready to jump on your command."

"My instruments are ready," came her disembodied voice. "Jump when you like."

Ellis nodded to himself then shut off the intercom. "Sound one more jump warning," he told Peters, "then jump."

The captain sat back in his chair, listening to the final jump warning being issued throughout the ship. Cartographers would be performing one last check of their instruments. He heard engineers and mechanics report as they performed last minute checks of the EQ drives. On a Navy ship, each deck would report its readiness for jump. That chatter was noticeably missing to the captain. Readiness was assumed rather than reported. The captain gritted his teeth, afraid that Kirsten Smart was right. Perhaps he should have inspected of each deck personally.

"Warning has been given, Captain," reported Peters. "We can jump on command."

Ellis licked his teeth and rubbed sweat off his forehead with his sleeve. Looking over at Yermakov, he saw an expression of relief. Ellis wondered whether the relief was that the jump was coming or that he did not have to give the order to jump. "Jump," Ellis ordered simply.

Laura Peters' thin hand seemed to move toward the console in slow motion. She touched a button and reality collapsed.

* * *

Clyde McClintlock sat in the little office just off the kitchen, listening. His eyes were closed, but still, he seemed to smell with his ears. He felt as though he was falling though space, though if he concentrated as completely as possible, he could feel that the chair was under him.

As a rule, jumping out of normal three-dimensional space was disorienting. Though, this jump was different for McClintlock, he almost felt he could get his bearings.

* * *

On the command deck, John Mark Ellis fought to keep lunch down. His mind wandered briefly to the food Clyde had brought to him a little while before. He wondered if he had, in fact, tasted the evangelist's cooking. Shaking his head, his mind came back to the fantastic sights and sounds around him. Like other jumps, his senses were confused. It did not seem odd that he could smell the color of Yermakov's red shirt nor hear the scent of new plastic.

For the first time, a jump lasted long enough that Ellis realized this was simply the manifestation of perceiving a new dimension. The ship was feeling its way along the same dimension that time traveled, just as an ocean-going ship might move horizontally or a helicopter, vertically. There were theories that suggested that one could make use of temporal dimensionality to travel to other points in history. In fact, though, it seemed that ships only traveled forward with the currents of time.

John Mark Ellis was startled when he realized he could almost see his console. He tried to reach for it, but could not. His neurons, used to working in normal space could not move his arm. He concentrated harder. However, the harder he tried, the less likely he seemed able to succeed.

Trying a new approach, he relaxed and did not try to move his arm. Instead, he just imagined the act happening. His arm was at the console. Unfortunately, his eyes were not registering the hologram as anything more than a mass of sounds. The captain watched the growl escape his lips. Blinking with some surprise, Ellis sat back and tried to listen. All he heard were teddy bears in the night and a vague sense of green.

* * *

The ship seemed to hit a bump. At least that was the perception that Clyde McClintlock had as the *Sanson* moved across one of the mysterious nodes that stood in the middle of deep space. "Cluster, where are you?" The whisper rattled his head.

* * *

Ellis felt the ship lurch as it passed a node where none should be.

The lurch took Ellis' mind from thoughts of song. Aboard the *Firebrandt* such a lurch would not have been noticeable. He wanted desperately to know where the node went. He seemed to sense that answering that question would help him find the Cluster.

Just as that thought came together, Ellis felt a tightening in his chest as reality converged and the *Sanson* returned to normal three-dimensional space. His stomach lunged for his throat. The captain grabbed his armrests and fought a desperate need to throw up on the deck. "We can't have been jumping for an hour."

"One hour three minutes, Skipper," said Yermakov checking instruments. His smirk made him look even more like a squirrel than before.

The captain took several deep breaths. That only made the nausea worse. "I take it the ship's okay?"

"You'll have my report." The first mate sniffed.

Ellis only had time to nod before he found himself running back to the lavatory. There, his lunch came up with a fury. He had not bothered to close the door. The captain reddened when he saw Kirsten Smart looking in at him bemused and a little concerned. "The jump was a success, Captain. Make the ship ready to go again day after tomorrow." She inclined her head. "You might go to sickbay before the next jump. They probably have something that will help the motion sickness."

A low growl rumbled down in the captain's throat. "Motion sickness, indeed," he muttered under his breath.

* * *

Kirsten Smart rubbed itchy tired eyes. She had just spent the entire day staring at map data. Standing, she stepped to the drink dispenser and ordered a cup of tea. Returning to her desk, she saved her work and turned on the holo news.

Clyde McClintlock's face appeared. "Still no word from the missing evangelist," said the disembodied voice of the reporter.

"I'll say," said Smart. She took a tentative sip of tea. "What's Ellis doing with that guy in tow?"

The door chime sounded. Kirsten turned off the news. It was Clyde with dinner. He placed it carefully on her desk. "Can I bring you anything else, ma'am?" asked Clyde.

Kirsten smiled knowingly, trying not to look at the bad hair dye job. Why hadn't she noticed it before? With a barely perceptible sigh, Clyde left for Ellis' quarters.

* * *

"They say the Cluster is out there in the void," said Clyde McClintlock. He sat opposite G'Liat at the table in Ellis' cabin.

Ellis sat on his hands on the bunk shaking his head. "The Cluster is, or belongs to, a three-dimensional entity like us. A fourth dimensional object passing through our dimension would not have as constant an appearance as it does."

"Why not?" asked G'Liat.

"If a three-dimensional object passed through a plane, it would appear different as different parts moved through. Even an object as regular as a sphere would appear to change size." Ellis pursed his lips.

The warrior rocked from side to side. "I see your point, though I'm not sure it's safe to reach any definitive conclusions."

The captain snorted. "I do think the deep space nodes hold part of the answer, though. I think the Cluster might be able to use them to navigate."

"Use them to navigate?" asked G'Liat, genuinely curious. "What makes you think that?"

"I listened to the lyrics, like you told me. I heard the color green."

"You heard it too," said G'Liat nodding. "But why associate green with the Cluster?"

McClintlock waved the warrior's question aside. "Where do the nodes go?"

"I think I might be able to use ship's sensor data to determine that," said Ellis with a smirk. "I think I can set up my console to operate under jump conditions. During the jump, I should be able to use one bank of sensors to scan a node as we pass."

The warrior narrowed his eyes. "That doesn't sound productive. You should continue to listen to the songs. I too heard the green," said the warrior trying to return to the original subject. "It seems a clue. Perhaps there are others."

"Some clue," grumbled Ellis. "Like you asked, why associate green with the Cluster. If we're not careful, we'll spend all our time trying to find meaning in all the clues. I think programming the sensors will provide more answers."

"I agree," said Clyde, slapping his knee. "But why not program the sensors to come on automatically? You might be able to move your arm, but I'd be surprised if the console would register the action."

"If I programmed the sensors, Ms. Smart would ask questions. I'm not prepared to answer those questions just now." Ellis dropped from the bunk to the deck. He stepped over to his duffel, pulled out a pedestal and sat it on the table between McClintlock and G'Liat. Turning it on, the hologram of Jerome Ellis standing on the bow of his boat appeared. His hair blew in the wind. The captain stood back and let them watch the holo for a few moments. "For his memory and for the other humans who've died," said the captain with a determined whisper. "I'll make the console work."

* * *

Putting words into action proved nearly impossible, though. The next day, Ellis spent hours in his office trying to recall how his panel appeared during the jump. From his experiences with jumps, he knew that squares often looked like circles. Unfortunately, as he tried to put his mind to the problem of making a panel that would look like something in the beyond, he found he could not recall exactly how anything looked during a jump.

After about seven hours, there was a knock at the door. Ellis turned off his console. "Come in," said the captain.

A lanky man entered the office. "I'm sorry to interrupt, Captain."

"Who are you?" asked Ellis, rubbing his eyes.

"Isaac Aubry," said the man. "I'm one of the ship's programmers."

"Oh," said Ellis. The captain indicated a chair across from him. "Can I get you a cup of coffee? How can I help you?"

"The computers seemed a bit slow is all," said Isaac. "That's really unusual. I did some poking about." Isaac pointed to the captain's holo terminal. "I found that lots of the compute cycles were going to that station."

"Oh," said Ellis again, too tired for a snappy come back. "I'm designing a new interface for my console."

"With 4-D codes?" Isaac back-peddled when he saw the captain's expression. "Sorry, but I got curious about what you were doing and checked it out. You should really encrypt your files better."

"I'll do that," said Ellis coolly.

"Still," said Isaac, only slightly daunted. "Check out Norton's book on 4-D programming. It's on the net."

"Okay," said Ellis. "Sorry I've been eating so much computer time."

"It's not enough to worry about. I don't think most people would even notice, but I get irked when I even notice a second's delay," said Isaac. He stopped and wrung his hands noticing the captain's expression. "Sorry, but lots of people play games in the beyond. Keeps them from getting motion sick. I just saw how much time you were spending on the project and wanted to keep you from reinventing the wheel."

"Thanks," said Ellis.

"I hope I haven't overstepped my bounds," said Isaac.

"No," said Ellis with a sigh. "Actually you've helped me a great deal."

With that, Isaac stood and left. Ellis reviewed the recommended reading and, at last came up with a design that simply consisted of one large red button to initiate scan. He would have to rely on feeling the bump to know when to begin scanning. When time came for the next jump, Ellis brought the display to life.

Yermakov shook his head when he saw the obscenely simple display. The captain simply sneered in reply and left to make his rounds of the vessel. At last, the jump warning was sounded and the *Sanson* leapt into the beyond.

Anxiously, Ellis waited for the bump that would alert him to the presence of one of the deep space nodes. In time, he felt the jolt. With a great force of will, he was able to reach the button. The scan initiated. Ellis held his breath, hoping he would learn something.

* * *

Returning to her quarters after the jump, Kirsten Smart browsed various on-line news archives. Searching for references to Clyde McClintlock, she discovered he had been a colonel on Sufiro's World. As she continued to work her way through the news archives, she learned about the Erdonium struggle. One thread leapt out at her from all the news archives. A commander in the Confederate Navy had negotiated peace. Unfortunately, the news archives failed to give the name of the Commander. Rather, they gave credit to his commanding officer, the admiral Kirsten had heard on the news, Strauss.

Kirsten sighed. Her intuition was nagging. She felt certain the commander must be Ellis. Looking at Ellis' record, she noted he was from Nantucket. It took only moments to locate the *Nantucket Beacon* on-line edition.

Searching for the last name, Ellis, Kirsten was surprised to find not an article about Sufiro's World, but rather an obituary. The obituary was for a man named Jerome Ellis, killed by the Cluster. Reading a little farther, Kirsten learned that Jerome Ellis was survived by a son: John Mark.

Kirsten Smart chewed on her thumbnail and wondered how John Mark Ellis, Clyde McClintlock and the Cluster all tied together. She knew that Ellis had met the Cluster and that the meeting resulted in his loss of a military career. She worried about what would happen if Ellis met the Cluster again.

With a sigh, she turned her attention to the reports. One report came from Isaac Aubry. Generally, she found programmers an annoying lot, however this one often worked with Quincy Markovitz, a cartographer whose work she admired. Her eyes moved along the report. "Maybe it's time I found out what Ellis is doing with 4-D code," she said to herself. "He may get motion sick, but somehow I doubt he's playing games."

* * *

On Nantucket, Manuel Raton and Suki Ellis poured over holograms of Titans. They watched as Titans danced computer algorithms and intricate holographic displays appeared. Coffin arrived with three cups of coffee.

"Okay," said Fire as she pointed to the hologram. "Watch this part carefully. I think they're pulling up an archive of some kind." Two Teddy Bear-like creatures flung their paws into the air and barred their teeth. They dropped to the floor and wagged their small tails in the air. Fire sipped her coffee. "Think you can do that?"

Manuel scratched his nose. "Play it one more time. I think we can pull it off."

Coffin smiled and stirred his coffee. The three watched the holographic movie one more time. Manuel gulped some coffee. "Let's do it."

Fire and Manuel stood up, each taking a deep breath. They marched around in a circle. After a three-count, they threw their hands into the air. Barring teeth, they growled slightly and dropped to the floor on all fours.

"You need to get your butts a bit higher in the air," called Coffin as the office door opened.

Dorothy Harriman, the gray-haired observatory director, gasped. Fire and Manuel stood up suddenly, straightening their clothes. "Did I interrupt something?" asked Harriman, eyes wide.

Coffin, Raton, and Fire all shook their heads quickly. "No," said Fire. "Nothing at all."

Harriman, her question suddenly forgotten, stepped backwards gingerly, closing the door quietly behind herself.

Grandchildren of Chaos

The African veldt, hot, dusty, and dry, had been one of the most alien landscapes the warrior, G'Liat, had ever visited. Traveling alone, he had battled a lion and killed it for his dinner. The lion was the most graceful hunter the warrior had ever encountered. Whenever G'Liat moved around humans, he mimicked the lion at the cost of some comfort, but gained a great deal of respect. Even more than the lion, G'Liat had been taken with the drums of Africa.

The rhythm of the many types of drums wove a pattern that made the warrior wonder if humans understood fourth dimensional reality, what they called the beyond, even before they needed it for space travel. G'Liat's body moved to those rhythms as he listened to a recording of the African drums while working on his assigned task for Kirsten Smart. His job was to map the deep space nodes where the gravitational forces of unknown objects interacted with the forces of stars in the galaxy; the same thing Ellis had hoped to accomplish.

Pungent incense burned while he worked. Looking at the perfumed smoke, he saw it travel upward and break into turbulent eddies. Humans, with their talent for metaphor, often worried about the deep space nodes. Too often, they thought of space, not as a vacuum, but as a medium like water or air. They were afraid that as they jumped from star to star within the galaxy, they would suddenly be caught in the turbulent wake of one of these nodes and swept off to some unknown place in the universe. Romantic fictions had even been based around the notion. Fortunately, thought G'Liat, gravitational forces decrease with distance and whatever caused those nodes was very far away.

The warrior pulled up a holographic display of the nodes he had mapped to date during the journey. The *Sanson* had made seven jumps into the beyond since leaving Earth. During those three weeks, Clyde McClintlock brightened. He spoke often of the cooks and their sensations of the Cluster in the beyond. On the other hand, John Mark Ellis' mood darkened. His beard was getting long and shabby and he spent all his time either in his quarters or in his office. The captain was growing frustrated. His surreptitious scans revealed nothing. Of course, Ellis only had access to one bank of sensors, not enough power to get clues to the distant origins of the nodes. G'Liat knew that Ellis was close to sensing the Cluster in the beyond without the aid of ship's equipment. With his natural sensitivity, Ellis ought to be able to lead

Sanson right to the Cluster. The warrior tried to get the captain to see, but was frustrated in his efforts. Ellis insisted that using the ship's technology was the answer. In the end, G'Liat decided Ellis would have to come around on his own.

The warrior put his worries aside for the time being and concentrated on the task at hand. He overlaid holographic maps of the deep space nodes from previous missions of the *Sanson*. The warrior's body seemed to list sideways. Gracefully as possible, he worked the human's clumsy interface controls and pulled more mapping data off the intergalactic network. Overlaying all the maps he began to sense a pattern.

He set the controls to display the maps in time sequence. Watching the animated maps, G'Liat noted that the deep space nodes had a limited lifetime. They would appear, travel through the beyond, then evaporate. Whatever caused the nodes was not only distant, it was moving.

The warrior rubbed his chest. Although he knew that a space vessel could not get caught in one of these nodes, he began to wonder if a specially designed ship like a mapping vessel could navigate one. He also wondered if any deep space nodes as strong as those within the galaxy had ever been charted and if so, how long did they last? Much as Ellis wanted to scan the nodes for himself, G'Liat suspected the answer could be found some other way.

G'Liat stood, deciding it was time to ask Kirsten Smart a few questions.

* * *

Suki Firebrandt Ellis and Manuel Raton stepped off a shuttle and walked across the gangway into the human pressure dome on Saturn's moon, Titan. According to her travel documents, Fire had come for the weekend to do some research in the vast Titan library. Manuel and Fire obtained lodging for the next couple of nights. Alone in their room, Fire and Manuel reviewed the dance steps and motions they believed would be necessary to get the information they wanted from the Titans' central computer. "Okay," said Fire. "Now, it's time for you to find where the Gaen Navy has its space suits hidden, and I will find out where the Titans have sequestered their central computer."

* * *

G'Liat stepped into Kirsten Smart's office aboard the *Sanson*. As he passed through the command deck, the warrior noted that Ellis was absent. Fleetingly, the warrior wondered where the captain was brooding. "How are you coming with your task?" asked Smart. She was a being that believed in coming quickly to the point of any conversation. G'Liat found that refreshing among humans.

"Quite well," said G'Liat, carefully modulating his voice to sound as human as possible. "I have charted all the deep space nodal points we've encountered to-date." The warrior sat down across from Smart's desk. He did not sit because it was more comfortable; rather he sensed it put the humans around him at ease. "I have a question or two."

"What Rd'dyggian wouldn't?" Smart smiled. "I have a question or two for you, as well. But, let's hear yours first."

"What do you know about theories regarding the movement of the deep space nodes?" G'Liat inclined his head, even though it hurt his stomach.

"Ask a dozen astronomers and you'll get a dozen answers," shrugged Smart. "My favorite theory is that they're caused by large planets that have broken away from solar systems."

"It's your favorite because you're a romantic. You imagine yourself being stranded with someone on one of those worlds." While the warrior judged Smart to be sentimental, it did not change his opinion of her. She was a strong willed in a way that seemed almost Rd'dyggian.

She shook her head. "At times, I think you're a mind reader, G'Liat."

"I am," said G'Liat without changing expression. "That's part of my particular specialty in communication. We've strayed from the point. The abandoned planets are not the most prevalent theory, are they?"

"Prevalence is relative," sighed Smart. "Still, I suppose what you're getting at is the theory that the nodes are caused by objects outside the galaxy." She shook her head. "The problem with that is that other galaxies are too far away to affect us very significantly."

"True," said G'Liat. "Still, there's more outside the galaxy than other galaxies. What about the globular clusters?"

Smart sat back, putting her hands behind her head. "The galactic halo theory. It's as good a bet as the abandoned planets and almost as impossible to prove. Don't tell me you have clusters on the brain, too."

The warrior leaned forward. "Who else has clusters on the mind?"

"Your friend, Ellis." Smart gritted her teeth, shaking her head. "The man is incorrigible. He's obsessed because that stupid clump of balls killed his father. Why can't he just get over it?"

"Death of a relative is a hard thing for humans to get over, especially when it's a close relative." G'Liat sat back and studied Smart. "Do you have a personal stake in his well being?"

The warrior caught a fleeting glimpse of some expression flashing across her face before she regained her composure. "Damn right I do," she said. "I have my career to worry about. He's falling apart and pretty much letting Yermakov run my ship."

"I see," mused G'Liat.

"Would you mind talking to him? I understand that the two of you are close. He's a Navy man. I had hoped he would bring a little discipline to this ship."

"You were the one who told him to back off," chided the warrior. "You've indicated you want a tight ship, but when he's tried to enforce discipline, you have told him to stop." G'Liat's purple mustache wiggled. "It's the contradiction that's driving him into a shell of sorts."

"I didn't want him to stop," said Smart standing. She put out her hands. "It's just that he was going about it the wrong way. If he kept going, he was going to alienate this crew so badly that they would never follow his orders." Smart let her arms drop to her sides. "I wanted him to get below decks and get to know the crew, but he's distanced himself so far I'm afraid there's no return."

"I'll talk to him," said G'Liat, gently. "I think I know what can be done to bring him around."

"I hope so. The last thing I want to do is break the spirit of a good man." She flopped down in the chair then looked up. "I think you said that you had another question."

"I was wondering if you've heard of any deep space nodes that are as strong as the ones we use to jump between star systems."

"Two or three," mused Smart. "There's one active now, as a matter of fact. Check the net for the Intergalactic Astronomical Union bulletins. Quincy can give you the detailed references." She folded her hands on the desk. "Who knows, we might even get you published in the bulletin!"

G'Liat rubbed his chest, in thought. "I'm not sure that my plots show anything remarkable to date."

"Probably not." Smart sat back. "However, we are going to pass by the granddaddy of deep space nodes in a couple of weeks. It just appeared a few days ago. It's not too far from where one vanished about a month back. Showing a correlation between the two would be publishable in more than the bulletin."

"I'll keep that in mind," said G'Liat as he stood to leave.

"Please remember to speak with Ellis," said Smart with a wrinkled brow.

* * *

John Mark Ellis sat in his office, next to Kirsten Smart's surrounded by a cloud of smoke. He realized that despite the corporate officer's ban on smoking anywhere outside his quarters, she rarely came into his office. Likewise, the ship's rooms were airtight. Only Ellis, and whomever else cared to venture into his domain, had to smell his pipe.

The captain still had an ample supply of the navy flake tobacco Coffin had given him. Amazingly, the tobacco had not been confiscated in Tokyo. The strong, slightly bitter flavor seemed to suit his mood. Somehow, he had expected to find the Cluster within a week of getting back into space. The fact that the ship had not yet encountered the Cluster disturbed him. Watching the news, no ships had encountered the Cluster since the Zahari about a month before. The captain puffed hard on his pipe, feeling like he should be relieved that the Cluster was gone. Instead, he was somehow disappointed, as though an old friend had gone away.

For a while, pouring over scans of the deep-space nodes had kept the captain busy. It seemed the more the captain looked at his scans the more they revealed the obvious. The nodes originated from large objects, but there was no way to know just which objects. Certainly, there seemed no way those objects could be charted.

Ellis barely looked up from his terminal when G'Liat entered the room. He just waved toward the seat in front of his desk and continued smoking and reading. The warrior sat silent, waiting. After a few minutes of furious puffing, the pipe bowl began to gurgle. Ellis removed the pipe from his mouth using the stem and gazed at G'Liat through the haze. "Where did it go? Do you know where it's gone?"

G'Liat's mustache wriggled rhythmically. Ellis thought the movement looked frighteningly predatory. "I have my suspicions. If I'm right, the Cluster will be back. If you'd listen to the songs, you'd know that."

"I would? Where will it come from?" Ellis' voice was gravely. "Why won't you help me find it?"

"Smart knows about your scans," said G'Liat. "She wants to know what you suspect. That's why she now has me scanning with more of the ship's resources."

"How the hell did she figure that out?" asked Ellis.

"The very fact that you don't know the answer to that, is why I can't help you. Not yet, at any rate." The nine-foot tall Rd'dyggian warrior stood and moved next to Ellis. He reached down and awkwardly opened a drawer with his massive six-fingered hand. "Why am I not surprised to find a bottle of whiskey?"

"I don't know," said Ellis with a blank expression. "It came aboard in my duffel bag. I haven't touched a drop since. I prefer Scotch to Tennessee whiskey."

"How well do you know your own history?" asked G'Liat reaching in to retrieve the bottle. "What do you know of Ulysses S. Grant?"

"He liked whiskey and cigars," said Ellis, shrugging. "So do I.

What's your point?"

G'Liat stared at the bottle and nodded. He removed the cap and handed the bottle to the captain. "Take a drink," ordered the warrior.

Ellis sat back, stunned. "I need my mind clear if we're going to meet the Cluster. You just said we're likely to."

"You need to relax." G'Liat inclined his head. "Your mind is not clear at all. It's clouded with obsession. That's why you hear, but don't listen, to the song. Do you know what you're going to do when you see the Cluster? Are you just going to put your mind in there again and see what happens? Why do you think I'm so reluctant to help you rush to the Cluster?"

"So, you do think the nodes are connected to the Cluster." As the warrior stood silent, Ellis accepted the bottle and took a long drink. Putting the bottle on the desk, he wiped his mouth with his sleeve. "I really haven't thought beyond finding the Cluster."

"Exactly." The warrior put an edge in his voice. "You're letting this ship go to hell. It would already be there if not for the competence of the crew. If we are to have any hope of contacting the Cluster, you must act like the captain you are. Don't think about what will happen when we meet the Cluster. Just be prepared to act and act deliberately. That is what being a warrior is all about."

"After great pain, a formal feeling comes," quoted Ellis, slumping back in the chair. "The Nerves sit ceremonious, like Tombs."

"What is your great pain?" asked G'Liat. His Rd'dyggian accent returned, along with genuine curiosity.

Sitting slumped, the captain took another swig of whisky. "When my father died, all I wanted was revenge against the thing that took his life." Ellis sighed. "Then I touched it and realized that it was an intelligence too. The Cluster was the same as Richard or you." The captain's chin dropped to his chest. "But I feel like my quest has caused me to betray my father's memory. I feel like I should be out to destroy this thing."

"Is that what he would have wanted?" G'Liat's accent was stronger than Ellis had ever heard it.

"I don't know. How can I know? He can't tell me." Ellis took a long swig on the whiskey bottle. He then put it on the desk and retrieved his pipe and tobacco. Unceremoniously, he dumped the burned ash onto the bare metal deck. "Ashes to ashes, dust to dust."

The warrior leaned forward. "To communicate with the Cluster, you must be yourself. To do that, you must relax and lead the people on this ship. If you follow my advice I will have really helped you."

"Lead the crew with half a bottle of whiskey in me?" asked Ellis with a weak grin.

"Get a good night sleep, first," advised the warrior.

"I'll do that, if you promise to tell me all you know." Ellis began rubbing out a flake of tobacco.

"I've told all I know." G'Liat resumed speaking in a human accent.

"Then tell me all you suspect, then." The captain tamped tobacco into the pipe.

"All I suspect is summarized in two places. First, look up what's known about globular cluster orbits, and then try to understand the theories of cluster gravitational interaction with the stars of our galaxy. The rest is in your dreams and the beyond."

"Are you suggesting that the Cluster came from a globular cluster?" Ellis' forehead creased. "Or, is that part of my deluded imagination."

"It is possible that you had greater insight than you realized when you gave the alien its name. Access your dreams and imagination. There's power there." G'Liat's face was expressionless. "Once you've done that, look at the results of human archeology on Titan. If you do that, you can draw your own conclusions." With that, G'Liat stood and left.

Ellis rubbed his beard and felt the skin of his face twitch as though wanting to see the light of day.

* * *

With no small effort, Kirsten Smart was able to download what declassified information existed in the Confederation Navy database regarding John Mark Ellis. For the most part, that information consisted of an image and a press release.

The image showed Ellis, as he was when he entered the Gaean Navy; all of his hair shaved off. Kirsten slapped the table. "They've shown this image on the news," she said to herself. She thought back, and remembered the image being shown in conjunction with the Erdonium crisis on Sufiro's World.

Kirsten grinned to herself, thinking that Ellis didn't look altogether unhandsome. The beard did seem to improve his features, though. Kirsten shook her head and rubbed her eyes. "Why am I thinking like this?" she asked herself.

As she heard her voice echo in the lonely room, she knew the answer. Obsessed as he was about the Cluster, Ellis was hardly a better confidant than any of the rest of the crew. If only Ellis would show some sign of lightening up, she might be compelled to open up to him.

Kirsten let her attention be drawn to the press release. It was from shortly before Ellis had received his promotion to Commander. It told of the first ship destroyed by a new alien species. For lack of a better name, the release credits Lt. John Mark Ellis with naming the alien, the Cluster.

* * *

On Titan, Manuel Raton and Suki Ellis arrived at their room shortly after local midnight. The two embraced, then sat down at a small table near a window that looked out on a darkened, cloud-enshrouded landscape. "Well?" asked Fire.

"I found the airlock from the dome to the surface. There's only one guard. He was pretty bored. He said that there were environment suit lockers and a hover transport outside," reported Manuel.

Fire nodded and bit her lower lip. She retrieved a sheet of paper from her pocket. "I think this is a map from this dome to the main Titan dome. Their central computer should be housed there."

"You think?" Manuel sat back and twirled his mustache. "That's pretty flimsy Fire-cita."

"You try reading through the records," said Fire sharply. "It's more like mythology than record-keeping."

"I'm sorry." Manuel folded his hands and twiddled his thumbs. After a bit he looked back into Fire's eyes. "You know, if we get caught, we could go to jail for a long time."

"Probably," said Fire. "The question is whether it's the Titans that will find us first, or the humans, after we steal environment suits and a hover." Fire moved to sit on Raton's lap. She unbuttoned his shirt and took his earlobe in her mouth. "We may not see each other for a very long time after tomorrow."

Raton stroked Fire's silver-black hair, his breath growing heavy. "I know, Fire-cita. Let's make the most of this night."

"We might not get much sleep," chided Fire, holding Manuel as much for security as out of passion.

"Who the hell cares?" Manuel pressed his mouth to Fire's. The two fell to the floor together.

* * *

That night, aboard the *Sanson*, Ellis slept off the effects of the alcohol. He awoke the next morning feeling surprisingly refreshed. Ordering coffee and a roll from the kitchen, he showered and dressed unhurriedly. With a deliberate force of will, he shaved his beard. Looking at the result in the mirror, he was vaguely disappointed. He remembered his jaw looking stronger than what he saw. "Is this who I am?" he asked himself. Shrugging it off as best he could, he stepped back out to the living quarters and began calling up the data files on globular clusters.

The information he found was not particularly surprising. As an officer graduated from the Academy, he had long known that the globulars made long elliptical orbits around the galaxy. Many times those orbits took the globulars through the plane of the galaxy itself. He rubbed his naked chin in wonder as he read that the clusters took between fifteen and thirty million years to complete their orbits.

Ellis turned his attention to the gravitational interaction of the globulars with the stars of the galaxy when Clyde McClintlock knocked on the door.

"Wow!" exclaimed the evangelist as he looked at Ellis' newly clean face. "I've never seen you that well shaved."

Ellis smiled and motioned for Clyde to take the seat opposite him. "I imagine I was pretty scruffy when I first showed up on Sufiro."

McClintlock nodded and laid the captain's breakfast out for him. The evangelist sat back to sip his own coffee. "The governor almost had me evict you from the planet," laughed McClintlock. The former colonel set his coffee down and looked at his feet as he thought of Governor Hill, the friend he betrayed. After a moment, he returned his attention to Ellis. "What are you reading up on?"

Ellis shook his head, while reaching for the sweet roll. "It's some stuff G'Liat recommended. Do you know there are theories that suggest those deep space nodes are caused by clusters?"

"Really!" Clyde McClintlock shifted to the edge of his seat.

"I mean globular clusters," corrected the captain. "It's suspected that as the globulars pass through or near the plane of the galaxy, the tidal interactions cause the nodes we've been seeing."

"What does that have to do with the Cluster?" McClintlock settled back in the chair.

Ellis read on in silence for a few minutes. "It's possible it holds part of the answer. Did you know that there's a globular in close approach now? It's passing through the plane of the galaxy even as we speak. The last time it was here was thirty million years ago."

Clyde McClintlock shook his head. "Are you trying to tell me that the Cluster is coming from some globular?" He set the coffee down and grabbed his wrist to stop his trembling hand. "Mark, if the Cluster came from that globular, then that means that Ezekiel couldn't have seen it."

"What?" Ellis peered over the display he was reading.

"The prophet Ezekiel, in the bible. He saw the Cluster only six thousand years ago," stammered Clyde.

"I'm afraid I'm not much of a Bible scholar," admitted Ellis, returning his attention to the display.

The evangelist and the captain sat in silence for a time. Ellis ate his sweet roll while reading. At last, the plate and coffee cup were empty.

Standing silently, trembling slightly, Clyde McClintlock gathered the dishes and left without further comment.

"Did you know that there's no evidence of any civilization on Titan before thirty million years ago?" Ellis continued to read. When he didn't get a response, he looked up and saw that the evangelist had gone. Like Clyde McClintlock, however, Ellis found himself trembling. He stepped to the window over his bunk and looked out at the stars.

At last he began to understand G'Liat's fears and see them as more than paranoia. There was evidence to suggest that the Titans – the benevolent leaders of the Confederation, virtually the founders of civilization itself – had first appeared the last time the Cluster visited the galaxy. Deep and disturbing questions filled the captain's mind. Taking a deep breath, Ellis wasn't sure he wanted to know the answers.

* * *

Instead of returning to the kitchen, Clyde McClintlock went back to his quarters. Since he had not been able to return home on Earth, he brought few personal effects aboard the *Sanson*. McClintlock fell listlessly into his bunk. He felt betrayed by the other man who had heard the words of the Cluster. How could Ellis, of all people, believe the Cluster was anything but God?

Clyde McClintlock closed his eyes tight. He tried, momentarily, to feel his way through the trail of logic that led him to believe the Cluster was God. The more he tried, the guiltier he felt of betraying his faith and those back on Earth who were relying on him to bring teachings from the Cluster. He also thought of the fact that it was Ellis who had defeated him on Sufiro. Revenge could be sweet. Deep down, Clyde knew what had to be done to blasphemers. He remembered from the teachings of his youth. If he died trying to kill the infidel, he would be invited into the Cluster realm.

Burying his head in the hard pillow, McClintlock cursed at the fact that he was not aboard a military ship. There he would have weapons. He felt the pillow grow damp as tears flowed. However, his spirits lightened slightly when he realized that he had an entire kitchen to his disposal. With his military background, he could make any weapon he chose. The only question was when to use it.

Sitting up in bed, a low moan escaped his throat. In the last few weeks, Ellis had become a friend. How could he think of killing a friend for an ideal? The idea made him shiver. He shook his head, trying to clear it. "Let Ellis do what he wants," mumbled McClintlock. "I'll be there to talk to the Cluster with the reverence it deserves. Let the captain beware if he tries to betray us."

* * *

A lone male guard stood watch over the airlock that led to the surface of Titan. Suki Ellis unbuttoned her blouse revealing ample cleavage. She wore tight shorts that accentuated her hips. Manuel Raton had worn tight pants just in case the guard had proven to be female. Fire took a deep breath then strutted out to the guard. She leaned on the door. "Must be lonely here?" she commented.

The guard turned. "Yes ma'am, it is." He licked his lips.

"Not many women on Titan duty?" she asked.

"Plenty of women," said the guard. "Just not that many interested in me." The guard looked down, almost sad. Manuel eased up and hit the guard on the back of the head. The guard crumpled to the floor.

Fire quickly attached her de-scrambler to the first door of the airlock. Within moments, the door slid aside. "It won't be long before they figure out we're here," she said. They pulled the guard inside.

After a brief search, they located the environment suit lockers. They stripped out of their tight-fitting clothes and pulled on the environment suits. Fire applied her descrambler to the outer door. Shortly, Manuel Raton and Suki Ellis found themselves on the surface of Titan. Fire was surprised that no alarms had sounded when she used the descrambler. She figured that no one must have been monitoring the doors remotely; assuming an attack would be rare. Their mistake, she thought and shrugged.

Fire and Manuel found the hover transport. It required no password to start. Apparently it was ready to go quickly in case of a crisis. The two set off across the ruddy surface of the moon, following Fire's map. She looked up in time to catch a brief break in the clouds. Fire caught her breath as she saw Saturn shining down from above.

* * *

Captain John Mark Ellis took several deep breaths as he rode the elevator to the *Sanson's* command deck. He was determined to regain his hold on both his life and his command. Putting his hands behind his back, he whistled the Battle Hymn of the Republic to help strengthen his resolve and to remind himself that he was, indeed, the captain. His heart skipped a beat when he felt the elevator stop.

The captain strode onto the deck as the doors opened. The crewmembers were all at their stations. Natalie Papadraxis stared at holographic flowers growing from her brightly colored console. Laura Peters was alert and working at her simply functional touch-pad. Simon Yermakov blew his nose into a handkerchief, then adjusted one of the brass control knobs on his holo-interface.

"Simon," called Ellis with confidence, rather than strength. "I was just down at the engineering deck. The crew there seems to be getting a little lax."

"What do you want me to do about it, Skipper?" asked Yermakov. As he turned to face Ellis, his jaw dropped open. He shut it quickly. "What happened to your beard?"

Ellis strode forward. Laura Peters nodded her approval at the captain's new look. Natalie Papadraxis seemed somewhat disappointed. "As to the latter question," stated Ellis, "it's none of your business. As to the former, your last report showed some instability in EQ engine number four. I want you to confirm that it's fixed properly. I don't want it failing while we're in jump." The captain stepped close to the mate, putting his hand on Yermakov's shoulder. "Tell Mr. Mahuk and the techs that they're doing a good job while you're down there." He patted Yermakov's shoulder and nodded.

Yermakov smiled sheepishly. He started to say something but decided against it. Instead, he stepped to the elevator and went below.

"Natalie, how well do your communications skills work during jump?" Ellis sat down, but kept his back straight.

"I sense a lot of things during jump," she said. "I often sense other telepaths and other ships that are with us in the beyond. Usually they're only there for a short time." She looked down at the floor and toyed with the end of her braid.

Ellis nodded. "Have you ever sensed Cluster ships out there?"

She thought about it. "Sometimes I feel a vast coldness. I've never been near a Cluster ship in normal space. Is that what it feels like?"

Ellis wasn't sure how to answer that question. He supposed the Cluster could be perceived as cold. However, he had always sensed warmth from it. Instead of answering, he asked another question. "Have you felt that coldness recently?"

"Not during this voyage," she said airily.

"Let me know if you do, please," he said. Ellis stood and patted Laura Peters on the shoulder. "Keep up the good work," he said as he left the command deck.

* * *

Fire and Manuel pulled up to the Titan dome. There was no airlock; not even a locked door. They simply pushed a button next to a bear-sized door and the door slid aside. The two looked at each other and nodded. They walked through the corridors, seeing few of the Teddy Bear-like creatures. When they did see a Titan, they ducked into a side corridor and waited for it to pass. It was believed that most of the Titans lived in caves, well away from the domes.

After a looking in a few rooms, they finally located the central computer room. The room was empty. There were no consoles or controls. There was only a simple star pattern on the floor. Fire and Manuel stepped inside and closed the door. They performed the dance they hoped would call the records of Cluster attacks on Titan ships.

A set of words written in the Titan language began to scroll through the middle of the room. Fire and Manuel held hands and turned in a circle, performing the translation algorithm to Terro-generic. Manuel whistled when he read the reports. Every Titan ship that had spotted the Cluster had avoided contact. False reports of destruction were filed.

"You were right," whispered Manuel. "They did lie."

"Let's find out what they know about the Cluster," said Fire. They danced another dance, awkward in their environment suits. They simply saw a report on globular clusters. "I think we need a little more shoulder shimmy," said Fire. Manuel giggled self-consciously, but stopped when he saw Fire's earnest look. They tried the dance again.

This time they were greeted with an animated presentation. They were looking at the heart of a globular cluster. Gasses, dust and plasma coalesced. From the center emerged first one, then a second Cluster. A third appeared from the primordial soup.

"It says here," said Fire, "that the Cluster is presumed to be an ancient lifeform. It formed from the extreme heat and pressure of the center of the globular cluster."

"When did it form?" asked Manuel, his eyebrows knitted.

Fire nodded. "According to this, it's believed that it might be the most ancient lifeform of all. It started as something like an amoeba – very primitive life. However, it has lived so long that it has acquired knowledge and self-awareness."

"How could that be?" Manuel folded his arms.

Fire's shrug was barely perceptible in the environment suit. "Plasma can fire off electrical impulses, not unlike an organic brain. If it lived long enough, if it was ordered properly in a matrix of sorts, I suppose plasma could become intelligent like a brain."

"Where do the Titans fit in?" Manuel started watching the door nervously.

Fire's arms swayed back and forth over her head. A new hologram formed showing a Titan next to a Cluster. Words began to scroll through the air. Once again, Fire and Manuel performed the translation algorithm and then read together. Fire's mouth dropped open. "The Titans and the Cluster are symbionts!" she exclaimed.

They turned at the whoosh of a door opening. A Titan filled the immense doorway, barring teeth and brandishing claws. "That is quite enough," growled the Titan. "I believe Teklar would like to have a word with you."

Coming to Terms

As Captain Ellis stepped into his office, the *Sanson* lurched. The captain swayed gently into the lurch and moved toward his desk and sat down. For the first time in the past several weeks he actually felt in control of his ship. Putting his palms on the desk, he closed his eyes and took a deep breath. He felt in-tune with all that was around him. While in the Navy he always sensed the watchful eye of the admiralty. Even though Kirsten Smart had an office next door, she was most interested in getting her work done. If anything, the captain was bothered by a sense that he had not done his job to the best of his ability. But that worry was easy to brush aside.

Silently, he cursed G'Liat for not bringing the information about globular clusters to his attention sooner. While the captain knew he could only blame his depression on himself, he felt the warrior could have saved him a lot of grief. Ellis sighed, wondering what G'Liat's reasons were.

A knock sounded at the door. "Come in," called Ellis.

Kirsten Smart blew into the office. She opened her mouth and began to speak but cut herself short. She looked closely at the captain's face, then shook her head. "What a shame," she said. Laughing lightly, she fell heavily into the chair across from Ellis.

Ellis' forehead creased. "What's a shame?"

"You actually cut your beard off." Smart snorted. "What have you been smoking in here, anyway? I thought most pipe smokers liked that cherry stuff. This room smells like a dirty ashtray."

"I thought you wanted the beard gone," said Ellis, shrugging. "As to the smoking, I can always switch back to cigars."

Another knock sounded at the door. Ellis acknowledged. Simon Yermakov entered the room. "I talked to the boys in engineering, Skipper. I think you'll find things in better shape down there." The first mate started to turn and slouch out of the room.

"Simon," called Ellis. Yermakov half turned. "Thanks." Then he added, "Will you be on deck for a little while?"

"Nowhere to go," said Yermakov with a sniff.

"When Ms. Smart leaves, I'd like to have a word with you." Ellis' tone was conversational. Yermakov nodded and left the room.

Kirsten Smart was watching the captain with her head inclined, a bemused expression forming on her face. "Something's come over you," she said. "You seem much more like what I thought I'd get when Meiji told me she'd hired a Navy man to command the ship."

Ellis took a deep breath and sat back. "I just had to learn how to relax."

"It suits you." Smart smiled warmly.

The captain nodded. "What can I do for you, Ms. Smart?"

"I just wanted to talk to you about McIntosh," she said. "Or, should I say, McClintlock?" Her tone darkened.

Ellis fought to keep surprise out of his expression. "McClintlock? What do you mean?"

"Don't play dumb," chided Smart. "Actually, I don't really care that our cook is Clyde McClintlock in disguise. While he can't cook worth a damn, he keeps the kitchen well organized. Nor do I care what his motives are, though he seems as fascinated by that damned Cluster as you and G'Liat. No problem, as long as none of you interferes with my job."

"You can rest assured that even though an encounter with the Cluster resulted in my resignation from the Navy, it will not interfere with this command."

"Your interest goes deeper than career." Smart bit her lower lip. "It's tied to family."

"How do you know?" Ellis' eyebrows came together. "I've never told you about it. We've hardly spoken, except professionally."

"Like your beard, that's also a bit of a shame." Smart leaned forward. "Sometimes alien warriors aren't the best people to come to when you're troubled."

"Be that as it may," said Ellis, folding his arms. "It doesn't answer my question."

"It's a small ship." Smart shrugged.

"G'Liat told you." The captain let a smug grin form.

Smart shrugged again and pursed her lips, playfully defiant.

"Anyway, I would hope we're actually helping with your job, not interfering." Ellis folded his hands.

"No matter what it is that you, G'Liat, and McClintlock are doing on my ship, the three of you are doing an admirable job," said Smart, nodding. "Even as tense as you've been, you've kept this mission going on schedule. That's what I need. Since it looks like you've settled in a little more, I suspect that you'll do an even better job." Smart sighed. "The problem with McClintlock is that he's always late with my breakfast. He says it's because he takes yours to you first. This morning, he didn't show up at all."

Ellis shook his head. "If anything, he left my quarters earlier than normal this morning."

"I really don't have a problem if he goes to your cabin before he brings my breakfast. I'm a late riser, but could you ask him to make his rounds promptly in the morning?"

"I'll try my best," said Ellis.

Smart smiled charmingly and stood. "Just one more thing. I understand that you cleaned McClintlock's clock on Sufiro. Why are you two such buddies now?"

Ellis shrugged and put on an innocent expression. "We were honorable enemies. I suppose we respect each other."

Kirsten Smart nodded skeptically. As she walked out the door, the captain noticed that her wide hips seemed to sway a little more than usual. Ellis shook his head, putting it off to not being observant enough during the last few weeks.

Shortly after Smart left, Simon Yermakov stepped back into the room. "You wanted to see me, Skipper?"

Ellis motioned for the mate to take a chair across from him. "Have a seat, Simon." When Yermakov was seated, Ellis opened the drawer of his desk and retrieved the whiskey bottle and two glasses. "Care for a drink?"

"I better not," said Yermakov with a sniffle.

"I've read that alcohol interferes with Proxom," said Ellis, pouring himself a drink.

"You know about the Proxom?" asked Yermakov, a little defiantly.

Ellis took a sip of whiskey. "I've been a little bothered by it, I have to admit. Why do you need it?"

"Why do you need to smoke a pipe?" Yermakov sat forward. "Doesn't the nicotine stimulate the brain much the same as Proxom? Could you command this ship if you didn't have that boost?"

The captain set the whisky down, positioning it carefully. "I don't know. The reason I asked you here is not to chastise you for taking Proxom. My reason is to encourage you to relax. You're awfully nervous and awfully defensive."

"Shouldn't I be defensive?" exclaimed the mate. "I've been on mapping ships for fifteen years. I know them inside and out. This command should have been mine. Instead, it was given to some Navy guy with a vendetta."

"What vendetta?" Ellis folded his hands.

"What happens if this ship encounters the Cluster? That's what worries me." Yermakov folded his arms across his chest. "Will the same thing happen to us that happened to the *Martha's Vineyard*?"

Ellis took a slow sip of whiskey. "I begin to understand." He set the glass down on the desk. Ellis did not want to justify his actions to Yermakov. He moved the glass around on the desktop and thought. Slowly, he realized he did not have to explain his actions. "What happened to the *Vineyard* was fate. Who knows why the Cluster attacks any ship?"

"I have a feeling you know better than anyone," grumbled the mate.

"Maybe I do. Still, my job is to captain this ship. You have my word that I will do nothing to endanger our mission." He felt a knot form in his stomach.

"What's your word worth?" asked Yermakov.

"I don't know," admitted Ellis. "Your job is to make sure I do my job."

Yermakov took a deep breath. Ellis saw a range of expression play across the mate's features. "It could be difficult," said the mate. "You're a strong-willed man."

"If you want to captain this ship some day," said Ellis with a deep frown, "you'd better be able to stand up to the likes of me."

Yermakov nodded. "I think I'm glad we had this conversation, Skipper," he said, slowly. "Anything else?"

Ellis pulled his drink close and looked into the golden liquid. "I hope not," he said.

* * *

When Clyde McClintlock finally arrived at the kitchen that afternoon, he appeared distracted. Morganna and the rest of the cooks had taken care of lunch and started dinner preparations without him. She watched and worried as McClintlock stared at the knives, as though evaluating them carefully. Although she had worked for some odd characters before, the evangelist was the worst.

"Can I help you find something?" she asked, stepping up behind him. McClintlock jumped, startled. "I'm sorry," apologized Morganna. "I didn't mean to scare you."

"I'm just a little preoccupied," said McClintlock with a nervous smile.

"Sometimes going through the beyond can do that to you after a while. It's a lot different on a mapping vessel than any other kind of ship I've ever been on," said Morganna.

"You've already told me all that. Have you finished the dinner preparations?" asked McClintlock hurriedly.

"I think the crew will like what we've got in store," she said. Morganna looked at McClintlock's eyes; they were glazed over. "Are you feeling okay?"

"You said that you don't believe the Cluster is God. If not, then what is it? Besides God, who else holds that kind of power?" McClintlock walked to his desk in a stupor. Morganna helped him into his chair. "I keep hearing people say that the Cluster is not God. First you, now the captain." McClintlock fixed Morganna with a gaze of steel.

The lead cook shifted uncomfortably under the evangelist's stare. "Maybe it is," she said nervously.

McClintlock smiled, making Morganna even more nervous. "We have work to do," he said congenially. "What can I do to help?"

Morganna almost suggested that the evangelist chop tomatoes. However, she decided that she really did not want to see him wielding a knife. "You can mix up the dough for the pie crusts," she suggested instead.

* * *

On Titan, Manuel Raton and Suki Ellis were surprised that they were placed into the same cell. A force field at the front of the cell held back Titan's cold, toxic atmosphere. In the cell was an Earth-like atmosphere. Their environment suits had been taken from them. "Too bad the only one who knows where we are is Old Man Coffin. I'm guessing he won't be mounting a jailbreak anytime soon," quipped Raton.

Fire sighed and shook her head at the comment.

Teklar, matriarch of the Titans, ambled up to the cell. She showed teeth capable of ripping huge chunks of ice and introduced herself. A second Titan appeared behind, but kept its distance. "I'm sorry to have kept you waiting all day," said Teklar.

Manuel's mouth fell open at the unexpected greeting. Fire pushed him aside. "I'm pleased to make your acquaintance," said Fire. "I'm sorry that we created a situation that has inconvenienced you."

"No time remains for pleasantries," stated Teklar bluntly. "You know our secrets with regard to the Cluster."

Fire's brow creased. "They are secrets you could not have kept hidden. Why didn't you reveal what you knew about the Cluster?"

"We were afraid," explained Teklar with a great heave of silver-gray shoulders. "We were slaves. We were afraid that the Cluster would just take us back into their fold and the galaxy would fall."

"The races of the galaxy could come together to help you," offered Fire.

Teklar fell back onto her haunches. "The other races in the galaxy might be candidate appendages; candidate slaves. The Cluster cannot be destroyed. An en masse action would simply attract attention. The

Cluster might stay forever. Surgery was required." Teklar paused, apparently reluctant to tell more.

"Surgery?" pressed Fire. "What kind of surgery have you been doing?"

"Your son, John Mark Ellis, has a certain passion for your species and a certain ability to relate to all species," began Teklar. It was time for Fire's mouth to hang open. "There was evidence that he had communicated with the Cluster and it did not take him as an appendage. We hoped he would be able to communicate with the Cluster, convey the sacredness of life and the Cluster would leave us alone."

"Does he know?" Fire's voice was a harsh whisper.

"No," said Teklar. "Though he might suspect. We've been monitoring his progress."

Manuel Raton stepped forward. "It's wrong to lie to the other beings in the galaxy. You can't let them die while you cowardly skulk away and hide from the Cluster."

"What would you have us do," growled Teklar.

"Tell the truth," growled Manuel in response.

"We would all be doomed." Teklar turned her head.

"Arrogant and selfish is what you are," said Manuel.

Fire waved him down. "Scared is what she is," she said quietly. Fire folded her arms. "What do you do if John Mark fails? What if the Cluster decides that they do want him as an appendage? How do you rescue my son who you've been using as a pawn?"

"G'Liat is with him. He is the most powerful Rd'dyggian warrior. He will keep Ellis safe." Teklar turned to face Fire again.

"But what if he fails!" called Fire. "You said the Cluster cannot be destroyed. Will my son be lost forever?" Fire's voice rose to a shout.

Manuel stepped behind her and gripped her shoulders, rubbing tension away. "She is right, you need a new plan. You, at least, need a backup plan." Manuel looked into Teklar's vast black eyes. "Even if everything fails, you need to let the rest of the galaxy know what may happen so they can prepare." Manuel's voice dropped almost to a whisper. "To do otherwise would be wrong."

Teklar was silent for a long time. "We would have to present this information slowly, carefully to avoid panic."

"However you decide. Do it," urged Fire.

"I will consider it." With that Teklar and her assistant turned and lumbered from the holding area.

* * *

John Mark Ellis returned to his quarters aboard the *Sanson* for the evening to find a flower sitting on his table. Cautiously, as though it might attack him, the captain approached the flower and saw that it included a note. Gingerly, he unfolded and read the note. It requested that he come down to the ship's garden. Rather than maintain air tanks, as many Navy ships did, *Sanson* maintained a garden to produce fresh air. The garden also produced a fresh supply of vegetables for the ship's kitchen. At first, Ellis thought about ignoring the note and going to bed. However, his curiosity got the better of him.

Stepping out of his cabin, Ellis saw G'Liat coming down the corridor. "How are things?" asked Ellis.

"You look much better," said G'Liat, congenially.

Ellis nodded. Something seemed wrong about the warrior. "You seem worried, though."

"I'm beginning to wonder if it was wise to invite McClintlock along with us." G'Liat looked around. "Were you headed out?"

"I was," said Ellis. "But I've got a minute, if you want to talk." The two stepped back into Ellis' cabin. "Haven't you been able to learn anything from McClintlock's encounter with the Cluster?"

"Not much," admitted the warrior. "The problem is that he's overlaid so much of his religious fervor over his own mental images that I can't really see what happened. Today, he seems more agitated than ever."

"He seemed fine, this morning." Ellis shrugged.

"I'll let you get on your way," said G'Liat, almost absentmindedly, after a moment's pause. "I think I'm getting old. I've almost forgotten how dangerous fanatics can be."

"I'll watch my back," said Ellis with a grin.

"That is probably good advice." With feline grace, the warrior stood and left the room silently.

Ellis sat for a moment and thought about the morning. He wondered if anything he had said would have set the evangelist on edge. The captain suddenly remembered that he had told McClintlock about the thirty million-year globular cluster orbits. Turning his attention to the flower on the table, Ellis shook his head. *Clyde McClintlock might be a loon*, thought the captain, *but he can't be so far gone as to let a thing like that worry him.* He carefully retrieved the note and flower. Eyebrows furrowed, the captain examined the note. The writing seemed feminine. Momentarily, he wondered if it could be McClintlock's despite the appearance. Doubting a trap, he put the flower in his lapel button and stepped into the corridor.

As Ellis rode down the elevator, he wondered who might have left the flower for him. He thought of Natalie Papadraxis who had looked disappointed that he had shaved off his beard. However, she did not seem like the type who would ask for some kind of clandestine meeting below decks. The same was true of Laura Peters. The captain wondered if he would ever understand women. His heart skipped a beat as the elevator stopped.

Stepping off the elevator, Ellis saw that the lights in the garden were dim. It was twilight cycle and soon would be night. Instantly on alert, the captain's eyes darted around the room. At first, the captain did not see anyone. Within a few minutes, his eyes adjusted to the semi-darkness. Looking toward a patch of ferns, he saw a short, broadly built person standing alone, wearing a flower much like the type he had. "Ms. Smart!" exclaimed the captain.

He stepped onto the soft bed of grass and walked through a row of beans over to where she stood. She looked at him with a nervous smile. "Are you terribly surprised?" Her voice was hushed and a little cautious.

"Am I surprised that you're in love with me?" asked Ellis, wide-eyed.

"I'm not in love with you," she laughed lightly. Ellis' shoulders dropped. He felt ridiculous at having made the assumption. "At least, I don't know whether or not I'm in love with you." She stepped closer to him and put strong hands on his elbows. "All I know is that I want you, at least once. You're an attractive man. Much more so, now that I see the real you."

The captain sighed. "It's the old story, I've shaved my beard and you can see what I was hiding, right?"

"Hardly," said Smart, shaking her head. "The beard was part of the real you." She took a step closer. Reflexively Ellis stepped back. "When you came aboard you were playing captain. Now that you've lowered your defenses, I see the man who gave up a career for a principal. That's attractive."

The captain swallowed hard. "So, now you want to have an affair? Would that be proper?"

"Propriety be damned," she said and moved her hands to take his. "Your palms are sweating," she observed. "Is the Navy man afraid of the corporate officer?"

"The Navy man's only been propositioned once before," he said. "That ended with him lying flat on his ass in the street."

Taking Ellis by the hand, Smart led him to a makeshift bench that had been set up. Ellis looked nervously at the elevator. "Don't worry," she said. "I changed the access codes so that only you and I can be here tonight." The two sat down and Smart put her hand on the captain's leg. She felt him tense. She moved her hands to his shoulders and began rubbing out tension. "The fact of the matter is, as far as I'm concerned we live in a sick society. People are afraid of intimacy in any form. I'm sure you've seen it."

"Why shouldn't people be afraid of intimacy?" asked Ellis defensively. "After all, Earth is overcrowded. Babies mean that many more mouths to feed. I won't even get into all the acquired immune disorders."

"There are risks," said Smart, gently. "However, I want you to relax and enjoy this night. You are the first man I've known strong enough to stand up to me in a long time. I'm only a little disappointed to know that you bent to my request to shave." She felt his shoulders relax some.

Ellis took several deep breaths. Though he did not find Kirsten Smart especially attractive, he began to sense that she was a kindred spirit; a person he could trust. Much as he had found Adkins on the *Firebrandt* attractive, he never could bring himself to approach her any way other than professionally. Smart offered him release that only an exotic dancer on Earth had offered before. In a way, the very offer made Smart seem much more desirable.

The captain found himself kissing Smart's full lips and looking into deep brown eyes. He did not resist as she unbuttoned his trousers and pulled them down to his ankles. Ellis finished removing his trousers. Then he reached over and helped the corporate officer remove her blouse. Ellis turned his attention to Smart's trousers.

Kirsten Smart lay back in the soft grass. Ellis knelt beside her and nervously took her right nipple in his mouth. He suckled her for a few minutes, then reached down to lightly touch the hair between her legs. Retracting his hand a little too quickly, he took a deep breath and gently explored her entire body with both of his hands. In response, she moved her hands along his body.

A low moan escaped Smart's lips as she steered Ellis' hips around. Gently, she guided him inside her and he lay for a moment, savoring the feeling. The two began a coordinated symphony of motion that Ellis did not think was possible. Soon, Smart shuddered, biting her lower lip. After a moment, she sighed lightly, her body exhausted. "I haven't felt this good in a long time," she whispered.

The two lay quietly on the grass. Ellis, for the first time since Sufiro, slept without dreaming of the Cluster.

* * *

Unable to rest, G'Liat walked the corridors of the ship. He allowed his natural loping gait to take over from time to time. It felt good to let muscles relax. At intervals, he let his massive hands strike out at the air. The warrior took a deep breath when he found himself in front of one of the ship's cartography labs. Straightening and resuming his leonine presence, he stepped into the room.

It barely fazed him to find himself standing in apparently empty vacuum – the stars of the entire galaxy surrounding him like a vast whirlpool. Across the room, Quincy Marcovitz looked up from notes he was writing.

"Working late?" asked G'Liat in deliberately conversational tones.

"Sleepless night," said Quincy. "You should have sounded the door buzzer. I would have restored the view so you could see the floor."

"No problem," said G'Liat. "I'm used to the chart tanks." With that, the warrior crossed the room to Quincy.

"I was bugged by something I saw earlier today." Quincy hit a button on his remote pad. Numerous blue spheres dotted themselves around the galaxy. "These are the charted positions of the strong deep space node we're scheduled to intersect tomorrow." Pressing another button showed a number of yellow spheres. "These are the positions of Cluster appearances. Note how closely correlated they are."

G'Liat imitated a nod. "Closer than I would expect from coincidence. I'm afraid your result doesn't surprise me."

"What's it mean?" asked Quincy.

"It means the search is nearly over."

* * *

Ellis awoke about six in the morning, ship's time. Kirsten Smart was snoring on the ground next to him. He stretched and looked at her lovingly. He could not help but wonder about her emotions. She said she did not, in fact, love him. However, she gave herself to him as no woman had before.

Sitting in the grass, the captain contemplated her words. She said that people were afraid of intimacy. He knew he had been so afraid of getting close to others that he never asked a woman to go to dinner with him. Most people around the Earth avoided real sex. The risk of infection and the fear of real closeness on an over-crowded Earth were simply too great. Men simply went to clinics and deposited sperm while women who wanted babies went to have it implanted. So, the population continued to increase.

Ellis, with his roots in the sands of Nantucket and the pioneer world of Sufiro, was glad to have shared a special moment with a real human being. Whether love existed or not, Ellis knew that their relationship would never again be purely professional.

Smart opened one eyelid and noticed Ellis was awake. She sat up and put her hand on the captain's shoulder. "Awake already?"

"We have to get to work soon," muttered Ellis. "The cooks will want to get down here in a couple of hours to get their veggies for the day." He reached over and kissed her. She returned the kiss with relish. "Perhaps we can get together again soon," he said.

She winked. "That's an interesting way to put it. Don't you think the crew will get suspicious if the captain and the boss are sleeping together routinely?"

"Do you care?" asked Ellis.

"Images don't impress me." She shook her head. "Your cabin or mine?" The two embraced again, then, business-like, they put on their clothes and went their separate ways.

* * *

Mark Ellis hummed all through his shower. The captain stepped out and dressed in a well-pressed white shirt and brown woolen trousers. When the knock came at the door, he expected McClintlock with breakfast. He was surprised when G'Liat stepped in, instead.

"You're up early," commented Ellis. In point of fact, Ellis had no idea what time the warrior normally arose. "Where's Clyde?"

"I don't know," said the Rd'dyggian, his accent thick. "He was not in his quarters last night." He turned to face the captain. "Neither were you."

"Must I be where you can find me at all times?" Ellis looked smug as he punched the command for coffee into his wall panel.

"We are approaching the time of the trial," said G'Liat sternly. "Our next jump is going to carry this ship near the strongest of the deep space nodes."

Ellis moved to the table with his coffee and sat down. "You suspect that node is the one that leads to the Cluster's home?"

"Most likely," said G'Liat. "I'm not sure we're ready. I let you waste a lot of time on that sensory equipment."

"You could have told me it was a waste of time," chided Ellis. He sipped his coffee.

"Maybe it wasn't a waste. It did put Smart on the trail of the nodes." Before Ellis could react, G'Liat asked, "Why do you associate the color green with the Cluster?"

Ellis, taken aback, sat his mug on the table. "The eyes of the woman in the Cluster vision. They were green."

"What else have you sensed in the beyond?" G'Liat folded his hands. "I believe you mentioned teddy bears at one point."

Ellis' brow creased. "I did."

"Stuffed toys that happen to look a lot like the Titans," commented the warrior. "What about your research?"

"I think you knew what I'd find," said Ellis dryly.

"Indeed," said G'Liat, sitting back. "Do you sense the convergence of ideas?"

"I do." Ellis nodded. "But what do I do with those ideas? You haven't given Clyde or me much training."

"You probably need training least of all. This morning, I see a man ready to face destiny." G'Liat stood and began to pace. Ellis had known enough Rd'dyggians to know that showing nervousness was an extremely dangerous sign. "It's Clyde I've wanted to learn from and prepare. I am afraid of what will happen when he confronts the reality of the Cluster."

"I don't like the sound of that." Ellis took another sip of coffee. "You are afraid?"

"I want to see what's in his mind before we see the Cluster. I need your help, he's been reluctant to let me try."

A knock sounded at the door. It was Clyde McClintlock with a plate of steaming pancakes for Ellis. "Ah, G'Liat, if I'd known you were going to be here, I would have brought something for you." He turned his attention to Ellis. "Captain, my assistant Morganna tells me someone was rolling around down in the vegetable garden last night."

Ellis felt his cheeks warm. "Well, I'm sure no permanent damage was done," he muttered into his coffee. After a moment, he looked up. "Clyde, G'Liat needs your help."

"He wants to look into my mind," said McClintlock bitterly. He dropped the tray of pancakes to the table. "The vision is mine and mine alone. You should never have let him desecrate your mind, either."

"It's the only way he can help us understand," pleaded Ellis.

"You keep speaking of understanding, Mark." McClintlock shook his head. "All we need to understand is in the book of Ezekiel. Yesterday you spoke of the Cluster returning. I agree with that. What I disagree with is the timing. I believe it was here six thousand years ago, not thirty million years. Hell, that was before man even walked the Earth."

Ellis folded his arms and looked at G'Liat. "There's nothing I can do," he said shaking his head. "If he doesn't want to allow you in, I'll support it."

McClintlock smiled. "You mean that, Mark?"

"You don't have to help us, Clyde," said Ellis somberly. "You said it succinctly. Our beliefs are different. I don't agree with yours. I won't force you to agree with mine."

"Thanks, Mark," said McClintlock with his hand over his chest. "Now, if you'll excuse me, I have to go prepare lunch." McClintlock turned and left the room.

"You might be endangering us all," said G'Liat, coldly. "I need him so I can find out what you two have in common. Not only that, he's potentially dangerous. If I go into his mind, I could diffuse that danger."

Ellis shook his head. "I could have told you what we have in common all along," said the captain, pouring syrup over his pancakes. "We are both men of deep feeling. As to diffusing the situation, we didn't have to bring him along." Ellis cut the pancakes with his fork and took a bite.

"Perhaps you're right," said G'Liat, folding his arms.

"Of course I'm right," said Ellis, smugly. He took another two bites from his stack of pancakes. "You've been so busy playing warrior teacher that you haven't been thinking."

"And you have?" asked G'Liat, sounding incensed. "You've been more obsessed than any of us. If it weren't for me, you'd still be wallowing in self pity back on Earth."

"You're probably right." Finishing his pancakes, Ellis wiped his mouth. "So, you plan to collect data on this node, right?"

"Ms. Smart ordered it," said the warrior, seeming less glum.

"Would you let me see that data right after the jump?" asked Ellis hopefully.

"You will get to see it at the same time as Ms. Smart," said G'Liat bowing slightly. "I just hope that data proves more useful than Clyde McClintlock."

The Chase

John Mark Ellis walked the decks of his ship with hands clasped tightly behind his back. As he walked, the whispers of the crew followed. He could never quite hear what they said, but he sensed a tension, not unlike the tension he was feeling up until a few days before.

He reached the second deck and walked into the kitchen finding everything spotless. The knives, hanging on the wall, sparkled. The cooks were beginning preparations for the next morning's breakfast. To the captain, it seemed like they were giving the food extra special attention.

Moving on, Ellis went to the infirmary. The place always felt too quiet to the captain. Two clean medicine cabinets, adorned with red crosses, stood silent vigil on one wall. A stretcher was strapped to another. Bottles of oxygen were strapped to a third wall. There were no doctors aboard *Sanson*. Instead, three members of the crew were trained as emergency medical technicians. Since *Sanson* was never designed for battle, the only real reason for an infirmary was in case a member of the crew got sick or hurt on a piece of equipment.

Stepping quickly out, Ellis came to the ship's stern and the central engineering section. This was the section run by Mahuk – the most devout Moslem Ellis had met in ages. For years, he had worked on Earth, designing mapping vessels. He only went into space himself when his wife died and his children were grown. "How is it with you, this fine evening?" said Mahuk, in a vaguely weary voice.

Ellis looked at the consoles and displays. "Better than I have been in a long time," said Ellis, conversationally. "How is it with you?"

"My engines are in good shape given how long they have been out in space without maintenance," sighed the engineer.

The captain turned his attention from the consoles to Mahuk. "Are you saying we need work on the engines?"

"We always need work on the engines. These drives are finely tuned to the subtleties of the universe. They don't run indefinitely." The engineer shrugged.

Ellis tried to decide if he should press the issue further. Instinctively, he went to rub his beard and felt vaguely disturbed to find that it was not there. Shrugging, he turned to step out of engineering control. "Good night, Mahuk," he called.

"May Allah go with you," said the engineer, turning back to his duties. Ellis thought he heard the engineer whisper, "May Allah go with us all."

The captain returned to his quarters. Stepping in, he found his pipe and tobacco on the table. Methodically, he rubbed out the tobacco and packed his pipe. After several minutes' work, he sat back and lit it. Smoke billowed around him and he let his mind float. Tomorrow morning, the *Nicholas Sanson* would jump near the node G'Liat suspected could take them to the Cluster's home. To the captain, it felt like the night before a battle. However, he was aboard a ship with no guns and no armor. Captain John Mark Ellis felt strangely exhilarated.

The door whispered open and Kirsten Smart stepped in, inclining her head. "Must you smoke that thing?" She reached behind and entered her code, locking the door.

"It helps me think," said the captain. "It gives my thoughts an order they wouldn't have otherwise."

Smart moved to the table and sat down. "What is there to think about, tonight?"

"We jump first thing in the morning. I'm worried about the ship." Ellis took a defiant puff of the pipe, then set it on the table. His stomach lurched as the ship listed gently to one side.

"Have you toured the ship?" asked Smart raising her eyebrows.

"Everything's in good shape," reported the captain.

Smart smiled and unbuttoned her jacket halfway. "I have some equipment that needs the captain's personal attention," she grinned as she pulled back the coat just far enough to reveal a tantalizing amount of cleavage. Ellis grinned while the corporate officer slowly continued to unbutton the leather jacket.

A knock sounded at the door. Ellis' shoulders dropped, but Smart shrugged and smiled. She pulled her jacket from one shoulder then the other. The knock sounded again. Ellis started to stand, but Smart shook her head. "Who says you have to answer it?" she whispered. Smart stood up and moved around the table and massaged the captain's shoulders.

Just as Ellis began to relax, G'Liat strode into the room. The warrior's black eyes first fell to Smart's naked chest, then to Ellis who stood and grabbed her jacket.

"I am sorry for the intrusion," said G'Liat. His voice was sincere, but urgent. "However, I have to talk to you for a moment."

Ellis returned the jacket to Smart, then sighed and closed his eyes. Opening them again, he retrieved the pipe and sat down. Re-lighting it, he looked up at Smart, who was buttoning her jacket. "Would you excuse us for just a moment?" he asked.

"No," said Smart simply. She sat down at the third chair. "If this affects the ship's operation in any way, I want to be here."

"G'Liat?" asked the captain. He returned the pipe to his mouth and sat expectantly.

The warrior stood silent for half a minute then sat. "All I wanted to do was ask you to keep your mind as open as possible during the jump tomorrow. I've been thinking about what Clyde has said. An open mind might be as effective as sensors."

"An open mind may be as good at what?" asked Smart, pointedly.

"At detecting deep space nodes," said Ellis around the pipe. "Is that all, G'Liat?"

The warrior nodded and stood. "For now," he said. G'Liat stepped from the cabin.

Smart stood and entered a different code into the door combination. She looked at the locking mechanism for a few minutes as if trying to figure out how G'Liat broke the code. Finally she turned back to the captain. "Deep space nodes?" she asked. "Why would you be interested?"

"Shouldn't I be interested?" asked Ellis. He took a deep draw on the pipe. "Look, G'Liat's a friend. He wants to understand these nodes and sometimes he has weird notions about how to sense them."

Smart put her hands on her hips. "It's so important that he breaks in here to tell you that?" She shook her head and moved back to the table. "I've heard the stories the cooks tell about the Cluster and how you can sense it in deep space. This has nothing to do with the nodes does it?"

"It is about the nodes," said Ellis defensively. She stood abruptly and turned her back. He removed the pipe from his mouth. "But it's about the Cluster, as well."

Smart turned around slowly and inclined her head. "We've talked about this obsession. I thought you were over it."

"The Cluster killed my father. That's not something that's easy to get over."

"There's more to it than that, isn't there?" She sat down again, putting her elbows on the table. "What would happen if we met the Cluster?"

He returned the pipe to his mouth and chewed lightly on the pipe stem. He puffed a few more times then returned the pipe to the table. "I want to talk to it, try to understand it," he said slowly. "There's more to it than malevolence. There's a whole lot more."

Smart watched the captain wide-eyed. Her eyes narrowed and lips pursed. After a moment, she let out a slow breath. "Talk to it?"

Ellis explained all he knew about the Cluster. He told her about Sufiro and what he and McClintlock had sensed there.

"But what about the incident with the *Martha's Vineyard*?" she asked, uncertainly.

"To be honest, I'm not sure whether it was my fault or not," admitted Ellis, shaking his head. "I won't let what happened at 1E1919+0427 happen to the *Sanson*, though. I promise."

Smart glared at the captain. "Why? That sounds awfully cowardly for a Navy man?"

Ellis' jaw dropped. His mind swam through a sea of excuses. Finally, he realized the truth. "I could never let anything harm you."

"Did you destroy the *Vineyard*?" she asked. Ellis shook his head and opened his mouth to speak, but she cut him off. "In fact, it sounds to me like you did the one thing that might have worked to keep the *Vineyard* from being destroyed."

"That's what I thought at the time," said Ellis, looking down at the deck.

Smart drew the captain's attention back by unbuttoning her jacket again. "I think you were right. You are under orders to protect this ship using every power at your disposal if we encounter the Cluster." She flung the jacket away. "Do I make myself perfectly clear?"

Ellis shook his head, lightly. "Perfectly, sir."

Smart looked down at her chest then back to the captain. "You've been in the Navy too long. Do I look like a 'sir' to you?"

* * *

Suki Ellis and Manuel Raton awoke in separate bunks in their cell on Titan. A hot breakfast sat on the table, waiting. Fire yawned and stretched. She poured a cup of coffee and helped herself to a piece of toast. Manuel stepped into a small alcove and relieved himself then joined Suki at the table.

"Good morning," came Teklar's voice from behind the force field.

Manuel and Fire turned in unison. "How long are you going to keep us here?" asked Manuel, coming to his feet.

"Until we determine whether John Mark Ellis succeeds or fails," answered Teklar.

Manuel's shoulders sank. Fire stood next to him. "What about informing the rest of the galaxy about the Cluster?"

"The first announcement was last night. It doesn't tell all we know, but it is the first, carefully planned, step." With that, Teklar turned and left.

* * *

John Mark Ellis arrived on the *Sanson's* command deck the next morning. Taking the chair next to Yermakov, he felt certain this was the day he was going to find the Cluster. He tried to analyze his emotions to figure out why he felt so positive. The reasons eluded him. Perhaps, it was nothing more than Smart's reassurance that she would back Ellis in whatever course he followed.

"I think we're ready to go, Skipper," said Yermakov. "Ms. Smart was in a little late this morning, but that's not surprising given the morning news."

The elevator opened and G'Liat stepped onto the command deck and moved to a position behind Ellis. "You should be at your jump station," snarled the captain.

"I'm performing some last minute calibrations. I'll be done in a few minutes," explained the warrior. G'Liat leaned close to the captain's ear. "Did you see the news this morning?"

"No," said Ellis. He tugged on his collar. "I was preoccupied."

"I'm not surprised," said G'Liat dryly. "The Titans made a rather remarkable announcement last night. I recorded the broadcast. You should take a look while I finish up."

Ellis nodded and excused himself. Entering his office, he started the recording. A hologram of a gray-coated ursine animal appeared over his desk. The Titan spoke heavily accented Generic. Ellis knew the creature as Teklar, leader of the Confederation. As often happened, Ellis couldn't look at Teklar without being reminded of his favorite teddy bear from childhood. He sat down at the desk, folded his hands and listened.

"For over a thousand years we have maintained that the way to keep peace in the galaxy is by the rule of Titan law. I think you will agree that our rule has been benevolent. However, beneficent as we have been, we have differed little from dictators. I propose that over the next year our rule be phased out and democratic elections be phased in." The recording ended at that point. Ellis guessed that G'Liat had chopped out all news commentary. The time scale proposed by Teklar was a long one. One Titan year was nearly thirty years on Earth. Still, thirty years to change a system of government that had lasted for thousands was incredible.

Ellis looked up to see G'Liat standing before him. "What do you think?" asked the warrior.

"It's incredible," gasped Ellis. "While many of my people have asked for this very thing, this is going to scare the wits out of many of the other peoples of the galaxy. What do you think?"

"I think it sounds like damage control," commented the warrior.

"Damage control?" asked Ellis, eyebrows lifted.

"They know the truth is about to come out," said the warrior. "Truth can be like a tidal wave. The Titans don't want to be swept under." G'Liat moved toward the door. "My calibrations are finished. We should jump soon."

Ellis nodded and stood, slowly. Back on the command deck, the captain sat down next to the first mate. "I see what you meant about the news." The captain took a deep breath then composed his thoughts. "However, what's been said doesn't affect this mission. Ms. Peters, are we ready to jump?"

"Yes, sir!" she called smartly.

"Then what are we waiting for?" asked the captain. "Let's do it."

Before Ellis completely registered the fact that Peters had activated controls, the universe seemed to contort itself and Ellis found himself floating outside reality. After the first long jump, he was better able to control the nausea that resulted from the disorienting effects. Even so, this was almost the worst of the jumps. More than any time before, it felt as though the ship was falling along a steep incline. The captain struggled desperately to keep his mind clear though he felt he was falling out of his chair. In front of him, the two women were gone. To the side, Yermakov seemed to vanish in a puff of smoke. The universe filled with a loud yellow.

In the midst of the yellow void was something. Ellis forced himself to concentrate on whatever it was. He felt, more than saw, orbs upon orbs in a spherical red symmetry. Red, his mind screamed, not silver; not green.

* * *

"Red?" questioned McClintlock, huddled in his quarters. Suddenly he realized he was seeing more orbs than were on the Cluster. Not only that, but the orbs were separated by some distance. The symmetries were the same, but the scales were radically different. It was not the Cluster he was seeing. Instead, he was sensing something very different, a globular cluster.

In a flash, he sensed a presence. The presence was vaguely metallic and somehow alive. Its appearance was almost momentary, but definitive. "I'm here, my Lord," called McClintlock. His voice disappeared as soon as it came from his mouth.

* * *

Metallic, alive, and home were the three sensations that rattled through Ellis' mind. He no longer felt like he was falling. Instead, it seemed as though the ship was climbing up a steep slope. Yermakov, Peters, and Papadraxis all reappeared in their rightful places and reality slowly faded in.

"Jump complete," reported Yermakov. "What a rush!"

Ellis shook his head then regretted it as he felt a wave of nausea hit. "Position report, Ms. Peters?" he asked with his eyes closed.

"Alpha Coma Bereneces system," she said.

"Nice place," said Natalie Papadraxis, dreamily. "They say it's even prettier than Earth."

Ellis opened his eyes. Although he had never been to the human colony at Alpha Coma, he felt he knew it well. It was the home of one of his heroes, Admiral Barbara Firebrandt; the woman credited with eliminating piracy in the galaxy. Briefly, Ellis wondered if he would find his place in the history books here.

"Mr. Mahuk is calling from engineering," said Natalie.

"Thanks," said Ellis as he reached over and activated speakers. "What can I do for you?"

"Captain, the port side EQ generator went out of alignment with this last jump. I'd like to put into port at Alpha Coma to do some adjustments," he reported.

Ellis took a deep breath and rubbed his chin. "How bad off are we?"

"We could do two or three more jumps," admitted Mahuk. "However, we aren't scheduled to be near another human colony until after the fifth jump. I wouldn't put these repairs off, Captain."

"I understand," said Ellis. "I'll talk to Ms. Smart and do what I can." With that, he turned off the intercom. Sitting back, he looked at Yermakov. "What do you think?"

"If we have to stop, I'd rather stop at Alpha Coma than either of the next two worlds." Yermakov shrugged.

Ellis stood and got the feel of the swaying deck. Stretching, he looked at the empty holographic viewer. "Give us a forward standard view," said the captain.

Natalie grinned and activated several switches. The sight that greeted the captain should have been terrifying. However, he almost expected it. Instead of the blue oceans and green continents of Alpha Coma Bereneces, the viewer was filled with silver orbs, hanging menacingly. "Standard view?" asked the captain, quietly.

Natalie sat with her mouth hanging open. Ellis turned to Yermakov who gripped the armrests tightly. Seeing everyone stunned, Laura Peters looked past Natalie's shoulder. "Standard view," she reported. "The Cluster is one hundred meters in front of us."

Ellis felt captivated by the image filling the viewer. He walked slowly forward and tried to put his hand up to touch the hologram. "What's our status?"

"All stop relative to galactic rotation," reported Peters. "Cluster is also stopped."

With a force of will Ellis retracted his arm. "Maintain position," he ordered. "Let's not do anything to get it mad."

"I think that's the most sensible order I've ever heard," said Yermakov, swallowing hard.

Kirsten Smart emerged from her office followed by G'Liat. They both gaped at the image of the Cluster filling the hologram. G'Liat stepped up to Ellis. "Have you tried anything?"

"Not yet," said Ellis forcing calm into his voice. "Last time I tried anything, a ship was destroyed."

"The time before that, a planet was saved," said G'Liat, gently.

"Fifty-fifty odds aren't that great," said Ellis, nervously. "I thought I was ready for this meeting." Looking back at the image of the Cluster, the captain felt an overwhelming sense of peace. "I think we should just wait."

G'Liat put his hand on the captain's shoulder. "You know what you have to do. Waiting could get us killed."

Kirsten Smart stepped up to Ellis. "Is that true?" Ellis stood, staring blankly at the viewer. "If that's true, you better do something."

Ellis swallowed hard.

* * *

Down in his quarters, McClintlock felt the deathly stillness of the ship and somehow knew the Cluster was near. "My Lord," he cried. Love and fear welled to the surface and tears spilled down his face. "Show them the error of their ways. You are the one true God in heaven!"

McClintlock felt his vision blur. He balanced himself against the table to keep from falling over. In an instant, the table vanished and Clyde McClintlock found himself in a desert. Ancient ruins stood in the distance. Within a few seconds, the evangelist recognized he was standing in the Holy Land.

Turning around, he saw a woman with piercing green eyes. The evangelist blushed momentarily when he realized she wore no clothes. However, he could not see any features of her body clearly. All he could focus on were the eyes. She held the bible and the Koran. She shook her head and lay them on the ground. Turning her back on the evangelist, she moved off toward the ruins.

* * *

"The Cluster's moving off," reported Peters. "It's slow, less than a kilometer per hour, but definitely moving."

"Match speed and follow," said Ellis. He moved away from G'Liat and Smart.

"Follow it?" asked Yermakov. "Are you crazy?"

"Possibly," said Ellis. He felt beads of sweat form on his forehead and palms. He sat down in the command seat.

Smart put her hands on her hips and glared at the captain. "I told you to do what you needed to protect the ship. I didn't tell you to chase this thing."

Ellis sat quietly and thought about his actions. His order to follow had been intuitive, however there seemed to be some sense to it. "Every ship that has been destroyed has either maintained position or tried to run away," he said. "Let's try following."

G'Liat moved to Ellis' side. "Do you sense anything?"

"Nothing definitive," said Ellis, shaking his head.

"Clyde," said Natalie Papadraxis, slowly. "Clyde is talking to it."

Ellis was on his feet. Natalie looked up at him with wide eyes. "Clyde is very agitated," she said. Natalie looked toward the viewer. "The Cluster is calm. I'm not sure it wants to talk to him, but he's the only one who hears it right now."

The captain fell back into the command chair. G'Liat's massive hand was on the captain's shoulder. Ellis shrugged it off. With deepening resolve, he looked at the image on the viewer and tried to project the same sensations of peace and tranquility he felt whenever he saw the Cluster.

Sitting in the command chair, Ellis began to feel the comfort of his home on Nantucket. Memories of his mother cooking breakfast and running on the moors with his father slowly filled his mind. "Home," said the captain, simply.

* * *

McClintlock sat in the sand, tears burning his cheeks. What he was seeing must be a lie, he thought. Impressions that the Cluster was nothing more than ancient life kept impacting his emotions and the evangelist simply could not accept those emotions.

Looking around, Clyde McClintlock realized he was back in his quarters. Nothing seemed to make sense any more. Somehow, Ellis must be making him see these visions. He could not accept that it was the Cluster.

"Why would Ellis want me to see false visions?" asked the evangelist, standing. "Why would he want to lead me on a false quest?" Suddenly the answer occurred to him. Only one being could deceive a true believer as thoroughly as this. Gathering resolve, McClintlock knew what he had to do to save his followers.

* * *

The crew on the command deck blinked in astonishment as the Cluster vanished from view. "It's jumped," announced Peters. "What should we do?"

"Maintain course and speed," said Ellis, in a daze.

G'Liat motioned for Ellis to stand. The warrior looked uncomfortable as he sat down in the captain's seat. Quickly, he ran a number of calculations. "We've been following a jump point in addition to the Cluster. If we jumped, we could follow it home. I've taken the liberty of plotting a specific course. We could go with your order, captain."

"I'm not sure I like the sound of that, Skipper," said Yermakov, sniffing. "I think we've gotten away lucky and we should get away from here as soon as we can."

"We'll do that," said Ellis bitterly, "as soon as you're captain of this ship." He turned to Peters. "Maintain course and speed."

"Aye, aye, sir," said Peters. "We are following the jump point."

"What do you think, Natalie?" asked Ellis, putting his hands behind his back.

"I don't think the Cluster would harm us if we followed. I think it wants something." Natalie folded her hands in her lap.

"It's been looking for something all along," said G'Liat standing from the captain's seat. "You sensed that in the beyond."

"But, if the Cluster's been gone for a month, what have I really been sensing?" Ellis rubbed his hands nervously.

"The beyond is time," said G'Liat simply. "Perhaps you sensed the future or the past. Perhaps you sensed the Titans in the present. There's more in the beyond than the Cluster."

"Prepare to jump," said Ellis calmly.

Yermakov swallowed hard. "I really must protest, sir," he said, standing. "You gave me your word that you would not endanger this ship. Is this all your word is worth?"

Ellis aimed his finger at the first mate. "Mr. Yermakov..."

Kirsten Smart marched toward Ellis and grabbed him by the elbow. She led him to the rear of the command deck. "For once, I think Simon is right, we should get out of here."

"G'Liat said you've wanted to know where the deep space nodes lead," countered the captain. "This is your chance to find out. You've been mapping known trade routes for years, this may be your one chance to make a mark in history; your one chance to explore something new."

"My chance for the history books or yours?" countered Smart. She looked into the eyes of the only true confident she had known in years.

"History books or not," said Ellis, his voice softening, "isn't this what science is all about? Do you back me or do you remove me from command?"

Smart took a deep breath and shook her head. "Mr. Yermakov," she called, "follow the captain's orders."

Yermakov bit his lower lip and returned to his chair.

"Maybe I could love you, after all," said Smart. She kissed her finger and touched it to his nose. With one last look at the command deck, she turned and entered her office to prepare for the jump.

Ellis looked longingly after her, then moved back to the command seat. He heard Peters sound the jump warning. G'Liat moved back to Smart's office. "All decks report ready," said Peters. "Mahuk is a little nervous about this, though."

"We're all nervous. If I'm right, though, we'll be back in this system after only two jumps," said Ellis. "Mahuk can repair his engines then."

"If you're wrong?" asked Yermakov, no malice in his voice.

The captain put his hand firmly on the first mate's forearm then looked forward. "Jump," he ordered, his voice cracking.

The ship tumbled down a figurative rabbit hole. The captain's mind could not focus on a sense of reality. There were no colors and no sounds. In a sense, the ship seemed to be moving through fourth dimensional reality faster than it ever had before. Time lost all meaning and the captain's brain could not keep up. In the end, Ellis simply blacked out.

* * *

John Mark Ellis awoke slowly. His limbs hurt and his head throbbed painfully. The other members of the bridge crew had also blacked out. Yermakov stirred slowly, his head slumped forward into his hands. Peters awoke next, looking vaguely green. Finally, Natalie opened her eyes and almost automatically activated the viewer. Bright, reddish light flooded the command deck. The hologram was crowded with stars.

G'Liat appeared behind the captain. He, like all the other crewmembers on the deck, was in awe of the sight before him. "I presume we're somewhere around the perimeter of the globular I told you about," said the warrior.

"Why the edge?" asked Ellis, holding his hands up to block the glare of thousands of suns. He was relieved when Natalie showed the presence of mind to cut the intensity of the image.

"I suspect if we were near the center, the gravitational forces would rip the ship apart," commented Kirsten Smart, who emerged from her office, rubbing her head.

Ellis grunted acknowledgment. "Where's the Cluster?"

Peters shook her head, woozily. "I'm sorry, Captain, I don't show it around anywhere."

Mahuk's voice burst through on the intercom. "You've done it now, Captain," called the engineer. "We burned out engine number four. We can't jump again until it's repaired."

"Then repair it," growled the captain.

"I would need a dry dock to repair the damage that's been done," reported the engineer.

Ellis pounded the armrest of his chair. "Do the best you can." The captain looked at his first mate. "Perhaps you were right."

This time Yermakov put his hand on the captain's forearm. "Damage is done, Skipper. We're here, we might as well find your Cluster." The mate's voice held only a small amount of bitterness.

Ellis looked toward Smart. "I told G'Liat we may get a paper out of this mission," she said. "If we survive, this will be the most famous voyage in the history of space flight."

"If we survive," said Ellis.

"Captain!" came a panicked voice from the intercom. Ellis thought he recognized it as one of the cooks. He believed the name was Frank.

"Natalie, why aren't you monitoring the calls as they come in?" asked Ellis, shaking his head.

"I think you'll find this one's important," she countered.

"Go ahead," sighed Ellis.

"Captain, I think you better get down here. Morganna's dead. She's been murdered."

Ellis looked up at Smart and G'Liat. Licking his lips he stood. "We'll be right down, Frank," called Ellis. G'Liat and Smart followed the captain off the command deck.

PART IV
Emperical Evidence

Globular clusters are almost spherical, appear to be dynamically stable and are very long lived. Unlike other clusters, globular clusters are very old. Globular clusters are believed to be relics of the formation of the Galaxy itself.

— Dr. Greg Stephens
From his Lectures

Confronting the Clusters

Manhunt

Captain John Mark Ellis entered the galley at a full run. Stopping suddenly, he supported himself against the wall to catch his breath. Looking over, he saw the cook, Morganna, a gaping hole in her abdomen, lying in a pool of blood. The captain sank to his knees beside her, remembering the dead cook on the *Martha's Vineyard*. "Not again," he moaned softly. He reached down and touched her hair. Looking up into Frank's craggy features, he held back tears. "Who did this?"

Frank shook his head. The cook did not try to conceal his tears. "I don't know; I wasn't here." He had to choke down a sob to get the words out.

Ellis looked to Smart. A variety of emotions played across her face: rage at the act, sorrow for Morganna, and concern for her ship. "We've got to find who did this," she said bitterly.

G'Liat examined the walls. His black eyes landed on a board hanging on the wall. "One of the knives is missing," he said simply. Turning, he knelt down by Morganna and examined the wound. After a moment, he looked up at Frank. "How big is the missing knife?"

Frank looked at the rack, but was too overcome with tears to speak. He simply moved off to Clyde McClintlock's office and fell into the chief cook's chair. G'Liat followed and grabbed Frank by the shoulders, shaking him lightly. "Someone is loose on this ship with a knife. Someone very dangerous," snarled the warrior.

Kirsten Smart moved to support herself on the office's doorframe. "We are sorry that Morganna's dead, but you've got to help us."

Frank shook his head and took several deep breaths. "It's a bread knife," he said after a moment. "About a foot long and serrated."

Kirsten Smart dropped into the other chair. "Painful way to die," she said looking at her hands. "Serrated knife'd rip the hell out of you."

Ellis forced himself to stand and stepped over to the door. "That's what it did," he said, somberly.

G'Liat stood up straight and looked from Smart to Ellis. "There was not much sign of a struggle. She only has the one wound. The killer attacked with a single thrust."

Ellis forced himself to look back at Morganna's body. Surprise was frozen in her lifeless features. However, G'Liat was right, there were no scratches or cuts except the one wound. Not even her hair was out of place. "Where was her jump station?" he asked, weakly.

"She should have been in her quarters. However, McIntosh wasn't here, so she stayed," said Frank.

"She was alone?" asked G'Liat.

"She should have been," explained Smart. "Company policy only allows one person down here during the jump for safety. She would have been locked here in the office." She shook her head and looked accusingly at Ellis. "Or, McClintlock should have been here. That nut should be lying dead, not a sweet woman like Morganna."

"She was surprised," said Ellis moving back to the cook's body. The captain knelt down again. "Morganna could have stopped someone from entering if she wanted."

Kirsten Smart stood and moved over to Ellis. "She knew everyone aboard."

G'Liat turned. "However, she would not have let just anyone have access to the knives."

"Or any of the cookware," piped in Frank. "She was very protective of her kitchen."

"It was someone who should have been here," said Ellis. Looking down at the floor he took a deep breath, afraid of the truth.

"McClintlock," growled Smart. "It had to be."

"I'm afraid you're right," said Ellis, a quaver in his voice. "But why?"

"He was in communication with the Cluster," stated G'Liat. "Who knows what it said. Who knows what that could have done to him."

"How are we going to stop him?" asked Smart standing. "We're a corporate ship. We don't have a security force."

"It's my fault," said Ellis. "I brought him on board. I'll stop him." The captain stood and made his way to the intercom. "Natalie," he said into the microphone. "Have Simon seal off all sections of the ship. Only I am to have universal access. Is that understood?"

"I'll let Simon know," said Natalie. "May I ask why? That's an awfully draconian command."

"I know it is," said Ellis. "We have a bad situation here. Also, contact all section heads. They are to contact me immediately if they see Clyde McIntosh."

"Will do, Captain." Natalie Papadraxis' voice held a note of uncertainty.

G'Liat came up behind the captain. "You'll need help if you find him. He's armed. You're not. We might doubt his competence, but he's a more experienced ground soldier than you, all the same."

Ellis turned, stepping past the warrior. He grabbed another knife off the wall and faced G'Liat. "Now we're both armed and I'm younger than him."

"Don't be stupid," growled Smart. "I may be mad that you brought him on my ship, but I don't want to lose you. The more of us that confront him, the better."

Ellis pursed his lips. "You're staying here," he said. "It's bad enough if G'Liat comes. I don't want you hurt."

Smart put her hands on her hips. "Make me stay," she said defiantly.

"I am a better warrior than both you and McClintlock," said G'Liat facing the captain. "You must talk to the Cluster the next time we confront it. I'll go with you to keep you safe. If you insist that I don't go with you, I'll find a way to keep you here while I tend to McClintlock."

The captain's shoulders dropped slightly. "Okay, but I want both of you armed. We don't know what state of mind he's gotten himself into."

* * *

Clyde McClintlock sat in a deserted corridor near the ship's stern on the second level. Tears streamed down his cheeks as he stared in disbelief at the bloody knife in his hands. His plan had been to find the evil one and kill him. Morganna, while not a strong believer, had simply gotten in the way. Taking a deep, shuddering breath, McClintlock thought how much he had wanted her to believe that the Cluster was God.

"I betrayed Rocky Hill, my people, and now sweet Morganna," cried Clyde to himself. "All because of Ellis."

Looking back along the corridor, he noticed a couple of drops of blood along the path he had taken from the kitchen. He smiled cruelly. "They will lead the evil one to me."

Just then, the doors used in case of hull evacuation came down sealing off the corridor on either side of him. McClintlock stood, dropping the knife. He pounded on the door leading back to the galley. Trapped in the corridor, he would never get the surprise necessary to trap Ellis. Looking around desperately he noticed an opening to the ship's ventilation system at deck level.

Retrieving the knife, he used it to unscrew the bolts holding the grill in place. He ignored the scratches he was leaving in the paint. Getting the grill off, he was just able to squeeze himself into the ductwork. Knife ahead of him, he shimmied further toward the ship's stern.

* * *

Mahuk and a grizzled mechanic poured over manuals in the

engineering section. Their goal was to find a way to repair engine number four without a dry dock. Ideally, the engine would be pulled from the ship and the damaged parts replaced. The problem was that they had neither the facilities to pull the engine from the ship nor many of the replacement parts.

"We can fabricate most of what we need in the shop," said Mahuk, looking up from the display.

The old mechanic shook his head. "What, and assemble the components in free fall beside the ship?"

"Why not?" asked Mahuk.

The old mechanic snorted. "It'd take the better part of a month to do that with no guarantee that it'd work."

"I know," admitted Mahuk reluctantly. "What do you suggest?"

The mechanic scratched his tightly curled white hair. "The real problem is that three engines just don't have the oomph necessary for us to jump. We could get the power we need by moving the power conduits from the measuring systems to the three remaining engines."

Mahuk shook his head. "Those power conduits are out on the hull. You'd have to go extra-vehicular to do that."

"We'd have to do that to rebuild an engine. It's the least of our worries," said the mechanic.

Mahuk frowned. "Not only that, you'd have to re-sync the engines so we could go into jump with only three." Mahuk pointed at the schematic. "Those engines are precisely tuned. Upping the power to them would be like strapping three quinnium warheads to our hull. One mistake re-synchronizing the engines and our component atoms would be scattered so far into the future that there's no telling whether there will even be a universe for them to wind up in."

The mechanic inclined his head. "But it could work?"

Mahuk sighed. "It could."

"I can't think of anyone better able to get the calculations right to make sure we don't blow ourselves up."

"I appreciate your confidence," said Mahuk wearily. "I'm not sure it's well placed."

The mechanic smiled. "Do you want to orbit the galaxy in this damned globular for the rest of your life?" The engineer shook his head. "Then we better get started on those calculations."

Both men set to work on the computer. Each became entrenched enough in their work that they did not hear the scraping of someone forcing their way though the ventilation system, nor the scratching as that person worked nuts lose on a vent cover.

* * *

G'Liat was the first to notice the trail of blood drops leading toward the vessel's stern, away from the galley. Each of the drops were about twenty feet apart, meaning there were only one or two per section. Ellis, Smart, and G'Liat followed the sparse trail. The captain led the way, using his access codes to open doors as they moved.

They finally came to the open vent cover. G'Liat examined the scratches, then looked into the shaft. "McClintlock would be just thin enough to get through here."

"None of us are, though," grumbled Smart. "Seems like a good way to get us off his trail."

"I'm not sure he cares if we follow," said Ellis. "He would have been trapped in here. I think he just wants to get the drop on us."

G'Liat nodded. "In fact, I think he wants us to follow." The warrior turned to Smart. "Do you know where this shaft leads?"

"It should follow the corridor. It goes back the way we've come or on toward engineering," she said.

"Or, I would guess it connects to all the rooms in between," grumbled Ellis.

"Maybe," pondered G'Liat. "Even if McClintlock could get into the shaft, I doubt he has much room to maneuver. He'd pretty much have to travel a straight line until he got to another vent opening."

"One that came out where he won't be trapped, like in the corridor," said Ellis.

"That would mean engineering, then," stated Smart.

Ellis stormed ahead, punching in access codes at each of the doors until they came to the engineering section. As Ellis opened the door, G'Liat shoved the captain lightly aside and pounced into the room. He motioned for Smart and Ellis to stay back.

A mechanic lay across a console, his throat cut, blood still oozing to the floor. The warrior scanned the room. Aside from the low-lying consoles in the middle of the room, there seemed only one other place McClintlock could hide.

The warrior turned around slowly to find the evangelist holding a knife to Mahuk's throat. "Don't come any closer, G'Liat," said McClintlock. "I have no intention of killing Mahuk. It's Ellis I want."

Ellis stepped into the room and dropped his knife to the floor. "Let Mahuk go," said the captain. "I'm here."

"No!" cried Smart. "He'll kill you."

"If I can, I will," said McClintlock with a slight inclination of his head. "I don't know if the evil one can be killed, but I'm willing to die finding out."

Ellis kept his eyes on McClintlock, but spoke to Smart. "Mahuk is your only way home." The captain took a step toward McClintlock. "Clyde, let him go."

McClintlock's eyes moved from G'Liat to Ellis to Smart. Just as Ellis saw McClintlock drop the knife and loosen his grip on Mahuk, the captain felt two hundred pounds of force shove him into Smart. The two tumbled like rag dolls into the corridor.

Ellis gasped for breath as he struggled to get back to his feet. He staggered to the door to see McClintlock swinging his knife wildly at G'Liat. Mahuk lay on the ground, a knife wound in his side. From a distance, Ellis could not tell whether it was fatal. Looking up again, Ellis watched in horror as McClintlock's flailing blade connected with G'Liat's head. G'Liat let out a low growl as yellow blood began to seep from his cheek.

The warrior stood and watched for a minute, then struck out with his massive six-fingered hand. The Rd'dyggian caught McClintlock's arm and squeezed. The knife fell impotently to the ground as the captain heard bones splinter and crack. McClintlock's expression turned from rage to terror.

"G'Liat!" yelled Ellis when he finally found the breath. "Don't do it!"

Seeming not to hear, G'Liat pulled McClintlock toward him. Ellis launched himself at the warrior and rebounded when the warrior did not move. The captain watched helplessly as the warrior's free hand closed around McClintlock's neck. After only a momentary struggle, the evangelist's body went limp and the warrior let him fall to the deck.

"How could you?" cried Ellis horrified.

"He was only human," said G'Liat. His Rd'dyggian accent was especially strong.

Kirsten Smart stepped in and knelt next to Mahuk. She felt for a pulse. "He's still alive," she said, relieved. She stepped to the intercom and told the bridge to re-open all sections and ordered the emergency medical techs to the scene.

"You may arrest me." G'Liat said to Ellis. "I will not resist."

"Why did you have to kill him?" asked Ellis, his palms upward.

"It was the only way to guarantee your safety and the safety of the ship," said G'Liat simply.

"You could have restrained him just as easily." Ellis sat cross-legged next to the lifeless body of Clyde McClintlock and closed the evangelist's eyes. "Mine Enemy is growing old – I have at last Revenge – The Palate of the Hate departs – If any would..." The captain's voice choked before he could finish the last of Emily Dickinson's verse. He looked into the alien warrior's black eyes. "Damn you," whispered the captain.

* * *

That night, Kirsten Smart arrived at Ellis' cabin. Ellis lay on the bunk staring at the ceiling. Smart sat down at the table. "How do you feel?" she asked.

"Like hell," he said. "How's Mahuk?"

"The med techs say he'll be okay. He was sliced pretty bad, but nothing major was cut." Smart smiled warmly, trying to tell the captain that everything would be okay.

"Does he have a plan for getting us home?" asked Ellis.

"He does, but he won't be able to perform the repairs himself, now. His repair plans involve re-routing some of the power conduits on the hull. Someone will have to go outside the ship to do it." She leaned forward. "But, there's not much of a hurry. I thought you'd want to try to contact the Cluster before we went back."

Ellis looked toward Smart. His eyes were red-rimmed. "G'Liat and Clyde were both my friends. Maybe that friendship was dubious, but I cared about both of them. In the end, each of them betrayed me. My heart's not much in this anymore."

Smart stood and walked over to the bunk. She took Ellis' hand and held it tightly. "I won't betray you," she said. "I think we should at least look around, while we're here."

Ellis looked at the ceiling. "I think we should get home." The two were swallowed by an uncomfortable silence for several minutes. "If Mahuk is well enough to write down instructions on how to repair the engines, I can go out and do the fix."

"That can wait until tomorrow," said Smart. She sat on the edge of the bunk and pulled off her boots. She swung her legs onto the bed and held the captain. "For now, let's sleep."

Ellis turned to look into Smart's eyes. "The military is supposed to desensitize you to death. Tonight, I just feel sick."

"That's the way it should be," she said. There was no malice in her voice. She just held the captain tighter and buried her face in his shoulder. He could feel the material of his nightshirt grow damp as her tears began to flow.

* * *

The next morning, Simon Yermakov helped Ellis into a space suit. The captain and two mechanics planned to leave the ship and modify it so that it could get back to the Milky Way galaxy where it could be repaired. As Ellis inserted his hands into the white gauntlets, he wondered how G'Liat was doing. He thought he should go talk to the warrior. However, something compelled him to continue getting ready for the mission outside the ship.

Yermakov placed the helmet on the captain's head and smiled as he locked it into place. "Looks like everything's okay, Skipper. Hope you can fix this thing. Being out in this globular gives me the creeps."

"I hear you," said Ellis. The captain motioned for the two mechanics to follow him into the air lock. As the inner door sealed itself behind them, Ellis brought up a list of modification instructions on his armband. He was reading the instructions as the outer door opened. Looking up, the captain's mouth fell open at the sight that greeted him.

Light flooded into the airlock from countless stars hanging against a backdrop of even more stars. Ellis was used to seeing clumps of stars hanging in a sea of black velvet, like the Milky Way streaming its way through a rare clear Nantucket night or constellations filling ship viewers. This, on the other hand, was completely different. The two mechanics were likewise taken aback by the sight. Ellis simply turned off the light on the helmet of his space suit and motioned for the two men to follow him out.

In the eerie light of all the stars, it was not hard to find the power conduits in Mahuk's instructions. The work of rerouting them was more difficult than Ellis had pictured. The conduits were not designed to be moved, so the captain and mechanics had to break numerous welds and remove quite a few bolts from the black Erdonium hull of the ship. By mid-morning, Ellis was sweating profusely inside his suit and longed for a shower.

By noon, the captain was starving and ordered the work crew inside the ship for lunch. Eating only emphasized the loss of McClintlock. The captain knew the warrior had been right and the evangelist had to be stopped. As Ellis took a bite of his sandwich, he wondered at the fact that McClintlock had seemed like nothing but a nuisance until he was gone. Taking a last sip of lemonade, the captain realized how much he missed the conversation, no matter how deluded, of a man who had shared the common experience of communicating with the Cluster.

After lunch, Ellis and the two mechanics returned to work. After about two hours, the conduits were welded securely into their new locations. The captain ordered the mechanics inside to run simulations and make sure the modifications would work. Ellis, on the other hand, felt compelled to stay outside the ship for a short time.

Holding onto the outside of the ship, Ellis stared into heart of the globular cluster and wondered momentarily where the Cluster had gone. As he wondered, he began to feel an emptiness and a sense that the last months had been wasted. Before he sunk into despair, though, he thought about Kirsten Smart and smiled. If nothing else, gaining her friendship had made this voyage worthwhile.

Just as Ellis started making his way back to the airlock he felt a presence. Looking over his shoulder, he gasped as a glimmer of silver appeared among the reddish stars. A metallic object smoved toward the *Sanson* at incredible speed. It did not take long for the captain to realize that a Cluster was approaching. The Cluster stopped some distance from *Sanson* and Ellis wondered what it was up to. Alone, out on the hull of his ship, the captain felt naked and vulnerable. Another glimmer of silver appeared and Ellis inclined his head as a second Cluster approached. The captain was frozen in place when he saw a third glimmer. As had happened every time before, Ellis could not tear his attention away from the alien vessels. Someone yelled something into his helmet speakers. He thought it was Kirsten Smart yelling for him to get inside.

Captain John Mark Ellis pushed himself away from *Sanson's* hull toward the group of Clusters. As he floated in their direction, he saw a fourth glimmer.

Prodigal Children

Once again, John Mark Ellis found himself in a room surrounded by antiquities. This time, though, the room seemed more orderly than before. Ellis noticed that he was free of the constraints of his spacesuit. In fact, looking down, he noticed that he wore no clothing at all. Fortunately, the room was pleasantly warm.

Looking around, Ellis found a nineteenth century French armchair. He felt the hard wood of the armrests admiringly, then sat down in the chair, making himself comfortable. As he looked around the room, he realized that much of what he saw was nautical. He saw old brass lanterns and compasses. A wooden ship's wheel hung on a wall. As he looked at the furniture, he realized that it was not merely nautical; all of it represented styles he had seen in homes on Nantucket. Despite sitting nude in a room full of very familiar antiques far from the normal range of human travel, Ellis felt quite comfortable.

"Only human. The expression has a certain irony," came a voice from behind the captain. The voice had a strangely resonant timbre. It only took Ellis a few seconds to realize that it sounded like a Titan accent. The captain turned to face the sound of the voice. The woman he had seen at 1E1919+0427 walked up behind him. She paused, examining the captain with iridescent green eyes. Moving around the chair, she sat down on a sofa, crossing thin, but as before, strangely nondescript legs.

A woman with blue eyes stepped from behind an oak armoire. Like the first woman, black hair flowed over strangely rigid breasts. Letting his eyes wander down her body, he saw that her soft-looking belly had no navel. "Only human does not seem so ironic to me."

"Imagination is power," said the woman with green eyes. "See how this one interprets our communication. It can turn emotion into visual imagery. The appendages never did that."

"The appendages?" asked Ellis, his eyebrows raised.

"Imagination?" There was a hint of laugher from the blue-eyed woman. "He sees us all the same."

"We are sensual creatures," retorted the green-eyed woman. "He interprets that sensuality in a most fascinating way; a way that is most useful and a way that I wish to explore further."

Ellis noticed a third woman standing in front of him. She had fiery red eyes and seemed to glare at the captain. Involuntarily, Ellis shrank from her gaze. "It understands details of our communication. It is dangerous."

The green-eyed woman turned to face Ellis. She uncrossed her legs and put her hands on her knees, evaluating the captain. Sensuality, but not sexuality, thought Ellis, reddening as he caught himself staring. Looking back at her face, he thought he caught a hint of a smirk. "We have searched for the appendages. Instead, we found humans, Rd'dyggians, Zahari, and others. Humans know the appendages and are close to them."

Ellis licked his lips. "What are you?"

A fourth voice sounded from behind the captain. "The intelligence is minimized without the appendages." Turning around, Ellis saw a woman with vivid violet eyes.

The captain folded his hands in his lap. He began to realize that the four women were not speaking directly to him. He was simply hearing what they had to say.

"The humans show promise," said the red-eyed woman. "Perhaps they would serve in place of the appendages."

Ellis held up a finger to speak, but was interrupted by the blue-eyed woman. "Too independent. So are all the others we have seen. Only the original appendages will do or we . . ."

The violet-eyed woman slunk around Ellis and sat down next to the green-eyed woman. She shook her finger. "The human hears and understands. More than just one human hears and understands, but the one among us hears exceptionally well."

Off in the corner of the room, Ellis caught a glimpse of something soft and furry. Standing, he moved over to retrieve the furry object. It had black button-eyes and a smile stitched onto its gray fur. The captain recognized one of the teddy bears he had owned in his youth. "The humans know the appendages," said the green-eyed woman.

"What do we do about the humans that are here?" asked the red-eyed woman, sitting down on a stool.

"Nothing," said the green-eyed woman. She folded her arms. "They are harmless to us."

"They will not be, next time," said the blue-eyed woman.

"We will continue to study them," said the violet-eyed woman.

Ellis gently laid the teddy bear down. "Study us?" he asked. "How do you propose to study us? We are intelligent life forms. We can talk; we can give you information. You don't have to destroy our ships."

"Your study is invasive, they will remember," said the green-eyed woman.

"So are your searches," countered the violet-eyed woman.

Ellis moved to the center of the group of women and stamped his bare foot on the hard wood floor. He was disappointed that he did not make a very loud noise. "Listen to me!" he shouted.

The green-eyed woman smiled wistfully and looked at Ellis. "We have been."

All four women stood in unison and moved off in separate directions.

Ellis suddenly felt like he was falling and flailed to grab at something before he realized that he was in his space suit floating away from the *Sanson*. He thought he caught a greenish glimmer off of a Cluster as it moved off. The captain chewed his lip for a moment before he activated his suit's thruster control and turned around to return to the *Sanson*.

* * *

As the inner door of the airlock opened, Mark Ellis found himself facing a relieved Simon Yermakov. The first mate stepped up to the captain and unlatched the helmet. "We thought we had lost you, Skipper," said the mate once the helmet was off.

"You seem glad to have me back," said the captain. "There have been points on this journey where I'm not sure that would have been true."

"It's always been true, Skipper," said Yermakov. "Would I ever get promoted if I returned from a mission without my captain?"

Just then, the door at the other end of the room opened and Kirsten Smart stormed in. "What the hell happened out there, Mark? Did you lose your mind?"

Ellis inclined his head. "What do you mean?"

"Four of those Clusters just pull up to our ship and you float out among them. All five of you just sat there for about an hour. I'm surprised your oxygen supply didn't run out." Smart shook her head. "Don't you ever try a stunt like that again," she chided.

With Yermakov's help, Ellis continued to strip out of the space suit. "Trust me, all I want right now is to get back to familiar stars," said the captain, sitting down to remove his boots. "Then I want a shower."

"Did you learn anything, at least?" asked Smart, her tone softening. "Were you able to tell them about our intelligence?"

Ellis looked at the floor. "The part that frightens me is that I think they've known about our intelligence from the moment they first attacked a human ship."

Smart sat down on the bench next to the captain. "So, your father was killed maliciously?"

The captain shook his head, slowly. "I don't believe so. It was more a mistake. That's what the Cluster tried to tell me at 1E1919+0427.

They are looking for a part of themselves abandoned in the galaxy the last time they were there. They found us instead." Ellis looked up into Smart's eyes. "However, they're curious about us. To them, we're somehow unique biological specimens. My father was killed in the name of science. The destruction of his ship was more a dissection, I think, than an attack."

"I don't much like the sound of that," said Smart, looking toward the far wall. "I never liked biology. Now I know why." She looked back at Ellis. "What are they looking for?"

"The Clusters call themselves the intelligence. The others are the appendages. I think we call the appendages, Titans," said Ellis, slowly.

"The Titans are part of the Cluster?" asked Yermakov, wide-eyed. "How can that be? They're on our side."

"I think they still are," said Ellis. "Look at it this way, my hand could be considered my brain's slave. It's pretty rare when a liberated slave wants to return to its master." The captain stood, stepping out of the suit. Yermakov handed him his shirt and trousers. Ellis dressed, then looked from Smart to Yermakov. "Let's go home."

* * *

Ellis, Smart, and Yermakov stepped out onto the command deck of the *Sanson*. The captain sat down in the command chair and activated the holographic interface. He pulled up reports of engineering readiness and checked them over. "Ms. Peters," called the captain. "Are we ready to jump?"

"At your command, Captain. We are maintaining position relative to the jump point," reported the pilot.

Ellis watched as Yermakov took his station and Smart made her way back to the office. "Sound jump warning," ordered the captain.

Klaxons sounded around the ship. Ellis gripped the armrests of his chair tightly. "Everyone's as ready as they're going to be," said Natalie with some tension in her voice.

For a moment, Ellis was tempted to ask if the communicator had sensed anything while he was out with the Clusters. Instead, he shook his head and looked at Laura Peters. "Jump," he said almost inaudibly.

Once again, the *Sanson* rocked and tumbled its way through fourth dimensional reality at speeds that seemed impossible. Ellis fought to maintain consciousness. For a while he did. Streaks of red, green, blue, and violet seemed to dance by the ship. Was it a coincidence, wondered Ellis, that the women of the Cluster all had eyes in the colors of the rainbow? Did the Clusters just pass the *Sanson* in the beyond? After a few moments of watching the colors swirl in front of him, the captain passed out.

***

Ellis opened one eye and looked around. Sparks flashed from the pilot's console. The captain opened both eyes and forced himself out of his seat. He pulled the unconscious form of Laura Peters away from her arcing station. In a daze, the captain searched the manual controls for the power shutoff. After a moment, he found it. The arcs of electricity settled out and the captain fell back into the pilot's chair.

Natalie rolled her head and blinked her eyes open at the captain. "You're not Laura," she said, groggily.

"Not last I looked," said the captain with a sheepish grin. "Any idea where we are?"

Natalie activated her station. "According to this, we're on the outskirts of the Alpha Coma Berenices system."

Ellis let out a long sigh of relief. "See if you can find us some open repair facilities."

"With pleasure," said Natalie. The communicator put her hand to her head and called out with the chip implant.

Looking over, Ellis noticed that Laura Peters was stirring. The captain helped her to her feet. "Think you can get the ship into dock?"

The pilot blinked a few times. "I should be able to manage it, sir, presuming the ship hasn't been too badly damaged," she said. "Where are we?"

"Alpha Coma," said the captain. "A good place to take a well-deserved rest, I think."

"It's about time, Skipper," said Yermakov, just coming around. The first mate sniffed and rubbed his nose on his sleeve.

***

As the *Nicholas Sanson* began limping toward Alpha Coma Bereneces, John Mark Ellis made his way to his quarters to wash up. Once done he put on clean clothes and sat down at the table in his quarters. Activating the computer interface, he dictated a short message to his mother. He told her what he thought he knew about the Cluster and the Titans and asked if she had learned anything. He finished the message with a word about his feelings for a woman that he met recently.

The letter home done, Ellis rapped his fingers on the tabletop and looked out the window over his bunk. Finally, with some resolve, he decided to see how G'Liat was doing.

The captain found the warrior sitting alone in his cabin. African drums played and pungent incense burned, filling the room with potent vapors. The captain sat down opposite the warrior. "How are you doing?"

"I am caged," said the warrior. "I want out."

"There's no guard on the door," said the captain. "I haven't decided if I'm going to press charges."

"My sense of honor prevents me from leaving," said G'Liat, simply.

"Why did you kill McClintlock?" asked Ellis. "You could have subdued him. It would have been very simple for you."

"We are all specist, Captain. Have you ever longed to hunt whales as your ancestors did? Be honest." G'Liat leaned forward.

Ellis swallowed hard. "I've thought about it."

"When you sort out your feelings on this matter, you will be a better warrior," explained G'Liat. "Once you've done that, you are welcome to return to Rd'dyggia. I will teach you more."

"I'm not sure I want to learn what you have to teach," said Ellis, looking at the floor.

"This is not the Captain Ellis speaking who sought me out." G'Liat leaned back revealing the deep cut left by McClintlock.

"No," said Ellis, simply. "The universe seems to have changed for me."

"That is, as it should be. The offer still stands," said G'Liat. The warrior stood and looked out the window over his bunk. "I saw you with the Clusters. Did you succeed in talking to them?"

Ellis remained silent for several minutes. "I succeeded in hearing what they had to say."

G'Liat turned, his hands folded. "Nine tenths of communication is listening. May I look into your mind? I would like to hear what they said."

Ellis shook his head slowly. "No, not this time. My thoughts are my own. They always have been. I realize now that's why you couldn't see the second Cluster vision. It's personal and I didn't want you to see."

"Indeed, your ability to block me is strong, perhaps unique." G'Liat looked toward the floor. "You hadn't known me long at that time. You certainly had no reason to trust me. Does our friendship mean nothing? I helped you learn the origin of the Cluster. Can't you let me see what you learned?"

Ellis looked into the warrior's large, black eyes. After a moment, the captain held his hand open toward the chair opposite. "Sit and I'll tell you the tale."

* * *

On Titan, Teklar again appeared at the cell of Manuel Raton and Suki Ellis. As she lumbered up to the force field, the environment suits materialized in the cell. "Ellis has met the Cluster. He has either succeeded or failed. Only time will tell." A computer disk materialized in the cell. "Ellis sent this message to you on Earth. We intercepted it. You may read it before you leave."

"We are free to go then?" asked Fire.

"Yes," said Teklar simply. "However, I ask that you speak to no one of your break-in here. It might prompt others to follow in your footsteps."

"Will you continue to tell the galaxy of the Cluster?" asked Manuel.

"The process has begun." Teklar inclined her head.

"Then we will be silent," Fire agreed.

"Where would you like to go?" asked Teklar.

Fire raised an eyebrow. She thought for a moment. "I'd like to see my son."

"It will be arranged."

* * *

That afternoon, Ellis returned to his own cabin on the *Sanson*. On his table he found a cigar tied with a ribbon. The captain untied the ribbon, bit off the end of the cigar and lit it. Sitting back in the chair the captain savored the fragrant smoke and realized how much he had missed his cache of cigars.

There was a knock at the door. "Come in," called the captain.

Kirsten Smart stepped in and sat down in the chair opposite the captain. "How do you like it?" she asked, pointing to the cigar.

"One of the best I've had." While Ellis had tasted better cigars, this one was special. "Where did you find it?"

"Isaac Aubrey found a box listed in ship's stores. He brought it to my attention. I have no idea how it got there," she said with a grin. "Still, I thought you would appreciate them."

Ellis lightly chewed the cigar as his eyes narrowed. "Thank you," he said.

Smart looked toward the floor. "I suppose once we get to Alpha Coma, you'll want to contact the Navy and see if they will give you your old job back. After all, you've found evidence that the Cluster may be more of a threat than you previously thought."

Ellis sucked the cigar for several moments and contemplated her words. "I'm not sure they'd believe me any more now than they did a few months ago." The captain took a draw on the cigar and exhaled slowly. "Besides, I've been thinking these civilian clothes are a lot more comfortable than a navy uniform ever was."

"Are you saying you want to remain captain of this crew of misfits and undisciplined louts?" asked Smart with a wink.

"I think this crew could use me," chided Ellis.

"What makes you think we'll have you?" she asked, playfully.

Ellis shifted the cigar to the side of his mouth with his tongue and grinned wickedly. "If I left, you could always promote Simon to the captaincy."

Smart nodded concession. "I think I'm beginning to love you."

* * *

On Saturn's moon, Titan, Teklar was reading a human parable. She paused to contemplate the words, "And bring hither the fatted calf, and kill it; and let us eat, and be merry: For this my son was dead and is alive again; he was lost, and is found. And they began to be merry."

She wondered if the Intelligence would feel that way if her people were to return to serve them. Would they rejoice if they offered help? She wondered if the Intelligence had stagnated as her people had. If so, she wondered whether the two could work together to become something greater. She closed the book she was reading and snorted, hating herself for even contemplating leading her people back to slavery.

Accessing the net, she looked over the reports from *Sanson*. The home of the Intelligence would be accessible off and on for about thirty years. Much as she hated thoughts of slavery, the leader of the Titans knew they could not hide forever.

Silent Earth

Repairs to the *Nicholas Sanson* proceeded under the supervision of the mostly-recovered Chief Engineer Mahuk. Space-suited repair crews swarmed about the ship like gnats around a light post. Many people on the repair crew shook their heads at what they perceived to be an amateurish job of rerouting the conduits. Many commented that it was a miracle that the ship had not simply vaporized upon leaping into the fourth dimension of spacetime. It would take nearly two weeks for the crews to return *Sanson* to her former grandeur.

John Mark Ellis, weary from his encounter with the Cluster talked Kirsten Smart into not pressing charges against G'Liat. "Under one condition," said Smart. "Tell him to go to Rd'dyggia immediately. I never want to see his face again."

Ellis proposed the terms to G'Liat. "I will go to Rd'dyggia soon, then," said G'Liat. "The planet is in grave danger if what you told me of your vision is correct." The warrior paused for a moment, thoughtful. "But what will you do if our paths cross again?"

Ellis bit his lower lip and considered the answer to the question. "I think that depends on what the Cluster does," answered the captain. With that he turned and left the cabin.

The captain arranged a military funeral for Clyde McClintlock aboard the ship. Only Laura Peters, Kirsten Smart and the captain himself attended.

"Lieutenant in the Gaean Navy, Colonel of the Tejan Army and Pastor of the Cluster's flock," eulogized Ellis. "One could argue that he was misguided. But Clyde McClintlock always did what he thought was right. May someone be able to say that of us all when we pass down the long dark road."

"Amen," said Laura Peters, somberly.

With that, John Mark Ellis consigned the body of Clyde McClintlock to space.

* * *

Later that afternoon, Ellis and Smart sat in her office trying to find words to explain their encounter with the Cluster for the official report. They struggled to rationalize two tragic deaths, serious damage to the ship and the discharge of G'Liat without pressing charges.

They took a break and stepped out to the command deck. In the hologram floated a three dimensional representation of the *Sanson*.

Captain and owner's representative stepped into the hologram and evaluated the progress of the repairs. They watched as a segment of conduit was lifted from the ship. Soon a new segment was brought in to replace the old. Satisfied, they returned to Smart's office to continue the report.

Two hours later, after reading and re-reading the report, both Ellis and Smart had raging headaches. Wordlessly, Ellis stood and walked to his office. He returned a moment later with a bottle of whiskey. Without explanation, he handed the bottle to Smart. She opened the bottle and took a deep swig then handed the bottle back to Ellis. He gulped a shot of whiskey, wiped his mouth on his sleeve, then took another gulp.

"When they read this report, we'll either be heroes or unemployed," stuttered Ellis.

"Or imprisoned," said Smart with a smirk.

The two held hands across the desk for a moment. Then, Kirsten Smart pushed the button that sent the report back to TransGalactic Corporation on Earth.

"Let's get the hell out of here," said Ellis, then took another drink of whiskey.

"Where to?" Smart's eyes were limpid pools of exhaustion. "We can't just up and leave the ship."

"Why not?" asked the captain defiantly. "Mahuk is supervising the repairs and everything is in order. As to where, there's someplace on Alpha Coma I've always wanted to go."

* * *

Old Man Coffin awoke to a swaying followed by a lurch. He blinked in filtered twilight, but not the filtered twilight of his room in the Ellis house. His nose was invaded by the smell of wet wood mingled with humanity. There was a pungent undertone. "Whale oil?" he half whispered. Wood creaked loudly and he lurched again. He looked at his hands. They looked like the hands of a man thirty years his junior.

Coffin climbed out of bed and looked around in the dimness. There were shutters over his bed. He threw the shutters open and was greeted by the sight of open ocean. He had to grab onto a beam in the wall to keep from stumbling during another lurch. He looked around the room. He was in the after cabin of an old wooden sailing vessel. Charts were laid out on a table. A black coat and pants hung over a chair. Almost involuntarily, he scratched himself and felt the surprising roughness of wool. There was a pounding at the door.

"Come in," said Coffin, softly, almost reverently. The pounding came again. "Come in," Coffin growled loudly.

A young boy, barely into his teens opened the creaky wooden door. "The mate's compliments, sir," said the boy. "He would like to know what course to make."

Coffin rubbed the stubble on his chin. He stepped over to the charts. There were not only antique charts of the oceans of the Earth, but star charts as well. The universe had opened up to Coffin. He could see anything he wanted to see; go anywhere he wanted to go. "My God," muttered Coffin. "What has happened? Have I gone crazy?"

He was reassured by a soft feminine voice, almost in his head, but not quite, as though it echoed from outside. The sense was strong enough for him to know that he was not imagining this. "This galaxy is new to us. Take us to any place, any time."

"Sir?" asked the boy standing in the doorway.

"Damn it, boy! The mate can wait while I get my bearings. Get me some coffee and let me review these charts!" The boy ran from the room, practically slamming the door in his haste to leave. Coffin took a deep breath and smiled. Not only the oceans of the Earth, but the entire galaxy, were his to explore. "Where do we begin?" he whispered.

* * *

Aboard the *Nicholas Sanson*, Natalie Papadraxis screamed. Laura Peters rushed to her side. "What's the matter?"

"The Earth!" Natalie cried. "The Earth has just gone silent!"

Laura held onto Natalie, attempting to quiet her sobbing.

* * *

In the *Sanson's* launch on the way to Alpha Coma Berenices, Ellis explained that his great grandmother was Lord Admiral Barbara Firebrandt, famous for virtually eliminating space piracy in the galaxy.

"Her husband was president of Alpha Coma, wasn't he?" asked Smart.

"Her second husband," clarified Ellis. "Her first husband was Bradbury Firebrandt, my great grandfather. Story is she married him for his name."

"Bradbury Firebrandt was a powerful man then?" asked Kirsten.

"No," sighed Ellis. "She just thought it was a great name."

Kirsten Smart rolled her eyes. While Ellis somewhat drunkenly piloted the shuttle to the surface, Kirsten looked up the location of Barbara Firebrandt's grave. She punched the coordinates into the little shipboard computer and heaved a sigh of relief when Ellis relinquished control of the launch to the computer.

The captain took another sip of whiskey and offered the bottle to Smart. She shook her head. "If I drink anymore, I'll upchuck."

Ellis nodded, realizing he'd better not drink very much more himself.

The communication's light snapped on the launch's console. "Laura Peters calling Captain Ellis or Ms. Smart." The voice was calm and professional.

Ellis turned off the audio with an irritated flick of the wrist.

"Why'd you do that?" asked Kirsten.

"If it were really important, Natalie would be calling. I'm sure Laura's just got some matter of procedure for us to look at. Let's let Simon do his job."

Kirsten somewhat unhappily nodded agreement.

Within half an hour, the shuttle settled in a small landing field an hour's walk from the cemetery where Admiral Barbara Firebrandt was interred. The lights of Alpha Coma's capital city, Shangri La, twinkled in the distance. The time was about three hours before local dawn. Ellis and Smart held hands as they made the quiet walk to the cemetery. Like children who didn't belong, they helped each other clamber over the wall surrounding the cemetery. By the wan light of Alpha Coma's moon, they searched for the grave of Barbara Firebrandt.

They found the grave behind a locked gate. Tourists could stand and view the grave through the gate. To the side was a palm scanner. A plaque explained that only those descended from Barbara Firebrandt could actually enter.

"It must have identifications on file," mused Kirsten.

"Must it?" asked Ellis, still somewhat wobbly from the whiskey. "It could be a genetic scanner."

"Try it," encouraged Smart.

Ellis put his hand to the scanner. Both gasped as the gate swung open. "Bingo," said Ellis, shaking his head slowly.

The captain crept forward and knelt reverently in front of the marble monolith that was Barbara Firebrandt's tomb. He read the words that recounted the highlights of her seventy-year career. The captain frowned in contemplation. "How I wish I could have known you."

"Dad said she was a bitch." Ellis caught his breath and turned at the sound of his mother's voice. She stood at the gate alongside Manuel Raton. Suki Firebrandt Ellis stepped through the gate and embraced her son. She turned and shook Kirsten Smart's hand. "You must be Kirsten." Fire grinned. "Glad to meet you."

Smart inclined her head. "Who are you?"

Ellis introduced his mother and Manuel to Kirsten Smart, then turned to face her again. "Mom, it's good to see you, but what the hell are you doing here? Last I knew you were returning to Earth to see what you could learn about the Titans. How did you get here?"

"I'm not exactly sure. The Titans brought us here. Somehow they knew exactly where you would be. As to the Titans' origin, I learned more than I bargained for," explained Fire. She told her son what she had learned, carefully leaving out details about how she actually learned it.

"Then it's true," gasped Ellis. "The Clusters are searching for the Titans." Ellis told his mother about his encounter in space.

Fire took a deep breath and let it out slowly. She turned away. "Mark, do you realize what this means?"

Mark Ellis stepped to his mother's side. "They might decide that humans are more interesting than the original appendages." Ellis hugged himself. "What exactly was the nature of the symbiotic relationship between the Titans and the Cluster?"

Fire shook her head. "I'm not exactly sure. The Cluster is immortal and only has limited capacity to change and grow on its own. It relies on the appendages for purpose somehow."

Manuel had stepped out of the tomb and was looking up at the stars. "You know, such a relationship wouldn't be all bad. Imagine all that you could learn from something as old as the Cluster."

Kirsten was pacing next to the tomb. "That's the trade off. The appendages gain knowledge."

Ellis let out a breath he didn't know he was holding. "But what would happen to the beings that gained all that knowledge all at once?"

Kirsten stopped pacing and looked Ellis in the eye. "All that power; all that ability gained all at once could be devastating."

Fire nodded, remembering her research. "There's no evidence the Titans have evolved since they escaped the Cluster."

"Being a symbiont of the Cluster means the end of evolution," said Ellis hugging himself.

"Might mean," corrected Manuel, holding his finger up. "We don't know for sure."

"I'm not sure we want to find out," said Kirsten.

All turned at the soft swishing of footsteps rustling through the grass of the cemetery. A clean-cut man in a business suit was approaching. Only tired eyes visible in the moonlight betrayed that he had been awaken early. He examined the open gate and looked at the assembled group. "I presume we must be cousins," he said.

Suki Ellis walked up to the man. She studied his red hair turning gray and chiseled features similar to her father's. "Maybe," she said cautiously. "I'm Suki Firebrandt Ellis and this is my son, John Mark." She held her hand out and the captain took it.

"Then it's true. My grandmother did have another family." The man nodded as if finally believing something he'd never dared before.

He held out his hand. "I'm Herbert Firebrandt. I'm a Senator here on Alpha Coma."

Fire and Mark shook the new arrival's hand in turn. They introduced Kirsten and Manuel. "What brings you out here at this early hour?" asked Mark.

"Something terrible has happened," explained Firebrandt. "Don't ask me how I knew, but somehow I felt I would find the answer if I came out here tonight."

"Answer?" asked Fire.

"What happened?" asked Kirsten.

"The Earth has gone silent," explained Herbert Firebrandt. "About an hour ago, several Clusters appeared around both the Earth and Titan. We lost all communication."

"How can we help?" asked Manuel.

Herbert Firebrandt shivered in the cold. "Come to my office and we'll see what we can do."

* * *

Herbert Firebrandt had an expansive office in the Alpha Coma senate building in Shangri La. On the walk back, Firebrandt explained that his grandmother once mentioned a mysterious third son who was on Sufiro. "She seemed embarrassed about him," Firebrandt said.

"I don't think Ellison Firebrandt is exactly the kind of son that an aspiring politician wants to admit to," said Mark, almost under his breath.

Entering the Senate building was like entering a beehive, abuzz with activity. Senators and aides rushed to and fro, exchanging information and worried glances. Firebrandt was stopped several times on the way to the office. The Senator introduced one man as his aide. "Bobby, make sure we're not disturbed," he ordered.

Herbert Firebrandt offered seats and coffee to everyone. Manuel and Kirsten declined, deciding to watch the sun rise over the city through the windows in the high-rise office building. Ellis, mostly sober, nursed his cup. Fire slowly sipped from hers. Herbert activated his holographic console and called up records.

"John Mark Ellis," muttered Herbert. "I knew the name was familiar. Little did I know we were related." The image of Ellis, bald and completely shaved, hovered over Herbert Firebrandt's desk. "You were a commander in the Confederate Navy before you resigned."

"Tell me something I don't know," said Ellis, just a little grumpily.

"There's still no contact with Earth or Titan. It's as though they've completely vanished – how's that for something new?" Firebrandt forced a smile. His look turned somber. "Rd'dyggia, Zahar, and Tzrn are getting nervous. They're afraid the Cluster is going to come for them. Someone needs to find out what's happened before the galaxy panics."

Fire snorted. "You know, I never really thought the people of Alpha Coma gave a damn for people back on Earth."

Herbert Firebrandt shook his head sadly. "Earth's the mother planet of humanity. What happens if she's destroyed? Will the Cluster come after us next?" The Senator turned his attention back to Ellis. "Who better to help us than the man who has the most experience with the Cluster."

"I don't see how I can help, I'm just one man," Ellis shook his head and put the coffee down on his desk.

Firebrandt smiled. "It's within my power to reactivate your commission, Mr. Ellis. Or, should I say Captain Ellis?"

Ellis' jaw dropped. He stammered for a moment, retrieved the coffee momentarily then set it back on the desk. In a whisper, he asked, "Do you have the authority to confirm my posting?"

"No," said Firebrandt bluntly. As Ellis was about to interrupt, Firebrandt held up his hand. "However, I can call in favors. The Admiralty of Alpha Coma can appoint you a Captain in our fleet."

"I'm a captain without a ship," said Ellis, shaking his head, somewhat overwhelmed.

Kirsten Smart stepped up behind Ellis and put her arms around his neck. "The *Nicholas Sanson* is at your disposal, Captain."

Ellis turned his face toward Kirsten's. "I know you don't have that authority."

"I'm the most senior officer who can speak for TransGalactic at present. My word's law in this matter."

Ellis wriggled out of Kirsten's arms and took her hands but looked at the Senator. "Surely the Alpha Coma Navy could provide a ship."

Herbert Firebrandt nodded vigorously. "I'm sure we can."

Manuel Raton stepped away from the window. He poured a cup of coffee for himself and then sat in the chair that Ellis had abandoned. "But the Cluster may not take kindly to a war ship showing up," he said. "They may destroy a war ship to prevent you interfering with their plans."

"Exactly," said Kirsten with resolve.

"Why wouldn't they destroy the *Sanson*?" asked Ellis.

"Just another civilian ship with more humans, more potential symbionts," said Kirsten, grimly. She pulled John Mark Ellis close.

"Why would you do this, Kirsten?" Ellis' voice trembled.

"Mark, I want to evolve with you one day at a time; not overnight."

Kirsten Smart's eyes were bright and a single tear threatened to escape.

Ellis gave her a squeeze then turned to face Herbert Firebrandt. "Is the plan acceptable, Senator?"

"It sounds good to me, Captain Ellis," said Firebrandt. "Report to me when you're ready to depart for Earth." The senator pulled more data up on his computer. "I see that the *Sanson* needs a few more days of repair. Rest assured that all of Alpha Coma's resources are at your disposal."

"Let's hope we regain contact with Earth before these next few days are up," said Ellis.

"Amen to that," said Firebrandt. "Godspeed, Captain Ellis."

Ellis saluted the Senator. He stepped from the office along with Fire, Manuel and Kirsten. They walked back to the shuttle, discussing the future and speculating about what had happened to the Earth. For the most part, Ellis was silent, lost in his own thoughts. He was a captain in the Navy again. A few weeks ago, it was what he had wanted. Now, he wasn't sure he wanted the responsibility of saving the Earth. However, the job was his and he wasn't about to back down.

At the shuttle, Ellis hugged his mother then took her hands. "I guess this is good-bye again."

"What do you mean?" she asked, shaking hair from her eyes. "Manuel and I are coming with you." Ellis inclined his head. "Well, it's not like we have a ride to Earth any other way and it is home after all. We're not going to sit here and let you have all the fun."

Manuel patted Ellis on the shoulder. "Besides, I don't think you could save the Earth without us." A broad grin brightened Raton's features.

Kirsten stood in the door of the shuttle. "What are you guys waiting for? Let's go." She disappeared into the shuttle. Manuel, Fire and Ellis followed. With a burst of jets, the shuttle lifted off for the *Nicholas Sanson*.

About the Author

David Lee Summers is an author, editor and astronomer living somewhere between the western and final frontiers in Southern New Mexico. His other novels are *The Pirates of Sufiro, Heirs of the New Earth, Vampires of the Scarlet Order* and the forthcoming young adult science fiction novel, *The Solar Sea*. His short stories and poems have appeared in such magazines as *Realms of Fantasy, SpinDrifter, Star*Line, Outer Darkness,* and *The Santa Clara Review.* David is also the founding editor of *Tales of the Talisman* Magazine.

Made in the USA